THE MAN
FROM
OAKDALE

THE MAN FROM OAKDALE

HENRY COLEMAN

with Alina Adams

Pocket Books

New York London Toronto Sydney

Pocket Books
A Division of Simon & Schuster, Inc.
1230 Avenue of the Americas
New York, NY 10020

First Pocket Books hardcover edition January 2009

POCKET and colophon are registered trademarks of Simon & Schuster, Inc.

For information about special discounts for bulk purchases, please contact Simon & Schuster Special Sales at 1-800-456-6798 or business@simonandschuster.com.

Manufactured in the United States of America

10 9 8 7 6 5 4 3 2 1

Library of Congress Cataloging-in-Publication Data is available.

ISBN-13: 978-1-4165-9360-7
ISBN-10:   1-4165-9360-8

For My Beloved Vienna,

A modest Valentine's Day trifle I whipped up the summer of 2008 to illustrate what our lives could have been like—if certain now-living people had stayed dead. And vice versa.

—H.C.

PROLOGUE

Lucy Montgomery had never kidnapped anyone before. She didn't know exactly how to go about it.

The one-and-a-half-year-old boy in her arms was no help. Johnny simply looked up at his twentysomething half sister with unabashed trust and a six-tooth grin. He stretched out one pudgy arm to offer her his plastic multicolored key-ring. Lucy kissed the tiny dents between his knuckles and shook her head to indicate no thank you.

Balancing the boy on her hip, Lucy flipped up the collar of her suede jacket to try and guard against the Christmas-time midwestern chill. She opened the back door of her car, disengaging Johnny's other hand from where it was glee-fully tugging strands of her dirty-blond hair from a hastily swept-up bun. She lowered him into the car seat she'd had the presence of mind to install a few hours earlier. It was about the only bit of planning she'd done. For everything else, Lucy was flying by the seat of her pants. As someone who had started college by filling out a spreadsheet with each class she intended to take over the next four years, involuntary spontaneity was not a state Lucy particularly relished.

But she'd had no choice in the matter. Lucy didn't want to kidnap her baby brother; she'd simply realized that she had to.

Johnny's mother, Jennifer, had died several months earlier. Though weak with pneumonia, Jennifer had signed herself out AMA—Against Medical Advice—in order to get home to her baby. More specifically, against Lucy's medical advice. The Oakdale Memorial Hospital Mortality and Morbidity Review Board had decreed that the death hadn't been Lucy's fault, which meant that Lucy wasn't legally at fault—but it also meant that not a day went by when she didn't fleetingly wonder what might have happened if she'd asserted her authority as a doctor and forced Jennifer to stay and get the medical care she'd needed.

Now, instead of the mother who'd loved him literally more than life itself, the poor little guy had three men fighting over the right to raise him: Paul Ryan, Jennifer's brother and Johnny's uncle; Dusty Donovan, Jennifer's widower and Johnny's adoptive father; and Craig Montgomery, victor of the most recent round of custody wars. Craig was Johnny's biological father—and Lucy's, too.

Lucy knew all three candidates very well. While each could conceivably have been an adequate parent for Johnny, having the three of them at each other's throats was intolerable. There was too much history there. Too many personal vendettas that had nothing to do with Johnny were being played out at the expense of the little boy.

Craig and Paul had once battled over a woman. She'd

ended up in a permanent coma. Dusty and Paul had fought over a woman, too. She'd ended up dead. Dusty and Craig had butted heads over Dusty's earlier relationship with Lucy. Lucy had barely escaped being buried alive. Dusty had blackmailed Craig. Paul had tried to kill Craig. Craig had tried to kill Paul. All of which explained how Lucy could say with unwavering certainty that she knew what happened to people who became collateral damage in these men's feuds, and why she refused to allow Johnny to grow up at the epicenter of such emotional, mental, and physical violence.

With the little guy strapped safely into his car seat, Lucy slid behind the wheel and smiled reassuringly over her shoulder at Johnny. As she did so, she caught a glimpse of her father's monstrosity of a house in the background. All houses, Lucy knew, had a tendency to look grim and foreboding in December twilight. Craig's home, however, carried the distinction of appearing equally sinister at noon on the Fourth of July. People said that dogs eventually came to look like their owners. Did that hold true for houses, too? Lucy wondered.

She started her engine. With a final shudder at the thought of Craig actually believing he could raise a well-adjusted child in such a house, Lucy drove off into the darkness. She hadn't told anyone where she was going—not even her grandmother, Lucinda, who'd begged for any sort of clue as to her final destination. When Lucy had refused to oblige, Lucinda had pleaded with her granddaughter to at least keep in touch—somehow.

Lucy had made no promises. No, that wasn't true. She'd made one, if only to herself. She'd promised that as long as

Craig, Paul, and Dusty were still battling over Johnny, she would never return her little brother to Oakdale.

With the departure of his children, Craig Montgomery lost his favorite battlefield. So did Paul Ryan. Both promptly shifted their combat zone. Dusty might have eagerly participated in the change of venue, but he was murdered soon after Johnny disappeared. (Surprisingly, neither Paul nor Craig was responsible for his death, though each did his best to make the other appear guilty of the crime.) Within weeks, Paul and Craig found yet another woman to fight over, Meg Synder. The fight led, rather predictably, to more heartache, more tears, more shattered marriages, more criminal charges filed, and more death.

But even the tug-of-war over Meg Snyder ultimately proved incapable of distracting Craig and Paul from their hunt for Johnny.

Although the two men claimed to hate each other, proclaiming that they were nothing at all alike, they did have one thing besides their disturbingly similar tastes in women in common: Each was determined to be the first to track down Lucy and Johnny.

No matter what it took.

Or who got hurt.

PART ONE

MONTEGA

1

Two years later

"It's official." Henry Coleman slammed his Al's Diner reservations book down on the counter. "Oakdale, Illinois, is the most fertile place on earth."

"Only if you are not married," Vienna Hyatt replied blithely. She flitted between the diner's dozen tables, sliding colorfully laminated menus onto every place setting in preparation for their usual dinner rush. In her distinctive Swedish-mangled English, she added, "I have been studying this interesting verity for many months now. I believe I have discovered the secret to Oakdale's baby boom. It only comes into effect if you are single. Very few married people here produce children. Have you also noticed this oddity?"

"Hmmm . . ." Henry opened the reservations book and ran his finger down the list of private kids' parties Al's Diner had hosted over the past few months. "Sage Snyder . . . Parker Snyder . . . Daniel Hughes . . . Liberty Ciccone . . . Nope, not a legitimate kid in the bunch."

Vienna had to reach across Henry, who was sitting at the counter, to file away her remaining menus. She didn't have to do it in such a way that first her breasts, then her hips, and, finally, the ends of her flowing ebony hair swished provocatively across his lap, but what fun would it have been otherwise?

"Am I supposed to be listening to anything you say while you do that?" Henry asked. Henry was an average-looking thirtysomething man of above-average height and below-average earning potential. He had ordinary brown hair, jug ears, chipmunk cheeks, and a smile that stretched from sideburn to sideburn. His girlfriend, on the other hand, boasted a face Plato would have described as "the golden proportion"—a nose no longer than the distance between the eyes, a small jaw, large eyes, and defined cheekbones. It was one that contained what modern-day scientists call "proportional physical symmetry." Not to mention one that men responded to by first staring, then stuttering, then attempting a strangled grunt, and finally blushing and running away in terror. As a result, Henry very rarely managed to actually listen to what Vienna was saying.

He tried his best, he really did. He loved Vienna so much that he even found her sometimes-incomprehensible accent charming. He genuinely wanted to hear what she had to say. But looking at her frequently proved too distracting. And, in this particular instance, her practically lying across his lap didn't help.

She turned around, resting the edge of her equally perfectly proportioned and symmetrical rear end against his thighs. That didn't help much either.

"And you know what other interesting fact I have also noticed?" Vienna asked as she kissed Henry on the forehead. She kissed the bridge of his nose. She kissed his eyelid and his ear and the very tender square of flesh where jawbone meets neck. He definitely liked the direction this was heading in.

"Do tell."

"You and I, Henry. We are single."

"You betcha. Single, footloose, fancy-free, fit as a fiddle and ready for . . ." Henry was trying to figure out a way to suavely maneuver himself and Vienna onto the counter without violating the Health Department's regulations against, well, having sex on counters, when Vienna's words finally penetrated his lust-addled brain.

"Hey! What's the big idea?" he exclaimed.

Vienna plopped awkwardly down on the counter. Henry did her one better in the slapstick department and actually slipped, hitting the floor with an ego-crushing thump. But he was up in seconds, eager to demonstrate that he had figured out what Vienna was up to.

"You're talking about us two Oakdale-dwelling single people having a baby. I thought we'd settled that."

"You settled it by buying me a puppy."

"Exactly. Pepper was for you to practice on. How did you like the helpless neediness, the constant 'accidents,' the all-night whining for your undivided attention?"

"That was you."

"Exactly." Henry had been shooting for droll. He'd have settled for amusing. Vienna did not look amused. He changed tactics to remind her, "You aren't even sure if you really want a baby. You're just reacting to the avalanche of babies all around us. It's peer pressure, that's what it is. A passing fancy. Like that entire first quarter of your life when you thought gorgeous locales, fabulous jewels, glittering parties, non-stop champagne, and strapping, wealthy men were the key to making you happy. Before you realized it was, in fact, a modest, heavily mortgaged diner in the charming American Midwest, complete with a debonair, though perhaps a touch less than strapping and a whole lot less than wealthy, chap."

"So you are saying that our love is also what you call a passing fancy?"

"No! What passing? No passing! Interception!"

Vienna stomped her foot. "You are trying to confuse me with your baseballing terms."

"What? Baseball? No, it's—never mind. Forget about my baseballing terms. You and I are the real thing. We're long-term."

"As in marriage?"

"As in long-term investments. Special. Fixed. Secured. A careful accumulation of only the most valuable properties to be nurtured and pampered throughout the course of a lifetime to insure ultimate, maximum payoff."

Henry figured he was safe focusing on money, Vienna's second favorite topic, as a way to keep them off her first favorite topic—marriage. Over the past year, Vienna had taken to channeling her frustrations over their lack of wedded bliss by doggedly trying to push all their friends into the bonds of matrimony. Which was fine with Henry. He liked to think of said friends as helpfully taking the bullet actually meant for him.

"If you do not take better care of those investments," Vienna said with a pout, "you might soon find yourself out on your precious, special, secured assets."

Henry wondered if that was a deliberate joke or an English-mangling malapropism. It was so hard to tell with Vienna, but either way, Henry had a feeling he was getting his assets handed to him in a sling.

"Admit it," he challenged. "You're not so sure about this parenthood thing yourself. You love our life the way it is. A baby would change everything."

Vienna hesitated.

Henry smiled. According to his favorite writer, nineteenth-century Irish wit Oscar Wilde, "She who hesitates is won." Would the man who also said that "one's real life is often the life which one does not lead" steer Henry down the wrong path?

"So it's settled," Henry barreled on, afraid to discover that what he discerned to be Vienna's hesitation was merely her pausing to refill her lungs so that she might unleash a torrent of fresh persuasion in his direction. "I don't want to hear another word about children," he said firmly.

The bell over the diner's front door jingled merrily. Probably just as well that they'd been forced to put their amorous activities on hold, Henry thought. One never knew when the Health Department might unexpectedly drop by.

Lucinda Walsh entered the diner in all of her dowager, stiff-haired, well-heeled glory. She wore a floor-length fox fur and made a point of carefully lifting the hem so that it just brushed the middle of her knee-high, black suede boots, and not the diner's recently swept, but obviously not very well, plebeian floor. At sixty-plus years old, Lucinda carried herself with the expected self-confidence of a woman who'd made her money the old-fashioned way—she'd married it. Then she'd waited for her elderly husband to die so she could drive his multimillion-dollar company to even greater, billion-dollar heights.

Lucinda looked critically from Henry to Vienna and back again. She said, "I need to speak with you about children."

"Craig Montgomery is a rotting, oozing pustule on the flesh of society," Lucinda announced.

"Guess we won't be naming a sandwich after him then," Henry muttered.

Thanks to Lucinda's colorful description, Henry felt a bit queasy as he handed her a menu. She, however, slid grandly into the nearest booth, accepted the menu, and skimmed it briefly before archly raising an eyebrow. "No wine list?"

"Our sommelier is in the Republic of Armenia this week for the annual master conference. Naturally," Vienna replied without missing a beat.

Lucinda raised her eyes to peer challengingly at Vienna. The younger woman met her gaze calmly and held it for a long beat. With the hint of a smile, Lucinda returned her menu to Vienna. "Naturally," she agreed.

"You were saying something about Craig Montgomery oozing and rotting," Henry prompted, less interested in what Lucinda ultimately had to say than he was in moving the conversation along before more customers arrived.

Henry suspected that Lucinda's choice of words wouldn't precisely complement their special of the day.

"And those are his good qualities," Lucinda snarled.

"Agreed. But Craig hasn't bothered anyone in Oakdale since he went on the run for bombing Paul Ryan's car."

"Disagreed!" Lucinda bellowed. She did have a most remarkable bellow. Not unlike a mountain lion protecting her cubs. While performing a speech by Lady Macbeth. For the hard of hearing.

"She disagrees," Henry translated helpfully for Vienna's benefit. English wasn't her first language, after all. Vienna nodded, either mesmerized or petrified.

"Craig is still tormenting a great many people in Oakdale, due to his relentless hunt for my poor granddaughter Lucy," Lucinda said. "His machinations with Johnny and the attempt to turn Paul into charcoal briquettes was only the most recent in his long, long, long list of criminal acts. Honestly, I don't know what my daughter, Sierra, ever saw in that man. Or what I ever did, for that matter."

Vienna blanched. "You and your daughter's husband—"

"Don't be vulgar, dear. It was before he was my daughter's husband."

Seeing that Lucinda didn't want to linger on the subject of her long-ago romance with Craig and that she was also less than pleased with Vienna's implied question, Henry hurried to redirect the conversation away from Lucinda's checkered past and back to Craig's. "Craig and Paul were also once in love with the same woman," he explained. "Meg Snyder loved Paul but she married Craig, then got pregnant by Paul and lost the baby. Then she dumped them both."

"Are you quite finished?" Lucinda wanted to know.

"Yes," Vienna answered for him.

"Thank goodness." Lucinda cleared her throat. "Lucy ran off with Johnny to protect him from Craig's brand of parenting. If anyone knows about its toxic effects, it would be my brilliant girl. She was named after me, you know. Lucy gave up her life for Johnny—even after I begged her not to—in order to save him from growing up as a perpetual pawn between Craig and Paul. It was no minor sacrifice. She had a promising medical career, a fellow who cared for her, a grandmother who would have given her no less than the moon if she had asked. For goodness' sake: Tell me what the point is of having children, of reproducing your bloodlines, if those same ungrateful offspring refuse to take advantage of your life experience to make their own road in life a little easier? Tell me!"

Henry and Vienna exchanged stymied looks and shrugged.

"Lucy was supposed to keep in contact with me!" Lucinda raged. "I insisted she do so! I could have helped her, I could have smoothed her way. Instead, she cut herself off from all of us, including Sierra, her mother. We don't even know where to reach the child to let her know that Craig is on her trail!"

"You haven't heard from Lucy?" Vienna asked.

"Not in months. It's as if a large hole opened up in the earth and swallowed my granddaughter whole, then stuck its tongue out to taunt me for good measure." Lucinda peered directly into Henry's eyes and proclaimed, "I want you to find Lucy for me."

"Me?" Henry yelped, sounding like a monkey protesting the theft of his last banana. While drinking a martini. "Why me?"

"Because the FBI informed me that my granddaughter's disappearance is an international matter, the CIA told me it was a family matter, and the Jokedale Police Department can't even get a lock on Craig Montgomery's whereabouts, despite his being at the top of their most wanted list. I guess that's what happens when the fugitive's sister is the chief of police. Margo keeps claiming she has a lead on Craig, but when it comes to closing the deal, he mysteriously escapes her clutches. I am tired of government-funded incompetence. I've decided to take matters into my own hands. To that end, I seem to recall that before you dedicated your life to playing Chef Boyardee alongside your Swiss Miss—"

"I am Swedish."

"And your people make a spectacular meatball, darling, don't interrupt—Henry, were you not the proprietor of a detective agency?"

"Well, yes, the Early Bird Detective Agency. But that was years ago."

"Splendid. Then it shouldn't be too difficult for you to transition from Early Bird Culinary Specials back to your previous line of work. You are familiar with all the players in this sordid family drama. Courtesy of your fiasco of a marriage to his sister, Katie, you and Craig were even relations for a short time, were you not?" Lucinda reached into her purse. "Will you take the job? Ascertain Lucy's and Johnny's whereabouts and relay them to me? Only to me and no one else, is that clear? Paul Ryan would love to unearth where

Lucy is hiding. His obsession with regaining Johnny is still running neck and neck with Craig's. Well, tough. He can hire his own minions."

"I'm sorry, Lucinda." Henry feigned a contrite expression. "We're very, very busy these days. The pepperkakor season is almost upon us again and—"

"Who or what, pray tell, is a pepperkakor?" Lucinda demanded.

"A pepperkakor is a ginger cookie," Vienna explained, thrilled to finally be contributing to the discussion. "We serve them here at Al's. They are a huge favorite in Sweden, especially during the Christmas holiday season."

"It's also my little pet name for Vienna," Henry waxed poetic. "Because she's sweet and spicy and, well, Swedish."

"Enough." Lucinda held up her hand, palm up. "I've lost interest." She took out a medium-sized manila envelope and tossed it on the table between them. "I'll pay you fifty thousand, plus all expenses. Here is ten thousand in cash up front to get you started. You will receive the remainder when you locate Lucy and Johnny."

"We will do it," Vienna said.

Lucinda beamed. "I knew you were good for more than just cuckoo clocks."

"That is the Swiss. I am Swedish," Vienna called after her. But Lucinda was already up and walking out the door.

"What are you thinking?" Henry asked Vienna the minute La Walsh was out of earshot.

"Well, at this very moment, I am thinking about how I will redecorate the diner for fifty thousand dollars. Plus maybe a padded expense or two," Vienna explained gleefully.

"This is ridiculous. We don't know anything about locating missing persons. Especially a missing person who really, really doesn't want to be found."

"But you ran a detective agency!"

"Ran it straight into the ground."

"This is not a problem. We will learn on the job, just like we learned how to run a diner."

"Speaking of which, who do you think is going to run our baby—sorry, bad choice of words . . . who do you think is going to run our fully mature bundle of . . . no, that's not it, either . . . Who's going to watch the diner while we go gallivanting around the globe looking for Lucinda's errant young?"

"It is not a problem. We will close up shop for a few days. Finding Lucy and Johnny should not take more than a week or two of our time. It might even be good for business."

"How do you figure that?"

"Absence makes the heart grow fonder, does it not?"

"That's for romance, not restaurants. And furthermore, who's going to take care of our puppy, Pepper? You know, Vienna, when you assume responsibility for a small, defenseless, drooling life-form, you can't simply pick up on a whim and jet off to glamorous spots unknown. Something to think about, huh?"

"Emma Snyder has offered to let Pepper stay at her farm anytime we like. She says the grandchildren adore playing with him, and Pepper loves running about in the fresh air." Vienna placed her index finger on Henry's nose and traced a line down to the spot between his collarbones. He tried to kiss her finger when it flicked across his lips, but Vienna was too quick. "Or would you rather that we forget about traveling and instead stay where we are so we can continue our earlier conversation?"

Henry put on his enthusiastic face and brightly asked, "So if you were Lucy Montgomery, where do you think you'd go?"

Vienna smiled. Henry could tell she was plotting something. But experience had taught him never to ask what.

2

"If I were Lucy Montgomery, where would I go?" Vienna sat in front of the mirror in their residential hotel room, leisurely brushing out her ebony hair. She'd sectioned the glorious cascade into twenty equal strands and pinned each up with a hairpin. With the precision and intensity other people reserved for tasks such as launching a space shuttle or corneal transplants, Vienna diligently unpinned one loop at a time and gave it a hundred loving brushstrokes. At this rate, though their bed stood a mere two feet from the vanity table, Henry suspected it would take him a minimum of an hour to move her the necessary distance. And that was only if she gave up and dropped the subject of Lucy Montgomery first.

"What do you say we start our new job tomorrow morning?" Henry reclined on a pillow against the headboard. He was wearing his finest burgundy smoking jacket and nattiest silver silk pajamas. If Vienna insisted on casting him in the role of intrepid detective, Henry preferred Dashiell Hammett's witty and effortlessly urbane Nick Charles to Peter

Falk's rumpled and confused Columbo, thank you very much. He'd have been willing to settle for Thomas Magnum in a pinch, but, Henry had to confess, his knees weren't really khaki shorts material. And all of his previous attempts to grow a bushy mustache had been, to put it mildly, unfortunate. He patted the matching overstuffed pillow next to him, smoothing down the amber sheets. "Tonight we can play a different game of hide-and-seek."

Vienna put down her hairbrush. She smiled at Henry through the mirror. He sat up at attention on the bed and smiled back. Vienna raised her arms, reached behind her neck, and unfastened another section of hair. She let it fall along her shoulder. She picked up her brush again and said, "A beautiful young woman traveling alone with a small child is not your typical tourist. She would be memorable even on a crowded commercial jet or attempting to cross a border. She is a wanted fugitive. Craig pressed charges when she disappeared with Johnny. This means that she could not just depart normally. I believe we should presume that Lucy employed unconventional routes to leave Oakdale, and that is the way in which we should look for her."

"Absolutely," Henry said, dramatically flinging back the covers. "Tomorrow."

"In that case, she could not have done it without help. Her family is very wealthy and connected. But since Lucinda says she has not heard from Lucy lately, and neither has Lucy's mother, Sierra, whom does that leave?"

Henry gave up. He pulled the covers back up with a lot less drama. He sighed and suggested, "Margo Hughes? She's Craig's sister, Lucy's aunt. Since she's also chief of police at the Oakdale PD, I'm willing to bet she knows all sorts of backdoor routes out of this town."

"Would a policewoman allow the kidnapping of a child, though?"

"Considering that Margo has personally handcuffed Craig for more felonies than your average sibling, I'd say probably. But I see your point. There's Katie—she's Lucy's aunt, too. And she's a bit more . . . shall we say legally lax, than Margo."

"She is also not nearly as good at keeping secrets."

"True. You want to get word out, you have three choices: Telephone, telegraph, or Tell-A-Katie. If I was going on the run, Katie wouldn't be my first choice of confidante."

"So no one on her father's side of the family. On her mother's we have got Sierra, obviously, Lucinda and—"

They both had the same thought at the same time. "Lily!"

The next day, Henry parked their car down the street from Lily Snyder's house and squinted meaningfully in its direction. He wasn't sure why he was squinting, but it seemed the correct expression to assume on a stakeout.

He mused, "You think Lucy's aunt is just going to blurt out what she knows about Lucy the second we ask her?"

"Of course not. If Lily was going to just tell anyone where Lucy was, I presume she would tell her mother, Lucinda, first, would she not? Or are they not on good terms?"

"You know how Lily and Holden have been married and

divorced and remarried like three times? Well, that's almost how many times Lily's had herself unadopted and readopted by Lucinda. Those two are crazy about each other. They just can't spend too much time together in the same room without getting the urge to throttle each other. You know, typical mother/daughter stuff. Ah, how that makes one long for the joys of parenthood." Henry snuck a sideways peek at Vienna, hoping his subtle jab hadn't been too . . . subtle.

"My mother and I get along gloriously," Vienna said, too wrapped up in her new endeavor to realize she was being baited. "If Lily is indeed keeping Lucy's secret from even her own mother, then I do not expect her to reveal it to us."

"So why are we here?"

"Because I expect to find evidence in her house that will help lead us to Lucy."

"And how do you expect Lily not to notice us surreptitiously digging through her drawers, loitering in her letters, and co-opting her communications?" Henry asked.

"Very simple. Lily is currently not home."

"My love now has X-ray vision?"

"No. Merely very good ears. When Lily and Holden came in for lunch yesterday, I overheard Lily say that her youngest daughter, Natalie, is in a ballet recital all afternoon. The whole family is to be in attendance. The house is empty. And I suspect pregnant with information."

Now it was Henry's turn to wonder if Vienna was the one baiting him. Well, two could play at that game.

"So, you say the house is barren, do you? Such a nice house, too. Look how it stands all alone on the corner.

Single, unattached. I'm glad they decided not to clutter it with unnecessary additions. So many people get overexcited about cosmetic alterations and they just don't think through the consequences of such a major change. Next thing you know, the entire foundation is crumbling. Okay, let's go in, take a look around. But try not to mess anything up. We want to leave it in sterile condition."

Vienna gave Henry a long look. He did his best to appear innocent—yet wise to her verbal machinations. Vienna sighed, then simply got out of the car without another word. Henry had to hustle to keep up with her. But it was a good thing he did, because, at the front door, Vienna stopped and pointed at the knob.

"You," she said.

"Whatever are you implying?"

Vienna rolled her eyes. Henry opened his wallet, got out a credit card, and broke into Lily Snyder's house.

"Thank you," Vienna said and waltzed right in. Henry followed. She said, "You look upstairs in the bedrooms. I will search the living room and the kitchen."

"Have you ever been here before?" Henry asked. "How do you know how the house is laid out?"

"I went on the internet last night and found a floor-plan on the website of this development's builder. I like to come prepared."

Henry gulped. "You're scaring me."

"Good." Vienna smiled and pointed to the stairs.

Henry obeyed dutifully. The first door on his right down the second-floor hallway appeared to be the master bedroom. Henry entered, bursting with confidence and bra-

vado. These quickly waned once he realized he had no
idea what he was looking for. Were they expecting to find
a map with Lucy's location circled in bright red pen? Or
maybe a stack of postcards inscribed "Having a wonderful
time in exile. Wish you were here. Lucy." Henry gave the
room a quick once-over, just to make sure. Nope. Didn't
spy any of those things lying around. He supposed that a
proper private detective would be digging into drawers and
under mattresses, but the idea of riffling through the Snyders' personal belongings didn't really thrill him. It was bad
enough when Henry and Vienna had owned a spa and the
good people of Oakdale had pranced through half-naked
and sweaty. Henry was still trying to dislodge from his reti-
nas the imprint of a prominent citizen wearing only a towel
and insisting that he speak to Henry immediately, peeka-
boo flesh be damned.

Instead of doing what Vienna had told him to do, Henry
passed the time shuffling through a variety of excuses for why
he hadn't. Then he conjured up a few backup lies about how
he had, but, oh, no, sorry, he couldn't come up with anything. He was working out a particularly intricate deception
that involved a previously undisclosed phobia of dry-cleaning
bags when he heard a car pulling into the Snyder's driveway.
A quick peek out the window confirmed that it was indeed a
Snyder car. Driven by a Snyder. Lily Snyder, to be precise.

Henry wondered if ballet recitals could be rained out.
And then he wondered why he was wasting his time wondering about such trivia when he should be wondering how
he was going to explain to Lily his presence in her house.
Or, rather, how Vienna was going to explain both her and

his presence, since she was downstairs, and most likely the interloper Lily would encounter first.

In a burst of unexpected chivalry, Henry's thoughts shifted from how he might protect his own posterior to the best way he might safeguard Vienna's (it was, admittedly, the more attractive of the two, and thus a greater loss to mankind if it was tarnished in any way). Considering the time crunch, Henry could think of only one thing.

He jumped out the window.

Well, perhaps "jumped" was a bit too Errol Flynn, or for those not born like Henry with the soul of a 1930s bon vivant, too Johnny-Depp-of-a-way to put it. It was more a case of one leg on the windowsill, then the other one, then a few squeamish moments of looking down at the ground, then a desperate two-handed grasp of the drainpipe and a part shimmy, part scramble down the wall, kicking up shriveled ivy and paint chips the entire way. Remarkably, he made it down in time to casually step up behind Lily just as she was slipping her key into the lock. Trying to unobtrusively brush the ivy and paint chips from his hair, he offered a laid-back, "Hey, Lily! What a surprise to run into you here!"

She turned around and faced him instead of heading inside. Through the crack in the door and over her shoulder, Henry caught a glimpse of Vienna madly scurrying upstairs and out of sight. Lily looked confused as she asked, "You're surprised to run into me on the porch of my own house?"

"Well, you and Holden have been spending so much time out at the farm lately, I didn't think you'd be here."

"But you were looking for me?" Lily replied, still confused. "Here? Where you didn't think I'd be?"

Most days of the week, Lily Snyder behaved exactly like what she was—a fortysomething mother of four. Her wavy brown hair was cut into a shoulder-length style that was both fashionable and practical, her earth-toned wardrobe was functional yet expensive, although you weren't supposed to think it was unless you really knew about high quality fabrics and good tailoring. However, every once in a while, Lily Snyder briefly morphed into her formidable mother, Lucinda Walsh. And when that happened, the unfortunate target of her ire knew to get to the point quickly.

So Henry got to the point quickly. "See, the thing is, I went to the farm, but Emma told me you all were at Natalie's ballet recital, so I came here, figuring you'd come back eventually, but here you are, and what happened to the recital? Tutu trouble?"

"Not exactly." Lily clearly didn't believe him, but she was just as clearly in too much of a hurry to explain why she didn't. Turning away, she strode into her living room and began looking under the sofa cushions while explaining, "Natalie is dancing the role of one of the mice in *The Nutcracker*, and she misplaced her whiskers. She's sure they're somewhere in the parlor, but . . ." Lily straightened up. "I'm willing to bet money they're somewhere in that disaster area she calls her room."

Lily turned to head upstairs. Henry followed, intending to intercept any potential run-ins with Vienna. Lily stopped halfway up. "Henry?"

"Yes?"

"What do you want?"

"Organic food," he blurted out.

"Excuse me?" Well, at least it made her pause. Henry wondered how fast he would have to talk to keep her from going all the way up.

"Vienna and I, we're thinking of starting an organic menu at the diner. You know—carbon footprint, food miles, Al Gore, save the whales, free the tuna, kumbaya? Vienna and I are nothing if not good, responsible citizens of the world. And since you ran that organic baby food company a couple years back, I thought you might have some pointers—"

"That baby food ended up sending a dozen children to the hospital."

"—on how to avoid that sort of thing." Never let it be said that Henry Coleman couldn't turn on a nickel and five pennies if need be.

"Not to mention the fact that it indirectly cost my mother her company."

"Right, right," Henry said absently, as if he hadn't been steering the conversation toward exactly this point on purpose. Never let it be said that Henry Coleman couldn't think on his feet while standing on spare change. "While you were up to your elbows in rancid mashed pears, Craig Montgomery tricked you into signing the papers that more or less handed WorldWide over to him, I remember that."

"I don't think I can help you, Henry." Lily continued her ascent up the stairs. "Sorry."

Lily might have been eager to find her daughter's mouse whiskers and head back to the recital, but Henry was motivated by a combination of true love and sheer terror. Plus, he had much longer legs. Three strides, and he bounded ahead of Lily, blocking her way just as she reached the top.

"I'll help you look," he offered. Before Lily could object, he streaked into Natalie's room in time to see Vienna duck into the closet. Thinking fast—and going with the obvious— Henry offered, "I'll check the closet."

Lily looked at Henry as if he was out of his mind. But then she presumably recalled some of his past less-than-sane moments—dressing up as a priest, dressing up as a chambermaid, dressing up as a pregnant woman named Henrietta—and decided that this wasn't so odd after all. "Sure, go ahead, knock yourself out. Natalie's costume was hanging in the closet. It makes sense that's where her whiskers would be."

"Great," Henry said as he all but dove in. "I'll get them for you."

Lily said, "Spoken like a man who doesn't have kids of his own."

In the closet, even though they were standing literally face-to-face, Henry made a point of avoiding Vienna's eyes as he blithely answered, "Nope. No, I don't. No kids."

"Well, take it from me: Your best bet for finding anything a child has misplaced is anywhere *but* the logical place." Lily sunk to her knees and proceeded to sweep her arm back and forth underneath Natalie's bed. "The most illogical place, however . . ."

"Good to know," Henry trilled while making a boisterous show of searching the closet anyway without stepping on Vienna or causing both of them to come tumbling out. Under different circumstances, the proximity might have been rather thrilling. It was kind of like playing Naked Twister. Only clothed.

In the meantime, to prevent Lily from wondering what exactly Henry was doing, in addition to keeping her talking about their original topic, Henry asked, "Craig tricking you like that, about signing over the company . . . May I ask why you ever trusted him in the first place? The man's a notorious scoundrel. He's embezzled money more times than anyone can count, including from his wife's business and his son's trust fund. He drugged your mother to make her look crazy, he paid some thugs to kidnap his daughter, he let Jennifer think Johnny was dead. The car bomb he used on Paul Ryan wasn't even his first attempt at moving up to a Class A felony. He did the same thing over twenty years ago to another guy."

Lily's head bobbed up from below Natalie's bed. She blew a loose strand of hair away so that it wasn't falling into her eyes. She said, "Craig wasn't always like that."

"True. I left out the part where he tried to slip his own wife a miscarriage drug. Or the times he kidnapped children who weren't even his."

"Craig did try to kill Steve Andropolous the same way he tried to kill Paul, gosh, has it been over twenty years ago now? Actually, now that I think about it, it was for the same reason, too. Twenty years ago, Craig was married to Betsy, but she was pregnant by Steve. More recently, Craig was married to Meg, but she was pregnant by Paul."

"Doesn't say a lot for Craig's prowess in the bedroom, does it?"

"But there was a time, when he was with Sierra . . . He wasn't . . . He didn't . . . You need to understand, Craig was Sierra's hero."

Henry prided himself on never being strapped for words. But he really couldn't think of a reply to that beyond, "Say what now?"

"They met in Montega. That's where Sierra was born and where she grew up. It's in South America," Lily added helpfully.

"I know. I read the papers."

"My mother sent Craig there. She told him that an old friend, Jacobo Esteban, had been killed by rebels. Jacobo was the leader of Montega, and Lucinda was very worried about his daughter, Sierra." As an aside, Lily added dryly, "My mother forgot to mention that Sierra was her daughter, too, but that's neither here nor there. Craig went, and he found Sierra while she was trying to bury her father all alone in the middle of the night. Craig helped Sierra escape from Montega. And later, in Oakdale, when she was married to this son of a bitch named Tonio Reyes—"

"Takes one to know one."

"No. Believe me. Tonio made Craig look like a saint. Craig got Sierra out of that horrible marriage. They had Bryant and Lucy together. They lived happily for years in Montega. After the rebels were defeated, Sierra was elected president."

"Sort of a Fidel Castro without the beard. Or the death squads."

"Sierra was determined to rebuild her country after the destruction, not to mention resettle the refugees who'd been forced to flee. Conditions were so bad even my mother was moved to adopt one of Montega's orphans—my sister, Bianca. She works for the United Nations in New York City now. Anyway, what I'm trying to say is Craig and Sierra really loved each other once. And they loved their kids. Craig was good to my big sister. And he was good to me. He was my friend. At one time, he was almost a father figure. That's why I trusted him."

Lily looked so sad. She'd obviously been crushed by Craig's subsequent betrayal. It was a sensitive situation, and Henry knew exactly what to say.

"Look," he pointed to the top of Natalie's bookshelf. "The whiskers."

Lily craned her neck, her joy at finally tracking down the missing costume part clearly overriding her sadness at the hell Craig had once put her through. Funny how life worked that way. "How the heck did they get . . . I don't want to know."

Henry reached up and retrieved them for her.

"You're a lifesaver." She kissed him on the cheek and hurried downstairs, a relieved Henry following. They said good-bye at the curb. Henry waited until Lily's car was completely out of sight before rushing back to the house.

Vienna poked her head out the open door, looking both ways to make sure the coast was clear. When Henry gestured that it was all right, she slipped out stealthily.

And then they hugged each other, jumping happily up and down in the middle of the street, exclaiming in unison, "Montega!"

3

"Montega! Of course it's Montega!" Lucinda roared, standing in the middle of her living room, surrounded by price-
less antiques. This time her roar was tinged by sarcasm, as if
they had stated the obvious. "Lucy has diplomatic immunity
in Montega. No one can stop her from leaving the United
States and heading there. Naturally it's where she went with
Johnny. Her mother even sent a plane for her!"

"Then why—" Henry began.

"Is this really what fifty thousand dollars' worth of private
investigation buys me?"

"Actually—"

"You think I'm going to pay you fifty thousand dollars
to tell me something I already know? Right before she left,
Lucy claimed she wasn't headed for Montega, but I knew
better. It was the only logical place for her to go. Sierra protected her for a while, but I realized she couldn't stay for
long. Craig still has friends there. And if not friends, then
stool pigeons. They'd have sniffed around, discovered Lucy,
and tipped him off eventually."

"Why didn't you tell us any of this before?" Henry asked.

"I didn't tell you that the sky is blue or that caterpillars turn into butterflies or that the capital gains tax is lower on long-term investments. There are some things I expect reasonably intelligent people to know or to figure out for themselves. Stating the obvious is a waste of my valuable time and, I presumed, yours. Lucy left Montega almost a year ago. She just disappeared one day. Didn't even tell Sierra where she was headed. I want you two to find out where Lucy is *now*. You didn't see Craig when he first realized she was gone. I was there. He was furious. It chills my blood to imagine what he might do to Lucy if he finds her first. I am counting on you to save my granddaughter's life!"

"We will get right on it," Vienna swore.

"You know," Henry said as he hefted his suitcase into the overhead compartment and turned to Vienna, who was already prettily strapped into her window seat, "when you told Lucinda we'd get right on it, I didn't realize you meant the first plane to Montega."

"Lucy Montgomery's last known location was Montega. It is only logical that we should attempt to pick up her trail there."

"And was it also logical for you to buy first-class seats?"

"They were the only ones left. Besides, we are professionals now. It is only appropriate that we should behave

in a professional manner. Oh, look." Vienna pointed at the
crowd of people awkwardly dragging their luggage past the
plush leather chairs and champagne flutes of executive ac-
commodations as they lumbered down the aisle toward their
own seats in the coach section of the plane. "Aren't riffraff
adorable?"

"That's Detective Adorable Riff to you," replied a familiar
voice with familiar bobbed red hair and apparently super-
sensitive hearing. "Meet my husband, Adorable Raff."

"Aw, geez." Henry suddenly envied chameleons their
ability to blend into the background; the skill would have
come in useful right about now. He groaned. "Beat it. It's
the cops."

Oakdale Chief of Police Margo Hughes had overheard
Vienna's observation. And she'd apparently brought along
her husband, former district attorney Tom Hughes, to arrest
them for Class A Snobbery.

"Vienna meant it in the nicest way possible," Henry assured her.

"I bet," Margo replied in a snarky tone. "What are you
two doing on a flight to Montega? And in first class, no less?
I didn't realize flipping burgers was so lucrative."

"Henry and I are considering reestablishing our efforts to
open a high-end spa in Oakdale. We have a very wealthy in-
vestor attached to the project. He is sending us to Montega
to study their operations."

"So you're going to Casablanca for the waters, is that it?"
Margo asked.

"I am afraid I do not understand."

"I'll explain it to you later, my little pepperkakor." Hoping to change the subject, Henry asked Margo, "And what takes you two to Central America?"

"Vacation," Tom said. "Margo and I realized we hadn't had one in . . . in . . ."

"Well, there was that time in the south of France," Margo recalled.

"Being chased by a drug-dealing, homicidal dwarf around a booby-trapped castle isn't exactly my idea of a vacation."

"How about our trip to Africa?" Margo asked.

"Ruined by the same dwarf."

"Pretty scenery, though."

"Yes, a lovely waterfall. Except I'm afraid I didn't fully appreciate all its charms while trying to frantically paddle around its deadly rapids. And convincing the local tribal chief not to make you his seventh wife was no picnic, either," Tom added.

"It's important for Americans to respect other people's cultures."

"In any case, that was over a quarter century ago. So we were due."

Margo noticed they were holding up the line of . . . uhm . . . riffraff and began to speak quickly as they were swept toward the back. "With Tom's job and mine and the kids . . . we needed to get away. We haven't seen his sisters, Frannie and Sabrina, in a very long time, and they both live in Montega, so here we are and there we go and see you two later!" They both disappeared behind the curtain delineating first class from coach.

"A quarter of a century," Vienna sighed. "Can you imagine having that rich of a history together? All of those memories. Children being born and birthdays and first days of schools and Christmas . . ."

"And homicidal dwarfs . . ."

"Do you think we will still be together and in love like that after a quarter of a century?"

Henry said, "My dearest, while I, more than anyone, appreciate those gifted lips of yours, perhaps two such perfect little buds were not destined for flambéing up spur-of-the-moment falsehoods. Going to Montega on a spa-researching expedition? Do you not recall what Lily told us? Revolution? Orphans? Carnage? Not exactly prime luxury spa territory. Margo's never going to buy it. We can't risk making her suspicious. Lucinda wants everything hush-hush to keep Craig from getting wind of our investigation. Not to mention that Lucy broke the law when she ran off with Johnny. If we track them down and then neglect to alert the proper authorities, that makes us accessories after the fact. Detective Hughes's day job is to arrest accessories. And I'm too cute to go to prison. Not to mention too big of a wuss."

Vienna stared at Henry for a long beat. Then she reached into her purse, pulled out a sheet of paper, and handed it to Henry. "Read," she ordered.

Henry read: " 'Welcome to www.TourismInMontega .com, your one-stop resource for all things Montega. Though ravaged by civil war in the mid-1980s, Montega has often been called "The Comeback Country of the Century." Under the administration of President Sierra Esteban, Montega was able to revitalize its international standing and World Bank ranking by turning Montega's renowned beaches, unsoiled wetlands, and picture-perfect scenery into a base for the continent's best resorts, hotels, sanitariums, and' " — Henry gulped audibly — " 'spas.' "

"Of course, spas. If Montega were still merely revolutions, orphans, and carnage, why would Margo and Tom choose to vacation there? And why would all of these other people on this plane be headed there?"

"I presumed that in addition to revolutions and carnage, they also offered a very favorable tax shelter policy."

Vienna raised an eyebrow. She crossed her arms. Henry cleared his throat again. He guiltily handed back the print-out to her. And then he threw his arms around Vienna and shouted, loud enough for even Tom and Margo to hear them way in the back, "I love this woman!"

He only wished he had a couch to jump on like Tom Cruise — without risking banging his head on the ceiling. And Oprah to bemusedly observe it all.

Vienna harrumphed. But she smiled while she was doing it.

Several hours later, as Henry was trying to convince the flight attendant that a fourth helping of filet mignon was not at all an inappropriate request and was this or was this not first class, Vienna tapped him on the arm, prompting him to turn around, which allowed the flight attendant to escape.

Vienna said, "Do you think Margo might have useful information for us about where Lucy could have gone? We agreed Lucy would not have confided in her aunt for fear of there being a conflict of interest. But is it not likely that Margo has investigated Lucy's disappearance? Even if she hit a dead end eventually, her research might still be of use to us. We need to question her. But in a subtle way, so she does not deduce why we are asking."

Henry said, "Excellent point, my pepperkakor. Perhaps you should scamper on back and inquire about what she knows; subtly, of course. I'm feeling a bit parched, myself. Another glass of champagne will help quell the discomfort."

"No. I am afraid I insulted her earlier. I think it would be best for you to do it."

"But . . ." Henry gestured weakly in the direction of the galley. "Free booze . . ."

Vienna said nothing. But she said it very pointedly. Henry slunk off. On the way out, he did manage to spy an unclaimed flute of champagne. He downed it quickly, setting the glassware back in place before exiting first class.

He found Tom and Margo all the way back in the twenty-third row. Though each was still technically in their assigned seat, the armrest was raised, and Margo had her legs draped across Tom's lap, while he had both arms wrapped around her shoulders and his face nuzzling at her neck. Henry took in the intimate scene and, after giving it a moment's consideration, figured nah, he wouldn't be interrupting anything by ducking his head under the overhead compartment and announcing, "So, fancy running into you two again."

With all those intertwined body parts, it was difficult to

see who exactly jerked in surprise at his greeting. Not to mention whose hands it were that seemingly attempted to encircle his throat. Without a doubt, though, it was Tom who demanded, "What the hell do you want, Henry?"

Henry took a defensive step back. "Sure is a funny coincidence us all ending up on the same flight like this. I figured since everyone's stuck in a holding pattern with nothing to do until touchdown"—he pretended not to notice the twin glares both Tom and Margo shot in his direction—"I'd take advantage of the serendipity to ask a few questions that have been plaguing me lately. For instance, Margo, as chief of police in Oakdale, do you find that there's a conflict of interest in primarily arresting people you know, are related to, or have dated at one point or another?"

Margo started at Henry. She shook her head as if to clear it. She said, "What?"

"I was just thinking about how difficult it must be for you when a friend or a relative breaks the law. You end up with a heck of a dilemma. Do you obey the calling of your badge, or do you look the other way and let someone you care about evade justice and skip the jurisdiction?"

Margo lurched forward, ending up balanced on her knees in the spot where the armrest once had been, so that her chin was practically atop Tom's head, her breasts in his face. All things considered, Tom didn't look too bothered by the situation. Margo, however, was on the warpath. Face-to-face with Henry, she hissed, "I know what this is about."

Henry gulped and wondered whether it was Margo's

superior detective skills or his own inferior subtlety skills that made so obvious so quickly the fact that he was fishing around for what she might know about Lucy and Johnny. "You do?"

"I know what everyone in town is thinking. Paul Ryan may have been the only one to actually come out and articulate it, but I know the rest of you suspect it, too. You all think I deliberately let my brother Craig flee the country so I wouldn't have to arrest him for setting the bomb in Paul's car."

Wow. Not at all.

"Wow," Henry said. "That's exactly what I meant. You and Craig. I suspect that. Yes, I do."

"Well, let me tell you something. If I'd had the concrete evidence against Craig last year, I'd have personally booked him and thrown him in a cell. Brother or no brother. But my hands were tied. By the time forensics was done and I'd gotten the appropriate warrants, he'd flown the coop. You think I'm happy about that? You think I enjoy knowing people are talking behind my back? Casting all sorts of aspersions on my professionalism?"

"Margo," Tom's voice wafted up from the vicinity of his wife's cleavage. "Calm down. We're supposed to be forgetting about work, remember? We're on vacation."

"It's just so hard," she lamented.

"I know."

"And it's just so easy to get caught up in the rat race."

"I know. We scurry around in the same maze, remember?"

"And then there's the kids."

"Oh, yes. It's been a heck of a year with the kids, I'm well aware of that."

With a dismissive wave in Henry's direction, Margo plopped back down next to her husband. He slid a comforting arm around her shoulder. She tilted her head until it was touching his, and both sighed sadly. Henry inched his way back down the aisle until he'd returned to first class, and Vienna.

As he took his seat and reached for another glass of champagne, she asked him, "Well, did you learn anything?"

Henry shook his head. "Nothing I didn't already know."

Lucinda had given Henry and Vienna her elder daughter's address in Montega with instructions to head straight for her estate as soon as they landed. Sierra would be expecting them.

"Well, maybe not exactly expecting," Lucinda had hedged. "I haven't actually been able to reach her on the phone for several weeks. But you two go on ahead, it will be all right. She'll put you up and get you anything you need to help facilitate your search for Lucy. Sierra is as frantic as I am. Neither of us can bear the thought of Craig finding our precious girl first."

As Henry and Vienna waited at the taxi stand, Henry appropriately outfitted in a Panama hat in honor of his south-of-the-border sojourn, Vienna looking admittedly much more fetching in a woven straw hat with a yellow ribbon to match her shoulderless sundress, they spied Tom, Margo, and their mismatched luggage heading their way. Tom and Margo spied Henry and Vienna, too. And set off in the opposite direction.

"Do you think it's something we said?" Henry asked.

"I cannot imagine," Vienna shrugged.

When their taxi driver heard that Henry and Vienna were headed for Chez Esteban, he embarked on a twenty-minute paean to the Esteban family, mentioning several times the valuable role he'd played during their struggle against the soulless, worthless, godless revolutionaries, and in Montega's subsequent rebuilding.

Since no reply appeared necessary or, frankly, wanted, Henry passed the driving time nodding thoughtfully in apparent agreement with the self-aggrandizing monologue while staring out the window. As they made their way over paved roads to dirt ones and back again, Henry, mindful of his professional responsibilities, prepared a fact-finding report for Lucinda in his head.

Palm trees.
Purple vegetation in the oddest places.
Really blue sky.
Blinding yellow sun.

It was a short report. But at least Lucinda wouldn't have to tell him the sky was blue. She'd be proud to note he'd figured that point out all by himself.

As they were getting out of the cab, Henry finally managed to get a word in edgewise, inquiring whether their driver might have any useful knowledge about the where-abouts of Sierra Esteban's daughter.

"There is a daughter?" the man asked, stuffing a wad of bills into his pocket and peeling off.

"Obviously," Henry observed to Vienna, "he was very close to the family."

Standing outside the cast-iron gates of Sierra's estate, Henry and Vienna peered through the bars like Dickensian orphans hoping for a spare crust of bread. They took in the sheer scale of the four-story, Iberian-style stone structure, only perhaps a quarter of which was visible from their posi-tion. Three-fourths of the towering structure was obscured, Henry presumed, for security purposes by vibrantly colorful flower beds, strategically planted shrubs, and an assortment of trees.

Henry and Vienna pressed the buzzer and gave their names and credentials to the security guard on the fuzzy black-and-white screen. The subsequent wait for approval felt as if the guard was not only calling Lucinda back in Oakdale to confirm their story, but also actually making the trip there—on foot—before granting them access.

With the midday sun blazing overhead and their lug-gage dragging behind them the entire length of the trudge from gate to front door, Henry and Vienna arrived at the entrance a tad bit less fresh than they'd started out. Hen-ry's Panama hat felt distinctly droopy, and he had to peel the front brim off his sticky forehead to get a good look at the gentleman greeting them inside the thankfully air-conditioned foyer.

If Henry hadn't been suffering from an obvious case

of heat exhaustion, his initial observation probably would have been a good deal more clever, but, as it was, he said the first thing that popped into his head before succumbing to sunstroke and gracefully fainting. "My—Sierra's butler sure does bear a striking resemblance to Craig Montgomery."

4

Another man might have felt a touch embarrassed about just how much time he seemed to spend unconscious. But not Henry Coleman. He viewed his soft skull as a badge of honor. Proof that he was the artistic, deep-thinking, sensitive Lord Byron type, obviously destined for a life more genteel, more refined, more . . . how to put this tastefully . . . well-funded . . . than the one he was currently forced to endure. He actually somewhat enjoyed passing out. It confirmed his high opinion of himself.

What Henry didn't like was coming to again. Reality was such a letdown after the euphoric dream state. When his eyes snapped open, the first thing he saw was the fresco ceiling of what he assumed to be Sierra's parlor. Blinding sunlight from the open windows burned his dilated pupils, and a cacophony of noise assaulted his tender ears. In all fairness, though, the plush settee he'd been laid on was quite comfortable.

Vienna sat by Henry's side, one slim, daintily manicured hand resting compassionately upon his bruised brow. The rest of Vienna, however, was turned away from the prostrate form of her weary lover to face the direction of the afore-mentioned cacophony of noise. The group now included not merely the former president of Montega, Sierra Este-ban, but also her presumptive butler, the one who so re-sembled her ex-husband—tall, lanky, long-limbed, so full of self-esteem he practically vibrated with it—and a pair of . . . Who were these ragamuffins supposed to be? Gardening staff? . . . who appeared to be dead ringers for Margo and Tom Hughes.

Margo was telling her brother, "End of the road, pal. Craig Montgomery, you are under arrest for the attempted murder of Paul Ryan. You have the right to remain silent. Anything you say, do, mock, or bon-mot can and will be used against you in a court of law. You have the right to an attorney—"

Craig turned to Tom. "You're an attorney. How much will it cost me to find out what exactly is going on here?"

Tom shrugged. "Get in line. I thought I was on vacation. Turns out my wife had other plans."

"Five minutes," Margo reassured Tom. "I'll settle this in five minutes, and then it's straight to paradise for us. I promise."

"Uh-huh," Tom said. He turned around, plucked a leather-bound volume off a shelf, and flipped through the several hundred pages of minuscule print. "*Crime and Punishment*, by Dostoevsky. How appropriate. I'll just get started on this, and you let me know when you're done." He settled down in a chair, whipped out his reading glasses, and pro-ceeded to peruse the pages.

Craig said, "You might want to brush up on international crime and punishment yourself, Margo. Montega doesn't have an extradition treaty with the United States. Go away. You have no power here."

"I've spent the last year calling in every international law enforcement favor I've earned in my career so I could track you down. I'm not getting on an airplane back to Oakdale unless I've got you in handcuffs in the seat next to me," she hissed back.

Tom looked up from his book and informed no one in particular, "She used to get that passionate about me."

Craig said, "Then you'd better ask Sierra for permission to become a permanent Montegan resident, because I'm not going anywhere with you. And you can't make me." The latter sounded less like a threat and more like a well practiced sibling taunt.

"No," Margo agreed, "but Sierra can." She turned to her former sister-in-law. "Presidential privilege. You can hand him over to the U.S. authorities even without an extradition treaty. You can help me put Craig behind bars and make sure he never hurts anyone either of us cares about again."

Sierra hesitated. Margo didn't understand the hesitation. To be honest, neither did anyone else in the room. Except Craig. He looked utterly confident.

When Sierra didn't reply, Craig strode over to his ex-wife, slung one arm around her shoulder, all but ruffled her bobbed blond curls like one would a child or a pet, and urged, "Come on, darling, tell them our wonderful news, don't be shy." He leaned over and kissed her deeply on the lips, only coming up for air long enough to announce, "Sierra and I are back together. And she doesn't want me going anywhere, do you, muffin?" Then he kissed her again, just in case anyone missed it the first time.

Henry had just about managed to get his head to stop spinning. This didn't help his efforts any. He sunk back onto the settee with a groan.

Margo heard and pointed in Henry's direction. "My sentiments exactly. What the hell is going on, Sierra?"

But Sierra's lips were otherwise occupied at the moment, and she declined to reply. So Vienna took advantage of the lull in drama to turn back to Henry and coo sympathetically. The cooing stopped abruptly, though, the second Craig paused his grand demonstration of love and devotion, leaving Sierra once again available to answer Margo's question.

"I . . . It's like Craig said. We've reunited. Oh, come on, Margo, don't look at me like that." Sierra's already immense blue eyes widened even further in an attempt to convey sincerity. "It's not like Craig and I haven't broken up and gotten back together before. We have one of those can't-live-with-you-can't-live-without you relationships. You and Tom understand all about that. How many times have you two been on the brink of divorce? I mean, you both even have kids with other people. But you always manage to make it work in the end."

"Tom isn't a selfish, criminal sociopath!"

"Sorry," Tom said, not even bothering to look up from his book.

"And neither is Craig," Sierra insisted. "He's changed."

"That's right. He has changed. He's gone from being the

sweet boy who rescued you to the son of a bitch who had your own daughter kidnapped and buried alive because he didn't like her choice of boyfriends!"

"Lucy did dump Dusty eventually," Craig reminded her. "So obviously that relationship wasn't meant to be. And I didn't even have anything to do with it."

"Because you were in jail for trying to run your last wife off the road!" Margo cried.

"Those charges were dropped. You heard Sierra. I've changed. I'm a new man. Or maybe I'm an old man. In any case, I'm the man Sierra wants. Right, precious?"

"Right," she said, and swallowed hard.

"I don't believe you," Margo challenged. "Something strange is going on."

"There's nothing going on," Sierra insisted.

"You mean, except for the glorious reflowering of our love," Craig prompted.

Sierra asked Margo, "Where are you and Tom staying in Montega?"

Tom looked up from his book. "We've got reservations at a five-star hotel a few miles down the road. Deluxe suite, private beach, room service, outdoor Jacuzzi. We were on our way there when Margo said she wanted to pop in. Just to say hello, she claimed."

"I'm so glad you did," Sierra exclaimed.

"Yes," Craig concurred. "Family is very important. Sierra and I both agree on that. As we do on so many other things."

"What I meant," Sierra clarified, "is I'm so glad you didn't go to the hotel."

"Yeah," Tom mused. "Room service, Jacuzzi, sun, sand, privacy. Who's got use for any of that?"

"Not the most recent owners, that's for certain." Sierra confided, "The hotel was sold to a chain a few months ago, and it has been a total disaster. They've overbooked, under-staffed, the beaches are filthy, and the food . . . the Health Department has been out there three times in just the last week. Believe me, you two do not want to go there."

"Oh, well," Tom said. "No hotel, no beach, no arrest warrant. This vacation has been a spectacular success. Come on, Margo. Good thing we didn't even get around to un-packing. Let's go home."

"No!" Sierra insisted forcefully. "No, no, please. I can't let you leave like this. Not after you came all this way. Mon-tega is known for its hospitality to visitors. Please, why don't you spend your vacation here? Henry and Vienna, too."

"Why them, too?" Craig demanded. "What's wrong with them booking a room next to the filthy beach? They're not family."

"Henry's in no condition to face the elements," Sierra insisted.

"It's hot," Henry agreed.

"It's winter," Craig noted.

"Global warming," Vienna patted Henry reassuringly on the shoulder.

"Actually," Craig said, "this has been one of the chillier ones on record. We've made it down to the low seventies at night."

"Global climate change." Vienna didn't skip a beat. "My Henry is very sensitive."

THE MAN FROM OAKDALE

Craig asked, "Why are you two even in Montega? Sher-
lock Hughes here, I get. But what's with Lady and the
Tramp?"

"Hey . . . ," Henry began, prepared to defend Vienna's
honor until he realized that Craig was actually paying her a
compliment. It was Henry he was calling a mongrel.

"We are here on spa business," Vienna said. "We thought
Sierra might be willing to help us explore our investment
options."

"I'd be happy to help," Sierra offered. "We'll spend the
weekend together. The six of us. Tom and Margo will relax,
Henry will recuperate, and Vienna and I will do some business. It will give everybody a chance to see that everything
is fine. That Craig has turned over a new leaf and we have
nothing to hide. It'll be fun. One big happy family. Family is so important, after all," she reminded her ex-husband.
"Right?"

"Right." Now it was his turn to swallow hard.

"What do you say?" Sierra faced her potential guests.

Tom closed his book and set it back on the shelf. "I fear
this entire palatial estate isn't big enough to contain my
joy."

The real butler, the one who looked nothing like Craig,
showed Henry and Vienna to their room. Henry discovered
that the notion of not having to go back outside, plus full
maid service, the promise of a six-course meal in a few hours,
and, oh, yes, the chance to even maybe accumulate some

useful information he could take back to Lucinda, helped greatly in his recovery. By the time the butler urged them to pull the bell cord if they needed anything, Henry was feeling more like his old self again. And his old self hated for a perfectly good Panama hat to go to waste.

He asked Vienna, "Shall we play a quick round of Henry Goes South of Vienna's Border?"

Vienna said, "I wonder why Sierra invited us to spend the weekend. Lucinda must have contacted her and told her that we were on the hunt for Lucy. I wonder what it means that Craig is in Montega. Do you think he is looking for Lucy here, too? Do you think Sierra is helping him? In that case, did she invite us to stay so she could throw us off the correct trail? I wonder how Craig convinced her to reconcile? I wonder if she really loves him? I wonder if she is willing to sacrifice her daughter to make him happy?"

Realizing that there'd be no South of the Border journey in his near future, Henry moved down the list of his manly needs.

"I wonder what's for dinner," he said.

Never let it be said that Henry Coleman didn't come prepared for an assignment. He might not have known where to start looking for Lucy, whom to question, or how to go about it, but he did know the most important thing—what to wear. In addition to his stylish Panama hat, Henry had packed several pairs of freshly pressed khaki pants, four matching, crisp shirts, two sturdy hiking boots, and a full evening suit with tails and pink cummerbund. When dining in a one-time presidential palace, it was imperative to dress appropriately.

Henry and Vienna stepped out of their room at the pre-scribed dinner hour. He had donned his tails and cum-merbund. She wore a floor-length pink satin gown with a plunging neckline and an even more plunging back. They looked so fantastic that Henry thought an orchestra should be playing. Vienna started down the hallway toward the stairs, but Henry beckoned her to return and suggested they use the back staircase instead.

"Why?" Vienna asked.

"Because they won't be expecting us to. Sierra is the one with inside information; Margo's the one with the warrant; the only thing we've got going for us is the element of sur-prise. We don't want to give that up. I say we snoop our hearts out on the way down to dinner. Some stealthy stair skulking. A little leisurely lurking. A bit of—"

"All right," Vienna chirped, clearly not understanding a word but willing to go along if it would make Henry happy.

They took the back stairs, pointedly peeking around every corner. On the third floor, Henry's plan paid off. They heard Sierra and Craig having a heated discussion outside a dark-ened guest wing no one appeared to be occupying. Without revealing his and Vienna's presence, Henry inched forward to get a better look.

"In case my facial expression wasn't sufficiently clear," Craig was saying, "I didn't appreciate the spontaneous house party you decided to throw for the weekend. You know I pre-fer having you all to myself."

He towered menacingly over Sierra, standing nearly a

foot taller than her. Although Sierra was backed against a wall, she refused to be cowed by him. "Learn to live with disappointment, Craig. After being trapped with only you for company the last few weeks, I needed to see some fresh faces."

"There was a time you wouldn't have minded it being just the two of us."

"There was a time when you didn't have to force me into it."

Craig sighed. "I know whenever a window gets broken in Oakdale it's standard practice to automatically assume I'm responsible. But you know better than that. You know I'm not the boogeyman everyone presumes I am. Regular people like their lives to be simple. Everything is right or wrong, black or white, good or Craig. That's what boring people believe because they've never had to deal with life being otherwise. But you and me . . . we've been around. We know that a person can do bad things for the right reasons and good things for the wrong ones. When you were fighting the rebels, living in the hills of Montega, battling for your life every day, every hour, I know you did things that pious, regular people would have considered reprehensible. But you were doing them for the greater good. I'm the same way. I don't wake up in the morning looking to do evil. But, if push comes to shove, I'm also not afraid of doing it. You understand that about me."

"I understand you, Craig," Sierra sighed. They were standing so close together that they were practically breathing the same air. Sierra could have reached out and kissed Craig if she'd wanted to. She also could have slapped him or kicked him in the groin. From the tension in her body, it was impossible to guess which way the standoff would go. "But that doesn't mean I forgive you."

And then she walked away.

Henry and Vienna hung back for a few moments to give Sierra and Craig a chance to arrive in the dining room before they made their own grand entrance. Once they did, they were pleased to see all eyes turn to them and gaze in awe at the fabulous figure they cut, although Henry was disappointed to note that he and Vienna were the only ones who'd taken the responsibility of dining with a former head of state seriously. The ex-president herself was wearing black slacks, a peach blouse, and strappy sandals. Craig and Tom were both in chinos and polo shirts. Margo was wearing jeans and a blue Oakdale PD T-shirt. With flip-flops, for Pete's sake.

Craig took in Henry and Vienna's evening wear. "Auditioning for the top of a wedding cake?"

"No." Henry spoke so quickly that the *o* practically beat the *n* out of his mouth. Which wasn't lost on Vienna. She let go of Henry's arm and took the available seat between Tom and Craig, leaving Henry to fend for himself.

Seeing his awkwardness, Sierra suggested, "Why don't you come over and sit next to me, Henry?"

He gratefully did as beckoned. From across the table, Vienna deftly unfolded her white linen napkin and laid it across her lap, avoiding Henry's eyes the entire time.

At least the dinner itself didn't disappoint: an appetizer of coconut-breaded shrimp, followed by curried sweet potato soup, an entree of Argentine skirt steak, and bread pudding for dessert. Plus fruits and vegetables picked specifically to accompany each course and featuring more colors and varieties than a 64 mega box of Crayola crayons. Personally, Henry couldn't understand how, when faced with a banquet so delectable, anyone could even think of using his or her mouth for a task other than eating, then asking for seconds. Margo, however, didn't appear to be suffering from such limitations.

She'd barely gulped down a single shrimp before she was asking Sierra, "So how exactly did my brother manage to worm his way back into your heart?"

"Oh, you know, Margo." Craig's large hand waved his tiny fork around dramatically for emphasis. "The usual. Flowers, candy, moonlight strolls—"

"Reminiscing about the time Sierra had you kidnapped and stashed in a monastery so you might reconsider your evil ways . . ."

Craig's expression didn't flicker. "If that's not a sign of true love, I don't know what is. It proved that Sierra thought I was worth saving."

Vienna said, "I think it is romantic, you two reuniting after so many years apart."

"Thank you." Craig beamed at Henry's girlfriend. Henry would have glowered in reply, but, oh, look, here came the soup.

"I think it says something momentous about a relationship when you are able to overcome your troubles and move on," Vienna added with a sigh. "For instance, I might never have forgiven Henry after he left me at the altar and said he did not love me enough to marry me and publicly humiliated me in front of all of our friends."

"You're kidding." Sierra put down her fork. "Henry did that?"

"Oh, yes. There we were, dressed in our wedding finery, preparing to recite our vows, and Henry decided that he could not put me in the position of loving him more than he loves me. So to prove that he does love me—just not enough, I suppose—he declined to marry me."

It took a moment for everyone at the table to process the story. Margo looked at Tom, Craig looked at Sierra, and then all of them looked at Henry. Their looks implied that they were all thinking, as one, "Well, at least we're not as bad as he is."

Once again, Henry felt the urge to shrink and disappear. But that would have meant giving up on the soup, so he fought the urge valiantly.

"But you two are back together? Not just professionally, but romantically, too?" Sierra clarified.

"Yes," Vienna said with a nod.

"This loser makes me look like a pretty good catch, doesn't he?" Craig piped up.

Henry expected Vienna to do what she always did and vociferously defend the loser she loved. Instead, she politely asked Sierra, "Why did you and Craig separate in the first place?"

"Which time?" Margo quipped.

"Hey, hey," Craig interjected. "First time doesn't count. I was presumed dead."

"True," Sierra admitted.

"And the second time, Sierra was presumed dead."

"Also true."

"Third time's the charm, though," Margo offered.

Sierra turned to face Vienna and answered her honestly. "We grew apart. We discovered we wanted different things out of life. I was very busy with the Montegan rebuilding effort—"

"Ah-ha!" Tom exclaimed.

Then quietly went back to eating.

"Hold on a second," Margo argued. "You two didn't split up because Sierra was busy working. You split up because my brother is a lying snake."

"Actually"—Sierra seemed reluctant but compelled to admit it herself—"the whole lying-snake-transformation came up later. At least where I was concerned. I can't speak for anyone else, but when we first divorced, it really was because I'd been working too hard and I had neglected my marriage."

Margo, Henry, Vienna, Craig, and Sierra turned their heads in Tom's direction, all expecting another "Ah-ha!" moment. He declined to oblige.

Craig said, "All of our previous separations were for trivial reasons. I said this, she said that, we both took our toys and went home. It was childish. We've grown up since then. Sierra and I finally understand what's truly important. After we lost Bryant—"

Henry whispered to Vienna, "Craig and Sierra's son was killed in a car crash a couple of years ago."

"—we both understood that to keep a family together, you have to be prepared to make sacrifices."

"Kind of tough to keep a family together," Margo noted, "when your daughter is on the run from you."

There it was. The elephant that had otherwise been shuttled to the periphery of the room had been rather unceremoniously yanked out to serve as a centerpiece. Craig's face darkened, Sierra lowered her eyes, and Henry and Vienna exchanged surreptitious looks of eager glee across the table. She even seemed to have forgiven him his panicked reaction to the wedding cake question.

"That," Craig said crisply, "was a misunderstanding I am very eager to correct."

"So Sierra, you don't mind that my brother has driven your only living child underground?" Margo asked her former sister-in-law. "It doesn't bother you that as long as you and Craig are together, you'll never see your daughter again?"

"That's enough!" Sierra Esteban rose from the table. The gracious hostess was gone. In her place stood Sierra Esteban, rebel leader and former president. Or maybe it was just Sierra Esteban, Lily Snyder's sister and Lucinda Walsh's daughter. In any case, she clearly could roar with the best of them. "Craig's and my relationship is none of your business. Please refrain from taking whatever professional and personal bad feelings you and Tom dragged along from Oakdale out on the two of us." Sierra sat back down. She smoothed out her napkin. She smiled pleasantly at her assembled guests.

"More wine?" she asked Henry.

"Always."

Sierra reached for the decanter and poured a splash of

burgundy liquid into his crystal glass. And then she smiled at him. It was a very friendly smile. Henry smiled back. Sierra patted his arm. And rested her hand on Henry's biceps a bit longer than was polite.

"Okay. That was weird," Henry thought.

He glanced across the table at Vienna to see if she thought it was weird, as well. But Vienna was too busy asking Craig, "So you never for a moment felt like giving up? You knew you and Sierra were destined to be together forever?"

"Oh, yes. She can't get enough of me."

"I admire that sort of passion in a man. That steadfast-ness."

"I find that loyalty, the ability to make a commitment and then stick to it, is almost the definition of masculinity. Wouldn't you agree, Vienna?"

"Definitely. There is nothing more attractive."

Henry wondered if Vienna would find it attractive if he walked over and planted himself between her and Craig while shouting, "Look at me. I'm the one you're supposed to find masculine and steadfast!" But he was interrupted by a strange sensation.

Sierra Esteban's hand was on his thigh.

For a moment, Henry thought maybe she'd mistaken it for an armrest. Or, from the way she was squeezing it, one of those rubber stress-reliever things. But then Sierra leaned over and whispered in Henry's ear, "Make an excuse and follow me."

He looked at her quizzically, but she wasn't even facing Henry anymore. She'd turned away to answer Tom's question about Montega's Supreme Court and their selection of judges. Henry threw a beseeching glance at Vienna, look-ing for some guidance about what to do. But she and Craig were playing a game of European Geography, trying to list all of the rich and titled nobility they'd each partied with. Margo was merely fuming in silence. Henry realized he was on his own.

A few moments later, Sierra excused herself to go check on their dessert's progress in the kitchen. Prior to stepping away, she and Henry locked eyes. Sierra was clearly sending him a message. Henry just wished his receiver wasn't on the fritz.

He waited what he thought was a reasonable amount of time before rising and preparing to excuse himself.

Before the words were out of his mouth, Craig looked up and said offhandedly, "I'd be careful wandering around the estate on your own, Henry. This place is a maze if you don't know what you're doing. People tend to get lost and are never heard from again."

5

Henry sat back down.

Even when Sierra returned several minutes later and shot him a quizzical look, he glanced down and focused on his freshly served piece of three milk cake. Just to be safe, Henry didn't risk looking anyone else in the eye for the rest of the evening.

Later that night, when he and Vienna were ensconced in their bedchamber under the silk sheets and goose-down blankets, Henry asked her, "Did you notice anything . . . odd . . . about Sierra's behavior tonight?"

"I did!"

"Oh, thank God. I thought I was imagining things."

"But I do not blame her. It is surely most difficult to resist a man as chivalrous, attentive, and dashing as—"

"True, true, but it's hardly good manners to throw herself at—"

"Craig Montgomery."

"Come again?"

Vienna sighed, "I think while he was in Oakdale, I was, as he said, seduced by the commonly held notion that any window to get broken is naturally his fault. I did not have the chance to get to know him, to evaluate him on his own merits. He is very charming."

"So was Ted Bundy."

"Are you jealous?"

"Don't be absurd. I laugh at jealousy." He cleared his throat. "Ha."

"Good." Vienna kissed Henry on the cheek. But made no attempt to go further.

"In fact, it's Craig who should be jealous of me."

"Really? Why is that?"

"Because . . ." Henry started strong, but somewhere between the first and second syllable, he lost his nerve as images of the weirdness at dinner scrolled through his memory. Something peculiar was going on in Montega. But there was no point in opening that can of worms with Vienna until Henry knew more about which direction they were wriggling in.

"Henry . . ." Vienna prompted him to finish his thought.

"Because . . . I've got you." Henry silently complimented himself on the excellent save.

"For now," the love of his life chirped. "I was just telling Craig how interesting I found his and Sierra's long-term commitment. So different from yours and mine." Vienna offered him her most dazzling, perfectly proportioned smile.

Then turned around and went to sleep.

After a mere four hours of tossing and turning, Henry did as well.

When Henry woke up, fate seemed in the mood to serve him a better hand by kicking off his morning with the sight of nude flesh. Vienna's scrumptiously nude flesh, as a matter of fact. He got a glimpse of thigh, a flash of navel, and a tease of cleavage. So what if the best parts were covered by a forest green bikini? The day was still young.

Of course then Vienna had to go ahead and ruin it all by saying, "Oh, wonderful. You are awake. Let us head down to the pool."

Henry sat up and managed to yawn, stretch, and ogle all at the same time. He was, after all, a Renaissance man. He pointed to the two pieces of her bikini and said, "I don't think those things were made to go in the water."

Vienna laughed sweetly at his wit. Then she picked up a towel, a hat, and a bottle of baby oil and continued toward the door.

"Put on your swim trunks," she urged.

"Oh, no," Henry stuck his legs out from under the blankets. "These pasty knees weren't made for UV exposure. In the words of that great hypochondriac Woody Allen, 'I don't tan. I stroke.'"

"Very well," Vienna shrugged. She slipped on a pair of sunglasses. "I will see you at lunch then."

Henry might have protested her departure if Vienna hadn't already been out the door. He noticed she hadn't taken so much as a robe to cover up with. Not that Henry intended to torture himself with visions of her oiled, shining, nubile flesh parading in front of Craig Montgomery's lascivious eyes. Henry had much better things to do. Like walk over to the window, peel back the heavy damask curtains, and peer down four floors at the outdoor pool area. There, armed only with a pair of binoculars, he could easily observe Vienna and her glistening flesh on parade. Not to mention Craig's obvious appreciation of the spectacle.

Sierra was down there as well. She sat on a lawn chair next to her ex-husband, wearing a pink one-piece bathing suit and a matching headband to hold the blond curls off her face. She was reading a book, and didn't even glance up when Vienna arrived and promptly claimed the lounge chair on Craig's other side.

Unfortunately, the bird-watching binoculars Henry had packed for the express purpose of meeting all his professional spying needs did not come equipped with an extra-sensitive microphone. So Henry couldn't hear what Vienna was telling Craig, or hear Craig's obviously flirtatious replies. He only had their body language to go on. (Usually his favorite reading material.) Down below, as the sun shone and the chlorinated waves lapped, Vienna was leaning in toward Craig, looking into his eyes and batting her lashes. "Boy, these binoculars are good," Henry thought. "When they promised the amateur ornithologist crystal-clear detail, they weren't kidding!"

Vienna's exposed bosoms were heaving in a manner previously reserved just for Henry. It wasn't pleasant, but he could stand that. It was when Vienna threw her head back and laughed in apparent delight at something Craig said that Henry couldn't take it anymore. It was one thing for him to put up with Vienna admiring a man who was taller, more successful, smoother, and capable of enduring heat above seventy-five degrees without feeling light-headed. But the laughing—laughing was Henry's domain. If Henry couldn't make Vienna laugh, he might as well throw in the towel. Though probably not the one Craig was currently using to wipe down her back.

Henry yanked the drapes closed, turned, and marched into the bathroom, where he pulled on his swim trunks, grabbed a white terry-cloth robe, his Panama hat, sunglasses, and orange Crocs. He slathered zinc oxide on his nose, the back of his neck and ears, and, just to be safe, a little dab at the hollow of his throat, which somehow always seemed to escape the protection of robe and hat. Armed for battle, Henry stepped into the hall, where he literally bumped into Margo, who was coming from the other direction.

She took in his outfit and asked, "What are you supposed to be?"

"Skin-cancer safe."

"Congrats. Now drop the act and tell me what's really going on here. Why are you and Vienna in Montega?"

For a moment, Henry couldn't remember the cover story. And then he blurted out, "Spa!"

"Right," Margo said. "And Tom and I are on vacation."

Hoping to distract her, Henry observed, "Your husband isn't a very happy camper."

"And your girlfriend is gorgeous." In response to Henry's blank look, she said, "What? Are we done trading obvious facts?" Margo rested her palm against the wall so that Henry couldn't move past her without getting a ninja chop to the throat. "You're up to something. Are you two working for Craig?"

"What? No!"

"Because I warn you, no matter how much my brother is paying you, an aiding-and-abetting charge complete with mandatory jail term isn't worth it."

"No one is aiding, no one is abetting, and no one is paying. Vienna and I want nothing to do with Craig."

"Really? Have you seen the two of them lately?"

"She's a friendly girl. And nonjudgmental. Vienna doesn't leap to conclusions about other people's motives on the flimsiest of evidence."

"I'm watching you," Margo said. "I came to Montega so I could finally close the Paul Ryan case and put Craig behind bars, where he belongs. You get in my way, and I'll eventually get around to taking care of everyone."

"Except your husband, apparently."

Henry took advantage of the redness slowly seeping through Margo's skin, which seemed to temporarily paralyze her response time, to duck around her arm and take off. Before she regained her senses and came after him.

Sierra might have paid no attention to Vienna's arrival, but the moment Henry stepped around the nine-foot-tall hedges that surrounded the kidney-shaped pool and closed the cast-iron gate behind him, she was out of her seat and by his side.

"Henry!" Sierra cooed. "So glad you decided to join us."

"Yes, Henry," Craig said as he glanced up from where he was standing waist deep in water, dressed in a bright red Speedo. "Come join in the fun."

Henry presumed that the fun to which Craig referred was Vienna languorously swimming the backstroke through the cerulean water. She had her eyes closed to the sun, and she was raising her arms up and around her head, her hair waving loose and tantalizing underneath, her lips parted in an enigmatic smile as she sensually reveled in the frictionless sensation. For a moment, both Henry and Craig just stared at Vienna swimming her laps, since it sure beat anything else either of them might have had to do.

"Do you play Scribbage?" Sierra asked Henry. "I've always thought, 'Henry, now there's someone who's probably a whiz at Scribbage.' We keep a set of dice just for that in the cabana. Come with me, we'll get it."

Hmmm . . . play Scribbage or continue to watch Vienna? A tough choice.

And one that Henry was spared making when Craig hefted himself out of the pool and briefly balanced on both tanned and toned arms before swinging one leg over and standing up on the deck. He grabbed a towel, dried himself off, and told Sierra, "Henry's our guest. He shouldn't be fetching and carrying. I'll help you get it."

Henry supposed a more easily distractible man might

have wondered why it took two people to transport a small box containing thirteen dice, a timer, and a little cup to spill them from. But he was too busy watching Vienna.

When Sierra and Craig returned with their Scribbage game, Henry was feebly attempting to entice Vienna out of the cool, crystal-blue water to play a board game beneath the blazing Southern Hemisphere sun. He might have succeeded if Craig's jumping back into the pool with an unnecessarily dramatic splash hadn't drowned out Henry's most persuasive verbiage.

For the next half hour, while Vienna and Craig frolicked in the pool, splashing, racing, popping their heads out to take slow, leisurely sips of ice-cold water through disturbingly phallic- shaped straws (did Vienna really have to enjoy her refreshment quite that much?), Henry slowly performed his imitation of a baked chicken, melting on the inside and crisping up on the outside, as he attempted to form coherent English, high-scoring words with a handful of engraved dice. If he'd known Sierra was going to be a ringer, Henry might not have bothered attempting even that meager task. While she whipped out *clandestine* and *ensnared* as if her life depended on it, Henry barely managed to eke out *sad, lost,* and *done.* Of course, keeping his eyes on the game instead of surreptitiously watching Craig and Vienna might have helped Henry accumulate a few more points.

Or at least to realize that, on her latest turn, Sierra had somehow managed to spell out: *Meet. Tonight. Midnight. North. Gazebo. Come. Alone.*

Goodness, but she was a skilled player.

And goodness, but Henry was up to his neck.
In . . . something.

"Sierra wants to meet you alone at midnight in the north gazebo?" Vienna asked. "I wonder what she wants."

They were both in the bathroom that adjoined the guest bedchamber, Vienna naked in the shower, washing the chlorine out of her hair, Henry too busy lathering aloe vera lotion on any slightly pink areas of his person to pay her much notice. He'd told Vienna about Sierra's perplexing invitation because, well, obviously because it had been the right thing to do. Henry and Vienna didn't keep secrets from each other. That sort of behavior was childish and immature. He most certainly hadn't done it because, following a morning during which Craig had hung on Vienna's every word, it was good for her to know that she wasn't the only target of inappropriate sexual attention on this trip.

Not that Henry was trying to make Vienna jealous.

He was, in fact, terribly pleased that she reacted so calmly to his revelation. He was darn proud that Vienna didn't seem to care one single bit that another woman might be trying to seduce him away from her.

"You must go to meet her, of course," she continued in that sensible, generous, confident way that made Henry so happy to be on the receiving end of her maturity and wisdom. "You must find out what she wants."

"She wants me," Henry mumbled. "Is that so hard to believe?"

"But for what purpose?" Vienna turned off the steaming water and stepped out of the shower. Henry didn't bother to offer her a towel. Or to sneak a peek. That would teach her. Two could play at this game. Vienna continued, "The fundamental riddle we are facing is whether or not Sierra can be trusted. Does she know that we have been sent by Lucinda? And if she does, does she wish to help or hinder us? I would broach the topic very carefully with her. In case Sierra is in the dark about our true purpose, especially if she is working with Craig, we cannot risk tipping her off prematurely."

Yes, yes, yes. Vienna was making perfect, logical, brilliant sense. But, as far as Henry was concerned, the real fundamental riddle they were facing was: "So you honestly don't care that I'm going off on an illicit rendezvous?"

"Of course I care!"

"You do?" Henry melted on the spot. He instantly regretted not having taken that peek and wondered how the situation could be rectified. Immediately.

"I am very excited that you might be able to ferret out some useful information about Lucy's and Johnny's whereabouts from Sierra. She is already fond of you. And I know how charming and persuasive you can be."

He was deeply and mortally offended. But a little titillated, too. "Are you suggesting I prostitute myself?"

"Oh, Henry," Vienna said. "Do not be silly."

She turned on her hair dryer, making further conversation impossible. And leaving Henry to wonder what exactly she found so silly. The idea that Henry might use his charms to elicit delicate information from a woman? Or that any woman would fall for it?

Tom and Margo decided to skip dinner at the compound that evening, explaining that they had plans with Tom's sisters, Frannie and Sabrina Hughes. So, over the mango delight, Vienna and Craig decided to fill the gap by performing their South American version of the classic film *Tom Jones*, with its notorious food-standing-in-for-sex scene. Henry decided he'd do his best to ignore them. That is, when he wasn't trying to finagle a third serving of beef picadillo without making eye — or any other body part — contact with a determined and quite creative Sierra.

Afterwards, Vienna intercepted Henry on the way to taking a much-needed post-gluttony nap (the better to be bright-eyed and bushy-tailed for his midnight rendezvous, my dear) by insisting that they commence with some serious sleuthing, posthaste.

"If it's all the same to you," Henry muttered, his face stuffed into a pillow, "I'll sit this round out."

"Oh, my poor Henry." Vienna made appropriate clucking noses even as she applied a fresh coat of pink lipstick and lowered the peasant blouse shoulders of her azure sundress for maximum efficiency. "You rest up, then. Wish me a happy hunting!"

Henry mumbled something as she went out. He was pretty sure "Happy hunting" wasn't it.

When Vienna returned to their bedroom ninety minutes later, she found Henry in the exact same position she'd left him in. He saw no need to tell her that he'd actually been pacing the floor for eighty-four of the ninety minutes, debating whether he should storm out and challenge Craig to a duel over his woman, then wondering what he would do if the mad Montgomery actually accepted. Unable to reconcile the twin urges of chivalry and fear, Henry settled for lurking by the door and, when he heard Vienna's soft footsteps padding down the hall, leaping back into bed and assuming an air of convincing indifference.

Vienna tiptoed in, not sure if Henry was sleeping. When she saw that he wasn't, she looked at him expectantly, waiting for him to ask what she'd found out. Henry, knowing that was exactly what she was waiting for, refused to say a word. He wasn't sure exactly why. All he knew was that it somehow made him feel better about his manhood. For a moment, he and Vienna simply stared at each other silently. Then, tired of waiting, she crossed to sit on the bed beside Henry, telling him, "I was right. The man of the house is always the best person to consult."

"Craig actually gave you some useful information?"

"Craig? Craig is too busy playing games. I went to find the butler. He is the one with the knowledge."

"Good thinking." Henry was truly impressed. And he allowed himself to show it. "What did he say?"

"That Lucy and Johnny were in Montega, staying here at the house in secret. But when Lucinda called last winter to say that Craig had fled town to look for Johnny, Lucy ran away again. She did not even tell her mother where she was headed, because the butler heard Sierra desperately calling people, trying to find her."

"So Sierra doesn't know where Lucy is either," Henry mused. "That means her asking to meet me tonight can't be about that."

He'd been hoping to remind Vienna of the potentially amorous trap he might be walking into tonight, thus giving her a second chance to express her outrage and dread. But Vienna simply nodded thoughtfully and continued with her own train of thought as if Henry hadn't spoken. "Craig, however, did not come to Montega directly after leaving Oakdale. He arrived here about a month ago. Sierra did not even wish to let him in at first. She threatened to sic the guard dogs on him."

Henry's first thought was, "Ack! Sierra expects me to go stumbling around in the dark on an estate patrolled by guard dogs?" He decided to leave it unexpressed for now. His second thought he decided to share: "So how did Craig and Sierra get from 'release the hounds' to 'we're madly in love again,' in the space of four weeks?"

"Well, Craig can be very charming."

"Yeah. Thanks for that. Shouldn't Sierra be immune by now? I mean, isn't that how vaccinations work? A little bit of poison over a short period of time so eventually your body builds up defenses against it? Why aren't Sierra's anti-Craig defenses kicking in?"

"You should ask her tonight," Vienna suggested. Henry noted that there was no outrage in her tone. Or dread.

"Or you could ask Craig." Henry wondered why his tone sounded so accusatory when he had nothing to accuse Vienna of. Did he?

She nodded thoughtfully, conceding his point without so much as a twinge of guilt, then mused, "I wonder where Craig went looking for Lucy in between his departure from Oakdale and his arrival in Montega? He knows his daughter better than we do. He must have had some idea of where she would go. If we knew where Craig traveled, it would give us information of where we might look. Or, at the very least, where we should not bother to look."

"Sounds like a lead you should follow. Why don't you go do that?" Henry leapt out of bed. "I've got to get ready for my date with Her Ex-Excellency."

"Make sure you wear your cologne," Vienna advised. "You know how I cannot resist your scent. I am certain it will have an effect on Sierra, as well."

"You know," Henry snapped, "would it kill you to show a little bit of concern here? I'm off to meet another woman. A woman who hasn't been able to keep her hands off me since we got here."

"I know. Is that not lucky for us?"

"So you don't care, not one little bit, that Sierra wants me?"

"Do you want her?"

"No!"

"Then why should I be concerned?" Vienna's logic was infallible. If infuriating. "You love me. I know this. If Sierra's fondness for you helps us to achieve our objective, why should I bother myself over it?"

"It's not just fondness, you know. She had her hand on my thigh. And when we were playing Scribbage this afternoon, let's just say her fingers were itching to fondle more than the dice, if you get my drift. She wants me."

"How wonderful for us!"

Henry opened his mouth. Then he closed it again. His gift for gab had galloped away.

"Wonderful," Henry repeated before going into the bathroom to change. When he stepped out again a few minutes later, bedecked in a blue jewel-toned shirt that set off his eyes in a most spectacular fashion, Vienna was gone.

Henry gave himself plenty of time to locate the helpfully named North Gazebo prior to his midnight rendezvous hour. The only clues he had to go on were (1) it was a gazebo, and (2) it was located in the north. Of course, the question, North of what? instantly sprung to mind. And even if he used his crack detective skills to deduce that it referred to the north end of the property, that would still require him to know which way that might be.

Having never been a Boy Scout—Henry had preferred to spend his formative years with indoor plumbing—he, alas, now only had a fleeting notion of how to locate the desired direction by following the North Star or checking for moss growing on trees. He did seem to recall that the sun rose in the east and set in the west. But seeing as how it was the middle of the night, that information seemed less than helpful. He settled for merely walking away from the main house, figuring he could always circle the entire perimeter of the property until he came to a gazebo.

He'd just passed the pool area, taking a moment to glare at the scene of Vienna's and Craig's hijinks earlier in the day, when Henry heard a rustling along the hedges that surrounded it. His first thought was; "Guard dogs!" His second thought was, "Worse. Margo."

"Greetings and salutations." She popped up almost as if she'd been waiting for him. "And what brings you out and about at this time of night?"

Henry bent down and picked up a pair of sticks. "Collecting firewood."

"We're in the tropics."

"Ah, but a slave to weather romance cannot be. Vienna thought it would be romantic to have a fire."

"Cut the bull, Henry. I saw you sneak out of the house."

He let his arms drop. The sticks hit the ground. "Yes, ma'am."

" 'Fess up. If you and Vienna aren't working for Craig, then who are you working for?"

"We are on a crusade to eradicate wrinkles, tense muscles, and torn cuticles."

"The spa."

"The spa."

"Try again. I put in a little call back home. You and Vienna are broke. Al's is barely in the black. You don't have the money to launch another venture."

"Isn't that an invasion of privacy?"

"Yes, it is. And if you'd like me to cut it out, I suggest you level with me."

"What level? There are no levels here. Everything is aboveboard and on the up-and-up. Now, please hand me my firewood. I have a very hot woman waiting for me to make her even hotter."

Henry held out his hands. Margo handed him his sticks. And when he, in an attempt to throw her off the scent, headed back toward the house, she followed him.

She followed him through the front door, across the foyer, up the stairs, and into Henry and Vienna's room.

Where they both found the love of Henry's life in bed.

With Tom.

6

Vienna, dressed in a gossamer silk white dressing gown, sat with her back against the headboard, a pillow propped under her elbow, her bare legs tucked beneath her. Tom, wearing a maroon robe over light blue pajamas, was lying on his side, his palm holding up his head as Vienna giggled and slipped a grape between his lips.

Margo found her voice before Henry did.

"Excuse me?" She marched up to the bed and grabbed the fruit plate, sending grapes, strawberries, and melon slices flying everywhere.

"Ah, there you are, Margo," Tom said pleasantly. "Done lurking in bushes?"

"Are you actually trying to be funny?" she asked, disbelieving.

"I think I'm succeeding. Why else would I have spent the last twenty-four hours laughing over my foolish belief that when my wife said she wanted to whisk me away to a tropical paradise, she actually meant that she wanted to whisk me away to a tropical paradise? And not just use me as cover to pursue a vendetta against her brother."

"So this is, what? Your subtle way of getting back at me?"

"No. It's merely my way of keeping myself amused while you're off defending truth, justice, and the American way. A beautiful, sexy woman decided to pay me some attention. It has been a long time. I wanted to remind myself what it was like."

"That's *my* beautiful, sexy woman!" Henry interjected, feeling that he should contribute something, even if Margo did seem to have the situation under control.

"Of course I am," Vienna agreed. "Tom and I were just having a little fun."

"Tom?" Henry wanted to know. "What about Craig?"

"Craig is with Sierra." Vienna rested a hand on her heart, seemingly offended.

"And Tom is with me," Margo snapped.

"Not at the moment," Vienna said sweetly.

"You'd better put a leash on her," Margo told Henry. And then she turned and walked out of the room.

Henry expected Tom to leap up and follow his wife, but he took his time, swinging first his legs, then the rest of himself, off the bed. He picked up a grape that was still left on the silver tray and popped it into his mouth. "Thank you for a lovely evening," he said to Vienna.

"Thank *you*, Tom," Vienna said.

Tom waved and left the room. As he and Margo made their way down the hall, Henry and Vienna heard Margo say, "Was that supposed to be your way of punishing me?"

"It was my way of getting your attention," came Tom's

reply. "You're not mad because you think I'd have gone through with it. You know I wouldn't cheat on you."

"You have before," Margo accused.

"I was drunk. And you packed less heat back then. You're just mad now because I've made a point you don't know how to counter."

The last thing they heard Margo say was, "Isn't there a prohibition against lawyers arguing with regular people?" before Henry shut the door and turned to face his own double dealer.

"What's the matter, Vienna? Craig's not enough for you?"

"Craig, Craig, Craig, why are you constantly talking about Craig?"

"Well, why are you constantly draping yourself over him and laughing at his lame jokes and going swimming with him and noticing that his physique is so much better than mine?"

"He works out regularly. And his jokes can be most amusing," Vienna explained. "I thought, at first, that Craig might be able to lead us to Lucy. But obviously he is as much in the dark as Lucinda and we are. I flirted with him when I thought it might get us some information. When I realized that it would not, I moved on to other sources."

"Like Tom?"

"Precisely."

"Give it up, Vienna. You and Tommy Boy making fruit salad had nothing to do with our looking for Lucy and Johnny. What would Tom Hughes know about it?"

"Tom," Vienna said patiently, "is married to Margo. Margo has just spent the past year working to bring her brother to justice. This means she knows where he has been. She knows all the places where he has already looked for Lucy. This is knowledge that could be useful to us. But I could not very well ask Margo for it. She would have grown suspicious. She would want to know why we were interested. Tom, on the other hand, might also know where Craig has been. Perhaps Margo has confided in him. And if you had not come back unexpectedly like this, I might have known it by now, too."

"So you were ready to sleep with the guy—"

"Stop being so provincial, Henry. I was doing the same as you with Sierra. No more, no less."

"So you were jealous!" Henry might have jumped for joy, but he didn't think that would convey the right manly image at this time.

"No. Well," Vienna said, "not *very* jealous."

Henry threw his arms around Vienna. "I love you."

With Henry and Sierra's meeting time looming, Henry and Vienna called a truce.

Henry said, "If you promise not to seduce any more men without running it by me first, I promise to do the same."

"You mean you promise not to seduce any women?" Vienna clarified.

"That too, if you insist."

They also agreed to get jealous more often, even if there weren't any legitimate grounds to do so. It would just be another way of showing each other that they cared.

To that end, Vienna immediately went into the agreed-upon jealousy mode and refused to let Henry meet Sierra alone. After all, who knew what nefarious plans Sierra had for him? Vienna also pointed out that she could be useful on his mission. Unlike Henry, Vienna knew exactly which way was north, thanks to the arrangement of the constellations.

Even employing Vienna's expertise, however, they arrived a few minutes late for their rendezvous. The long-sought gazebo proved to be a hexagon-shaped glass enclosure tucked into a murky corner of the sprawling property. There definitely seemed to be a figure waiting inside, but frosted panes and ivy crawling up the sides made peering in difficult. Henry and Vienna split up, hoping for a peek. They figured that if this was some kind of ambush, forewarned was forearmed and all that.

"Do you see anything?" Henry hissed to Vienna.

"I think so," Vienna whispered back. "It is a woman who is waiting inside, I think. Long hair, brown, or maybe a dark auburn."

"Are you sure?"

"Well, I suppose it could be more ginger-colored or a golden red."

"That's not really important," Henry assured Vienna. "What's important is that long red hair means it definitely isn't Sierra."

"Unless she is wearing a wig," Vienna suggested. "Role-playing? Or a disguise to fool Craig. I wish I could see her face more clearly. Can you see her?"

Henry craned his neck. "I think so. Oh, no . . . I think she heard us. She's moving toward the door."

"No, she's not," Vienna said. "She's over here by the window."

"She's headed for the door. Get out of the way, get out of the way!"

"What are you talking about? She's not moving. I see her. She's not—"

The door opened. A woman with hair that wasn't exactly auburn or ginger—more of a classic red with a bit of warm chestnut blended in—stepped out and looked around, clearly following the sounds of their voices. There was nowhere for Vienna to hide.

And so she didn't bother. Vienna simply stood straight up and acted as if she had every right to be out at midnight, peering through strands of ivy into a secluded gazebo. In fact, Vienna's look suggested it was the interloper who had the explaining to do.

The redhead said, "I was expecting Henry Coleman."

Vienna did not so much as glance in Henry's direction, for fear that it would give his location away. She was being so valiant that Henry figured the least he could do was contribute to the effort. He stepped out of the shadows and announced, "I'm Henry Coleman."

In the great scheme of name declarations it wasn't exactly up there with "I'm Spartacus!" But Henry figured all heroes had to start somewhere.

The redhead nodded. "Sierra said you'd been told to come alone. Well, I guess it doesn't matter. Come in." She stepped aside and beckoned for Henry and Vienna to enter the gazebo, where they came face-to-face with another redhead, who, just like Vienna had described it, was, in fact, standing by the window.

The first redhead said, "I'm Frannie Hughes. This is Sabrina."

"You're Tom's sisters!" Vienna realized at once. "Tom did not tell us you were visiting here."

"Maybe you kept him too busy to chat," Henry couldn't help mumbling under his breath.

"Tom doesn't know," Frannie admitted. "We had him and Margo to dinner at my apartment earlier this evening, but we didn't tell him we'd be here tonight. Under the circumstances, it's better if he doesn't know what's going on."

"Tom also didn't tell us you were twins," Henry noted.

"We're not," Sabrina said.

Henry and Vienna silently took in the identical red hair, the huge brown eyes, and the smattering of freckles along two patrician noses.

Frannie explained, "We're actually cousins."

"Identical cousins." Henry finally felt like here was a deduction he was capable of making. "Like on *The Patty Duke Show*. Got it."

"Well, not exactly. We're also half-sisters."

Sitcoms had never prepared Henry for this. "Run that by me again?"

"Tom, Sabrina, and I have the same father."

"Dr. Bob."

"But we all have different mothers."

"Cousins," Vienna repeated. "So your mothers are sisters!"

"Were," Sabrina said. "Kim is my mother, but Frannie's mother was Kim's older sister, Jennifer. She's dead now."

"Kim's sister, Jennifer . . ." Henry felt like he needed to pull out a piece of paper and jot down a family tree. He clarified with Frannie, "That means your other half sister is Barbara Ryan. Which means Jennifer Munson was your niece. Which means her son, Johnny . . . never mind. We weren't talking about him."

Frannie said, "We know that Johnny is the reason you're here. Well, Johnny and Lucy both. Lucinda called Sierra to tell her, and Sierra told us."

Vienna told Henry, "So Sierra does know why we're here. That is why she invited us to stay." And then Vienna asked Frannie and Sabrina the obvious question. "Why would Sierra tell you?"

"It's rather complicated."

"More complicated than how you two are related?" Henry wondered.

"Not really."

"Then I think we'll be able to keep up. Why isn't Sierra here?" Henry went on. "She's the one who wanted to meet me."

"She couldn't risk it," Sabrina said. "Craig is always watching her."

"One more time: Why?"

"He thinks she knows where Lucy is."

"Does she?"

"No."

"Then why is he hanging around? And why is Sierra pretending that they're back together? Are they back together? I'm very confused," Henry confessed.

"Sierra wanted us to meet you so we could help you find Lucy."

"You know where Lucy is?"

"Yes," Frannie said.

"How wonderful," a male voice boomed from the doorway.

Craig Montgomery stepped out of the shadows, grinning broadly despite the presence of a very grim Sierra by his side. "Now you can enlighten us all."

7

Vienna glared at Sierra. "You set Henry up! You were never truly interested in meeting with him!"

"Well, of course," Craig drawled. "Think about this logically. You and I flirting is the result of two attractive people at their sexual peak occupying the same space at the same time. Sierra and a troll like Henry? It's farcical!"

"My Henry is no troll!"

"Thank you," Henry said. He looked at Sierra. "I don't get it. What's the point? You were just having a little fun? This is how you and Craig get your kicks?"

"Let me go," Sierra hissed as she wrenched her arm free, making everyone realize that Craig had been holding it, rather tightly, behind her back. She turned to Henry. "This isn't what I had in mind when I asked you to meet me."

Frannie said, "Sierra is telling the truth."

"Perhaps you'll find it inspirational and do the same," Craig said as he advanced on Frannie. "Where is Lucy hiding my son?"

"How does Frannie know?" Vienna asked.

Craig indicated Sierra. "Care to do the honors?"

"Bite me."

"Maybe later." Craig turned to Henry and Vienna and explained. "My ex-wife and her cohorts, The Wonder Twins here, have been in cahoots to keep me from my children. They didn't think I'd be smart enough to figure it out."

"You wouldn't have if my mother hadn't decided to take matters into her own hands by sending Henry and Vienna down here," Sierra fumed.

"I've always had a soft spot for Lucinda. How well I recall the days when, speaking of her hands, she couldn't keep them off me." Craig informed Henry and Vienna, "Lucinda and I had a brief fling in my younger days. Before I met Sierra. What can I say? Chemistry is chemistry. Right, Vienna?"

"You are a horrible, immoral man!" Vienna replied.

Sierra corrected, "You don't know him well enough to say that. But you are perceptive and you are right."

"Okay." Craig clapped his hands and rubbed them in anticipation. "Enough with the witty banter. Let's get down to business. Either Ms. Hughes: Where did you send my daughter?"

"Go to hell, Craig," Frannie snapped.

"Ladies, ladies, ladies . . ." He raised an eyebrow in Henry's direction. "Henry included—"

"My Henry is not a lady!" Vienna protested.

"Thank you," Henry said.

Craig continued, "Do I need to spell everything out for you? Very well. Follow along closely. If anyone wants to take notes, I brought a pad and pencil. Let's review: After taking my leave of lovely Oakdale—"

"Because you were wanted for attempted murder," Sabrina reminded him.

"—I did a brief tour of the Continent, sampled the delights of Asia, even poked my head into the Middle East for good measure, hoping to locate the crevice into which my daughter had wriggled herself and my son. Unfortunately, my beloved sister, Margo, apparently mighty peeved that people should think she actually showed a flash of family loyalty for a change, decided the best way to disprove that accusation would be to hound me from place to place. No sooner would I get settled in than up would pop Margo, extradition order in hand. It's what finally drove me back to Montega, and into Sierra's arms."

"Yeah," Henry asked Sierra, "how did that happen?"

Sierra looked grim. "He blackmailed me."

"I prefer the term 'persuasion.' With threats."

"Craig told me if I didn't give him amnesty in Montega, he would . . ." She exchanged a nervous look with Frannie and Sabrina. "He blackmailed me," she repeated.

"Oh, come now. Don't you want Henry and Vienna to hear the brilliance of my plan? They might learn something. You know how I love to enlighten young people." Craig explained, "Here's something I bet you didn't know about Montega. It gets seven hundred and fifty millimeters of rainfall a year, its major export is pears, it ranks number seventeen in education worldwide, and, oh yes, it breaks international law on a daily basis."

"Let it go, Craig," Sierra said. "They don't need to hear this."

"But I need to say it. What fun is it to commit heinous deeds if you can't boast about them to terrified captives? Are you unfamiliar with the Supervillain's Handbook?"

"Fine," Sabrina said. "Talk as much as you like. We don't have to listen."

"Oh, yes, you do." Craig blocked the door with his body so that neither Sabrina nor Frannie could reach the exit. "You two have a big part coming up in this tale. You wouldn't want to miss it."

"Unhand those women," Henry said, because it seemed to be the sort of thing a man in his position should say. Unfortunately, everyone—Vienna included—turned to give Henry such a puzzled look that he was left with no choice but to mutter, "Please?"

Craig ignored the entire outburst and went on. "It just so happens that international law frowns on countries handing out new identities to global criminals."

"They're not criminals," Sierra hissed through clenched teeth. "They're refugees. There is nothing criminal about helping people who've been chased out of their own country and are seeking refuge somewhere else."

"Actually, there is. Especially when the people in question are wanted criminals. And when the version of refuge you offer is Montegan passports giving them completely new identities."

"First of all, these wanted criminals, as you call them, are primarily political prisoners, freedom fighters and their families, who stood up against repressive governments and nearly got killed for it."

"You say semantics, I say semiotics, and yet you're still breaking international law," Craig stated firmly.

"And I didn't see you getting nearly as upset about the global injustice of it all back when you used your position as my husband to offer new passports and identities to real criminals—for a price. You disgust me!"

"I know. It's something I've managed to overcome and move on from."

Sierra announced to everyone, "Craig knew the only way I'd let him stay in Montega is if he forced me into it."

"Not true. I first tried to seduce you into it."

"Fat chance."

"Exactly why I switched tactics."

"He told me that unless I protected him from his well-deserved murder charge—"

"Attempted murder," Craig corrected. "Practically a misdemeanor in some places. And a lot less than what most of your poor refugees were accused of back home."

Sierra continued, "He would tell the world about Montega's underground railroad. If Craig blows our cover, it would put the lives of hundreds of people in danger. Frannie, Sabrina, and I have worked too long and too hard to let a personal vendetta shut us down. Craig also tried holding the resettlement program over my head when he thought it could lead him to Lucy and Johnny. But he was flat out of luck there. Lucy had a hunch he might try something like that. That's why she made sure I didn't know where she was going when she left Montega—that way, I couldn't betray her. To her own father. Even by accident."

"A good plan," Craig said. "I'd expect nothing less from my Lullaby. She's a smart girl. She gets that from me. I figured, even if you weren't involved, Lucy had to have had help from someone in Montega to get out of the country undetected. I had no idea who that might be, however. Up until tonight."

Craig turned to Frannie and Sabrina. He was smiling again.

"What's good for the goose," Craig said, "usually works on the pretty little goslings as well. Sierra was willing to pretend to have reunited with me—oh, the horror—in order to keep your exile pipeline flowing. How far are you two willing to go to protect it? Or should I put it in more personal terms? How far are you two willing to go to keep from being brought up on charges in front of an international tribunal?" Craig looked from one sister to the other. He wasn't smiling anymore. "Tell me where the hell you two sent my children, or I will blow this operation of yours wide open."

Craig left the gazebo first. He told Frannie and Sabrina he'd give them twenty-four hours to consider his offer.

The sisters took off soon after, whispering something to Sierra that neither Henry nor Vienna could hear. Which left just the three of them.

Sierra sighed. "My plan worked spectacularly well, wouldn't you say?"

"How did Craig find out?" Vienna asked.

"He was suspicions of you and Henry from the start and has been keeping an eye on you, but you know what, it doesn't matter. He forced me to come here and confront you all, and now he's dragged Frannie and Sabrina into his obsession. Lucy was right to take Johnny away from him. I am so proud of the stand she took. Even if it means I might never see her again." Sierra looked close to tears.

Henry wondered what to do. The only thing he could think of was to pat Sierra on the shoulder and mumble, "There, there."

Luckily, Vienna's sense of empathy was a bit more evolved than his own. She cooed, "You must miss your daughter very much."

"I do. It's funny, she's lived away from me since she was fifteen, so it isn't as if I've never been apart from her. But it's different when you know she's just a phone call or an email or even a plane ride away. When I don't even know where she is . . . it's like one of your limbs has gone missing. You don't think about your arms or your legs all the time. But you take for granted that, when you do, they'll be there. Same thing with your children. They're a part of you. It's impossible to imagine their being gone. That's what happened with my son, Bryant. After he died, I'd still catch myself thinking, 'Oh, that's so interesting. I should tell Bryant.' I miss him so much. But I'm not worried about him anymore. With Lucy, I miss her. But I'm also terrified that she might be suffering. She might need me, and I can't help her."

"We'll help her," Vienna said. And she looked at Henry expectantly.

"Sure," he said, having no idea what Vienna was thinking. "We'll help."

"We have to help Sierra," Vienna told Henry after they returned to their room.

"Uh, yeah, considering that you already promised we would."

"We cannot let Craig get away with this."

"I'm open to any and all suggestions."

"Let us go talk to Tom and Margo."

"Except for that one. Are you out of your mind, my little pepperkakor? After what you pulled with Tom tonight, you think Margo is going to want to chat with the two of us?"

"This is not about us. It's about Sierra and Lucy. For goodness' sake, Henry, Tom and I—it was nothing. You heard him. He knew we were just fooling. It was business. No reasonable person would take it seriously."

"I take a woman trying to seduce my husband very seriously," Margo said. "I'm funny that way."

Vienna and Henry had knocked on the Hugheses' door, politely at first. Then, in response to Margo's muffled, "Go away!" they'd identified themselves.

"It's Vienna."

"And Henry."

"Oh. In that case, go to hell."

When they'd indicated that they would not be doing so at this time, Margo had tromped over and flung the door open. She stood before them, dressed in sweats and an Oakdale PD sweatshirt, her arms raised. A palm on either side of the doorframe indicated how much she didn't want to let them in. Over Margo's shoulder, Henry could see an unmade four-poster bed. And Tom curled up uncomfortably on a sofa as far away from it as possible.

"What?" Margo wanted to know.

"Nothing," Henry yelped instinctively. "We were just leaving."

Vienna grabbed him by the arm before he could flee. "We need to talk to you. It is very serious."

Which is when Margo responded with her observation that she took women trying to seduce her husband seriously, as well.

"But we were being silly!" Vienna insisted.

"Am I laughing?"

In the corner to which he'd been banished, Tom yawned and stretched. "Vienna," he said. "This isn't a good time."

"It cannot wait. We must come in." She pushed her way past Margo, who seemed so shocked by the impudence that she somehow forgot to slap Vienna silly.

Henry took advantage of the lull in action to follow Vienna inside. He shrugged apologetically at Margo and repeated, "We must come in."

"Okay, look, Vienna." Margo slammed the door shut. "I get it. It was all a goof. Ha, ha, ha, how very French farce of you, how very uptight American of me. You didn't mean anything by it. You were kidding, Tom was kidding."

"Oh, I was not kidding." Vienna put on her most serious face.

"You weren't?" For a moment, Tom seemed pleased by her declaration; then Margo glared at him, and he went back to chastened. When Margo looked away, a little bit of the expression returned to his face.

"I was very serious about trying to discover what Tom knew about where Craig had been looking for Lucy."

Tom looked a lot less pleased and a lot more confused now.

Henry tried to help by explaining, "Vienna had this idea that it might help us to track down Lucy if we knew where Craig had already looked for her."

Tom asked, "And you thought I'd know?"

"Since when are you two looking for Lucy?" Margo demanded.

Henry told Tom, "Vienna's theory was that Margo might have told you. And that the information might be easier to pry out of you than out of her." Henry told Margo, "We're not looking for Lucy. What prompts you to ask?"

"Cut the crap, Henry."

"Yes, ma'am, cutting the crap, right away." He looked at Vienna, shrugged, and admitted, "Lucinda hired us. That's why we're here. Both she and Sierra have lost touch with Lucy."

"I knew it," Margo said. "Spas, my ass."

"We need your help," Vienna said.

"You picked a fine way of buttering me up."

"Craig is blackmailing Sierra. That is why she is pretending to be back together with him, and that is why she will not let you arrest him and take him back to Oakdale," Vienna explained.

"Well, I'm glad to hear Sierra hasn't completely lost her mind, at least."

"Also, he is blackmailing Tom's sisters, Frannie and Sabrina."

"Frannie and Sabrina?" Tom looked befuddled. "We just saw them for dinner a couple of hours ago. What do they have to do with any of this?"

Henry quickly filled them in on the role both Ms. Hugheses were playing in Sierra's humanitarian efforts. And how Craig was threatening to punish them for it.

"That son of a bitch," Margo said. "Just when I thought he couldn't sink any lower."

"You can stop him," Vienna said.

"Sure. If Sierra agrees, I can have him on the next plane back to the States. But if he's blackmailing her, that's hardly going to help the situation."

"There is another way," Vienna said. "You can arrange to have the charges against him dropped. You can tell the district attorney that your evidence is flawed and there is not enough of it to issue a warrant. This is something you have the authority to do, is it not?"

"In theory. But what good would it do? The point is to lock Craig up and throw away the key."

"No. Right now, the point is to free Sierra, Frannie, and Sabrina from him. You are the only one who can do that." Vienna laid it all out. "You can have the charges against Craig dropped in exchange for him handing over the evidence that he has against Sierra, Sabrina, and Frannie."

"No," Margo said. "No, no, no. Everyone already thinks I let him get away scot-free. This will just prove that I gave my brother preferential treatment. Paul Ryan will be screaming for my head before the plane touches down in Oakdale."

"But," Vienna tried to reason, "if you cannot bring him back to Oakdale anyway, and if people are already saying those things about you, then why not do it? It will not change anything."

"And it's to save Frannie and Sabrina," Tom said quietly. "They're family."

"So you want me to put my professional reputation on the line in order to protect your family." Margo looked from Tom to Vienna and back again. "You two have a heck of a way of asking for favors."

Tom said, "Not that I'm keeping score or anything, but I've pulled your sister Katie out of more legal jams than everyone in this room has fingers and toes." A quick digit count proved he wasn't exaggerating. "Frannie and Sabrina are your family, too. And it is your brother who's causing all the trouble."

"Please, Margo," Vienna said. "It is the right thing to do."

Margo sighed. "I'll think about it. Now, I've mentioned this before: Get the hell out of my room."

"Get the hell out of my room, Craig," Sierra told her ex-husband. The bedroom she was referring to was not the one they'd shared all the years they were married. After she and Craig broke up, Sierra had moved to an entirely different wing of the mansion, hoping to keep the bad memories—as well as the good ones—at bay. "The charade is over. Everyone knows we're not actually back together. Which probably means they're reconsidering those plans to have me committed and deprogrammed. In any case, you've got no excuse for being here anymore."

"How about me wanting to see my wife?"

"I'm not your wife anymore, either."

"But you were. Not just once. Twice."

"Youthful indiscretion. Both times. Now go!" But instead of turning to face the door, Craig settled down on a chair directly across from where Sierra was standing by the window.

He asked her, "How in the world did you and I get here, Sierra?"

"Well, I was quietly living my life, fulfilling my duties as a member of the Montegan parliament, trying to get over the death of my husband whom you so conveniently managed to get killed—"

"That was an accident."

"—and deal with the fact that your selfish actions drove my last living child underground, when you showed up one day and threatened to destroy everything I'd worked my entire life to build."

He paused. "It didn't have to be that way."

"That's right. You could have left me alone."

"Or you could have taken my side. For once. For a change."

Sierra shook her head. "Lay off it, Craig. I took your side plenty of times. I defended you to the world even when the things you did were indefensible. When people told me the kinds of things you'd done before I met you, I was the one standing on the rooftops, shouting, 'Oh, no. Not Craig. He's changed. He's a good man now.' "

"I was. Or at least I tried to be a good man. For you."

"Save it." Instead of looking at Craig as she spoke, Sierra chose to address a spot to the side of him, ensuring that they never made eye contact. Ensuring that he couldn't get to her. "I know I bought this act once before, but the statute of limitations has run out." In a deliberately jovial tone, she added, "By the way, you may be interested to know that I'm not blaming you for my blindness. There are always two people in every con. The one who does the fooling, and the one who wants to be fooled. I realize I wanted to believe that you'd turned over a new leaf. I wanted to believe that I was the woman who'd inspired it. I was flattered. And I played right into your hands."

Craig looked at her sadly. "Is that what you honestly think? That every good, positive memory we ever made together was part of some cynical plot on my part?"

Sierra wavered, though she still refused to meet his gaze. "Maybe not all of them . . . But I can't help it, Craig. When I look back now, I can't see the past clearly. It's like I have these pictures of when we were happy, but every time I look at the man you used to be, the man you became steps in the way and blocks my view."

"I did that?" Craig asked. "I didn't only mess up our present, I ruined our past for you, too?"

"Yes."

"So there's nothing good left of us?"

"Lucy was the last part of it. Your little Lullaby. And you've destroyed her, too."

"Damn it, Sierra!"

"I'm sorry. I know I'm being cruel. But, to be honest, you haven't exactly given me a reason not to be."

"When did I become this monster in your eyes?"

"I don't know, Craig. Maybe it was when you had Lucy kidnapped, then planted evidence to implicate my husband. Or maybe it was when your insane plan got Alan shot trying to rescue our daughter."

"I was afraid I was losing her," Craig said. "Lucy isn't just your last surviving child. At the time, she was mine, as well. I wanted my Lullaby back. I wanted to be her hero. Just one more time. Like it was when she was a little girl."

"So you had her kidnapped and almost killed."

"You've never made a bad decision, Sierra?" Craig challenged. "You never, say, impulsively married a wife-beating nutcase who practically kept you prisoner while still finding time to entertain a cadre of mistresses on the side?"

"Don't compare my marriage to Tonio with what you did to Lucy. Marrying him was a mistake. But it was a mistake that affected only me. I didn't drag other people into my screwups."

"How about me? When you married Tonio, you dumped me. You broke my heart. That doesn't count as dragging other people into your screwups?"

"What do you want, Craig?" Sierra demanded. "What's the point of this trip down memory lane? You wanted to remind me that there was a time when we were on the same side? Fine, consider me reminded. Yes, there was a time when I believed that you were better than Tonio. It still doesn't change anything."

"I thought more than anyone, you would understand why I've done the things I've done."

"Oh, I do understand. Someone—your own daughter!— has finally outsmarted the great Craig Montgomery. And you can't stand it."

"That's not what I meant. I thought you would understand why it's so important for me to get Johnny back. He's my son, Sierra. My only living son. You can hate me all you like. You can pretend that you never loved me and we were never happy together and that every word you ever heard coming out of my mouth was a lie and a con."

"That's not what I said. You're twisting my words."

"But don't you dare insinuate that I didn't love Bryant. Don't you dare suggest that it didn't kill me to see him lying on a slab in the morgue—"

"Stop it!"

"No! Our son—our idiosyncratic, funny, loving, lovable son—is dead. He's gone. Because of a dimly lit road and a thoughtlessly unfastened seat belt and a cell phone that rang at the wrong time. We lost Bryant for absolutely no good reason. Is it so wrong of me to want to fill a little bit of the gaping hole he left behind with the son I do have left?"

Sierra was trying her best not to cry. Because if she cried, she might not be able to get the next words out. And it was imperative that she get them out. Clearly and calmly. "It is wrong, Craig. You can't replace Bryant with Johnny."

"I can try."

"You shouldn't. It isn't fair to Johnny, for one thing."

"It isn't fair for a boy to be raised by his own father? A father who never even got the chance to show how good a parent I could be before Johnny was taken away from me? A father who wants to love him and guide him so that maybe—maybe—he won't make the same mistakes I have? The same mistakes that Bryant made? Is it so wrong for me to want to protect him?"

"This isn't about Johnny. You're not concerned with what's best for him. This is about what's best for you. What you want."

"I want what you took away from me!" Craig exploded.

Sierra startled. Craig's standard facial expression tended to run the gamut from cocky to smug. Neither of those allowed for any genuine emotions to peek through the façade. To be honest, Sierra preferred it that way. A Craig not in control was a Craig not wearing his mask of invulnerability. And a vulnerable Craig was a little too much like the man she'd once loved. A little too much like the man she was seeing now.

"I want a family!" he cried out, springing out of his chair and approached Sierra. "I want one person—just one, I'm not being greedy—who doesn't think that I'm evil personified. I want to come home and I want someone to rush to greet me so they can tell me about their day. I want to wake up in the morning with something to look forward to, instead of with a sense of dread. I want to be somebody's hero. I want to be somebody's whole world. I want to feel like if I disappeared, someone, anyone, would miss me. You have that. Hell, even Paul Ryan has that. Everybody has it. Why shouldn't I?"

"Because . . . Craig . . ." Sierra struggled to find the right words. Strangely, for once, she thought Craig might actually listen. "You hold on so tightly to the people you care about that it suffocates them. You try to force us into loving you, instead of just letting it happen. You drive people away."

"They don't understand," Craig mumbled. "I thought you would, but you don't."

"I do. I know how badly you need to be loved. But the way you go about it—"

"I thought you might want to help me. I know you miss Lucy, too. Why don't you want to help me bring her home?"

"Because Lucy was right to take Johnny away. The man you've become—you shouldn't be raising that little boy."

Barely an arm's length away from Sierra, Craig froze in his tracks. With the slightest flick of an eyebrow, the twitch of a muscle, the vulnerability was gone. So was the smug cockiness. In its place was a pure, cold, unforgiving anger, the likes of which Sierra wasn't sure she'd ever seen from him before.

"You're wrong," he told Sierra. "You're all wrong. I'm going to get my son back. And to hell with all of you."

8

The next morning, it was Margo's turn to bang on Henry and Vienna's door and wake them out of a sound sleep. When they didn't answer fast enough, she barged in and pulled back the covers. Henry slept in the nude.

Margo did not appear to care. Or notice. Or be impressed.

"I'll do it," she said. "I'll have the murder charges against Craig dropped in exchange for the info he's got on Sierra, Frannie, and Sabrina. But only if I get to be the one to tell my brother the good news."

Henry and Vienna were happy to let her. Their only request was that they'd get to watch. And that the grand announcement would take place in the drawing room. Henry had always wanted to attend a mystery's denouement in a drawing room, except he'd never known anyone who'd had a drawing room. Henry considered himself very lucky that Sierra's wouldn't go to waste, for he might otherwise have felt compelled to commit a crime just so they could all have gathered in it.

Margo offered Craig the deal in front of Sierra, Henry, and Vienna. Grudgingly, she told him her terms for having all the charges against him dismissed. Craig listened patiently, not saying a word. He stared hard at Margo and Sierra. Henry and Vienna, he ignored completely.

After Margo laid out the conditions, he merely said, "Give me until dinnertime to get everything together." He was halfway out the door before he turned to expressionlessly tell Margo, "I love you too, sis."

She didn't say anything. She didn't appear to have heard. But the moment Craig left, Margo rushed out of the room as well, struggling valiantly to hold back the tears.

Approximately eight hours later, it was Craig who reconvened them all in the drawing room with the announcement that he was ready to deal. Craig handed Sierra a stack of documents, mostly original IDs, side-by-side with copies of newly issued Montegan passports, all stolen from her personal records as a form of insurance—and potential extortion—at the time of Craig and Sierra's divorce.

"It's all there," he assured her. "But I wouldn't expect you to take me at my word, so go ahead and check."

"Oh, I will," Sierra swore.

It wasn't until midnight that she, along with some fax and internet confirmation from Frannie and Sabrina, was able to authenticate each document and make sure that nothing else was missing from their archives. While the ringing and whirling and "You've got mail"-ing was going on around them, Henry passed the time by roping the household staff into a poker game employing several different currencies "to make things interesting." At the end of it, Henry believed he was ahead, though a helpful calculation of the Montegan exchange rate by the butler suggested that might not exactly be the case. Henry resolved to ascribe the miscommunication to a language barrier—the butler spoke such excellent English that Henry was having trouble keeping up—and declared victory nonetheless. Henry also declined to inquire as to why the rest of the staff insisted on smirking as they collected their winnings.

Meanwhile, Vienna declined to take part in even so much as a game of hearts. She preferred to mill aimlessly about the first-floor rooms, pausing periodically to check out the framed portraits on the walls, many of which featured either paintings or photographs of Lucy and Bryant Montgomery at various ages. There they were sailing in the summer. There they were skiing in the winter. There was a preteen Lucy winning her first blue ribbon at a horse show, and there was Bryant at six, trying to look serious as he posed behind a chessboard while his eyes were obviously peeking off elsewhere. There were both kids at their baptisms. There they were at their high-school graduations. And there Craig and Sierra were, the proud parents, arms around their accomplished, golden-haired offspring, always beaming and smiling at the kids even when it was obvious that relations between the two of them were, at best, strained. Of course, Vienna pretended that she was no more interested in the family pictures than she was in the other decorative artwork hung about the place. And, of course, Henry pretended to believe her.

Finally, an exhausted Sierra hung up the phone and, more resigned than actually pleased, gave Margo the confirmation that Craig had indeed fulfilled his part of the bargain. All of his evidence against her, Sabrina, Frannie, and, most importantly, their refugee clients was accounted for. An equally exhausted and resigned Margo, with a sigh and a most impressive presentation of profanity, then handed Craig freshly faxed papers testifying that the charges against him for Paul Ryan's attempted murder had been dropped. And she told him she was ashamed to be related to him.

"Oh, but you won't be when you hear what a clever boy I've been," Craig assured Margo. "Thanks to you, I'm now free to leave Montega and travel the world. Which is good. There's just so much tropical paradise a man can take before he grows stir-crazy. I know Sierra will miss me—"

"Oh, cut it out, Craig," Sierra admonished. "Show some class, for once."

"But a man's got to do what a man's got to do." He turned to Henry and Vienna, acknowledging their presence for the first time. "I understand it is you I have to thank. You've made it possible for me to resume my hunt for Lucy and Johnny."

Gulps, as a rule, were barely audible sounds. But when four people performed them simultaneously, the effect was hard to ignore.

"Isn't it grand?" Craig waved his arms theatrically. "Now that I know all three of us are on the same trail, I can simply sit back, relax, and wait for your expert sleuthing skills to lead me straight to my long-lost children. After all, I've got nothing stopping me anymore."

It did not take Henry and Vienna long to realize that Craig Montgomery was obviously an acolyte of the "show, don't tell" school of making his point.

The following morning, after waking up extra early for the chance to wave good-bye to a departing and sullen Tom and Margo, Craig gleefully popped in on Henry and Vienna. While Henry was having an in-depth discussion with the downstairs maid about how exactly he preferred his shoes to be shined, Craig inquired, "So, any good leads on Lucy yet? You don't mind if I listen in, do you? Never know when a useful piece of information might pop up."

When he saw Henry pick up the phone, Craig offered, "If you're making plane reservations back to Oakdale, make sure to book me a seat on the same flight. Much more efficient that way, don't you think?"

"Okay," Henry said, slamming down the receiver. "I get it. You're rubbing in the fact that Vienna and I have made it possible for you to continue your *Les Misérables*, Inspector Javert hunt for Lucy and Johnny."

"Don't forget the part where I don't even have to do the heavy lifting anymore. I'll just follow you and the lovely Vienna, and reap the rewards of your labor."

"Don't you think this approach would work better if you were a tad more subtle?"

"This is me being subtle."

"Wouldn't you have had more of an advantage if you hadn't told Vienna and me you intended to follow us?"

"Oh, I suppose. But it wouldn't have been as much fun. You should see your body language right now. Frustration, defeat, impotence—"

"Hey, hey, hey. No on the impotence."

"I meant strictly professionally, of course." Craig smiled. "You all tried to outsmart me, and it blew up in your faces. What kind of man would I be if I didn't take full advantage of the opportunities to mock you?"

"Not Craig Montgomery, that's for sure."

"At your service!"

Safe in the bosom of their guest room and, well, Vienna's ample bosom, Henry griped, "We can't let Craig get away with this. He's making fools of all of us."

"We deserve it. I was so concerned over what he was doing to Sierra, I did not think through the consequences of Margo dropping the charges. But at least he no longer has leverage over Frannie and Sabrina. They know where Lucy is and were ready to confide in us before Craig appeared."

"Good point, but we can't let him keep following us. We might lead him straight to Lucy and Johnny. Which is the exact opposite of what Lucinda wanted. We've got to lose him."

"No," Vienna said. "We have got to catch him."

Twenty-four hours later, while adjusting the pillbox hat and veil that matched his pink Chanel suit and pumps, Henry wondered out loud, "Why is it whenever any of the women in my life have a plan, I end up dressed in drag by the end of it?"

"Because you make a most hideous woman, darling." Vienna, dressed in an identical ensemble, tugged on the veil so that it covered most of Henry's face. "It makes the rest of us feel better about ourselves."

"I don't even think you have a plan," Henry said. "I think you just want to have a little fun at my expense."

"Oh, I have a plan," Vienna reassured him.

The next day, Vienna, dressed in her pink Chanel suit and veiled pillbox hat, and Henry, wearing crisp linen slacks and a white shirt, wheeled their respective travel bags into the library to say good-bye to Sierra and thank her for her hospitality. Sierra assured them that they were welcome any time. Perhaps the next time they came, they could honestly take advantage of her country's world-class spas. She offered them her driver for the ride to the airport. Henry and Vienna gratefully accepted.

They loaded their luggage into the trunk and climbed into the back. They asked their chauffeur to drive slowly. They didn't want Craig, following along two car lengths behind them in his own vehicle, to lose their trail.

Halfway to the airport, Henry and Vienna asked their driver to speed up in order to catch the fading yellow light. They made it through the intersection just in time to leave Craig stranded on the other side. And then, in a completely unexpected development, two uniformed Montegan policemen popped out of nowhere, blowing their whistles and setting up a roadblock. They told all the drivers who were still waiting to cross that they would have to turn around and use alternative routes.

When Henry hung up his cell phone after complimenting Sierra on her marvelous local police force, he mused to Vienna, "It's good to be an ex-president."

Once at the airport, Henry and Vienna split up. She went to the nearest counter and purchased two tickets to Oakdale, U.S.A. Meanwhile, Henry retreated to the men's bathroom and proceeded to pull out an extra-large pink Chanel suit from his traveling case. Though safe in a stall for now, he did wonder how he'd explain himself when it was time to make his grand exit.

Having lived in Montega with Sierra for over a decade, Craig prided himself on being well-versed in the country's customs, climate, cuisine, and curses. But apparently, on that latter score, he was woefully behind the natives, who, during his pursuit of Henry and Vienna, managed to teach him all sorts of new and colorful expressions. First, the cops refused to accept Craig's logic that it would hardly bring about the end of the world if they allowed just one more car to cross before erecting their roadblock. And then it was the ultrasensitive citizenry, who took disproportionate offense to Craig's using their backyards as shortcuts to try and make it to the airport on time.

He got there too late to catch Henry and Vienna, but he figured their plane couldn't have taken off yet. He was only fifteen or so minutes behind them, after all.

Craig dropped his car in a no parking zone right in front of the entrance—learning even more new colorful Montegan expressions along the way—and hustled inside. He ran up to the first counter; knowing that no airline employee in this day and age would give another passenger's confidential destination or ticket information, he pleaded, "My wife, her name is Vienna Hyatt, she was wearing a pink Chanel suit and matching hat. I was supposed to meet her here. I'm late. Which way did she go?"

Craig figured that once he saw the flight number at the departure gate where she was waiting, he'd purchase a ticket for the same flight. One of the best things about living in the twenty-first century was that the media had convinced everyone men were stupid and helpless. So no one was surprised when a man acted all flustered and confused. Especially in comparison to his obviously wiser and more capable wife.

The check-in clerk pointed left. "That way, sir."

Craig took off. He scanned all the waiting areas in the

direction in which she'd pointed, but he couldn't locate Vienna. He grabbed a passing skycap and repeated, less winded this time, "Have you seen a woman wearing a pink Chanel suit and hat? My wife. I was supposed to meet her, but I forgot what gate."

"Where are the two of you heading?"

"I don't know," Craig said. The skycap raised a suspicious eyebrow. Craig improvised, "It's supposed to be a surprise. We like to plan these little challenges for each other. Keeps the marriage fresh, you know what I mean?"

"No."

"Have you seen her?" Craig asked.

"That way," the skycap said. And pointed right.

Craig cursed the check-in clerk and ran to the other side of the airport.

No Vienna there, either.

He stopped a cleaning woman and rolled out the same story again, this time throwing in the detail about mystery keeping their marriage fresh before she even asked.

"That way," she said and pointed forward, down a completely new hallway.

Craig employed some of his newly learned curse words, earning a look of disgust from the cleaning lady, and realized that his only option was to check out the departure gates he couldn't see from the public areas. But the only way he could do that was to go through security. And the only way to do that was to buy a ticket.

He purchased one to Oakdale, inadvertently stumbling on a bit of luck when the check-in clerk, while punching the buttons to print out his ticket, told him, "You'd better hurry if you want to catch up to your wife. That flight leaves in twenty minutes."

So they were headed to Oakdale! Craig practically did a little dance in place.

Stupid of Henry and Vienna, thinking they could out-smart him.

He pushed his way through security, infuriating several families with small children—that's what they got for at-tempting travel with the toddler set; was it Craig's fault they were weighed down with car seats and strollers?—as well as the Rent-A-Cop who insisted that Craig take off his shoes to pass through the metal detector.

Finally, however, Craig arrived at the gate. In a second stroke of luck, the flight had been delayed for half an hour, which meant they hadn't even started boarding yet.

Everything was going Craig's way. Except that there was no sign of Vienna or Henry.

Craig checked the adjoining waiting areas, hoping they'd merely chosen to sit in a less crowded location. He popped his head into the cafes, though Craig had a hard time imag-ining either of them chowing down on fast food judging by how Henry had slurped up the five-star cuisine at Sierra's place. Nothing. Where the hell were they?

"Excuse me," Craig asked the woman selling magazines and candy closest to the Oakdale departure gate. "Have you seen my wife? She's wearing a pink Chanel suit."

The woman nodded. "Over there. Buenos Aires depar-ture gate."

So that was their plan. Craig had to hand it to them. Vienna and Henry weren't complete amateurs, after all.

Obviously they'd purchased tickets to Buenos Aires earlier, then bought ones to Oakdale just that day, in order to throw Craig off the scent. They'd used the Oakdale ones to pass through security, then pulled out the backups once they were inside. Clever. Just not clever enough.

Craig craned his neck around the corner. He surveyed the waiting passengers. "I don't see her there now," he said.

The woman shrugged.

Needing confirmation that Vienna and Henry were indeed headed for Argentina, Craig questioned a waitress at the cafe, asking if she too had seen them enter the area designated for Buenos Aires. The waitress confirmed that she had noticed a beautiful woman wearing a pink Chanel suit, but that woman had been waiting over by the Paris, France, gate. To make matters worse, the guy who drove the luggage cart had last spotted her in the Tokyo, Japan, departure area. And then a little boy who overheard Craig asking insisted he saw a pretty lady in a pink suit next to the sign that said San Jose.

"California or Costa Rica?" Craig asked.

"I dunno." The boy shrugged.

Craig didn't know what to think, except that, for a small country, Montega had a huge international airport. He was running out of time and had to make a decision quickly. Seeing that the Buenos Aires flight was the next scheduled departure—and the only one that had already started boarding—Craig decided to gamble that he'd missed seeing Henry and Vienna get on board. It was the only logical explanation.

Vienna couldn't have disappeared into thin air any more than she could have been waiting in four different areas at the same time. Craig pushed his way back out through security and exchanged his Oakdale ticket for one to Buenos Aires.

"But I thought you and your wife . . . ," the clerk began.

"We love being spontaneous," Craig snarled. He grabbed his ticket and ran like hell to make the flight.

Only once he was irrevocably on board, the doors safely closed and the 747 cruising at altitude, did Vienna, Henry, Frannie, and Sabrina all step out of their respective hiding places, each of them wearing an identical pink Chanel suit with matching hat.

"To Vienna!" Back at the compound, Sierra proposed a champagne toast. "You're a genius."

"My genius," Henry cooed as they clicked glasses.

"Most important question," Frannie asked. "Do we get to keep the suits?"

"Yes!" Sierra crowed. "Absolutely. A souvenir of our triumph over Craig. They cost a fortune. And they were worth every penny."

"To Sierra!" they happily toasted this time.

Sierra looked at Frannie and Sabrina. "I never got the chance before now to thank you both for what you did for Lucy. I am so grateful she had you to turn to. I only wish I could have been the one to help her."

"Lucy understood," Sabrina reassured her. "It was her idea for us not to tell you where she'd gone. It was for your protection as well as hers."

"Well, thank you, in any case. Thank you, Sabrina, thank you, Frannie, thank you, Vienna, thank you, Henry. You're all the answer to a mother's prayers."

Vienna said, "Unfortunately, once Craig figures out that we have sent him on a wild greylag—"

"That would be goose, for the rest of us," Henry interrupted.

"—chase, he is going to go back to hunting for Lucy. She and Johnny are not safe. It would be better if Henry and I found her first."

Frannie agreed. "The only problem is, we're not sure where she is."

"I thought you two arranged to get her out of the country," Sierra said.

"We did. We issued her and Johnny new passports with new identities. She is traveling under the name Cindy Bryant. Cindy, a nickname from her full name, Lucinda Marie. And Bryant for—"

"Her brother," Sierra said softly.

"Lucy picked it herself. They are legally Cindy and Dustin Bryant now. Lucy said Dustin is Johnny's middle name."

Henry nodded. He explained for the women's benefit, "After his stepfather, Dusty Donovan. Jennifer married Dusty before she died. She wanted him to be the one to raise Johnny. But Craig sued for custody and won."

"Dusty?" Vienna asked. "The same Dusty whom Lucy was dating when Craig had her kidnapped?"

"Oakdale is a very small town," Henry explained. "You'd be amazed by how many people do all their dating exclusively in the same family. Well, obviously, not within their own family. Well, maybe in the case of the Snyders. Never mind. You know what I mean."

"So Lucy is playing mother to the adopted son of a man she once loved, who married the woman who had a child with Lucy's father?"

"It's a very, very small town," Henry repeated.

Vienna asked Frannie and Sabrina, "Where did Lucy and Johnny travel on their new passports?"

"Sweden," Sabrina said.

"Sweden!" Vienna's eyes lit up. Then dimmed briefly. "Are you sure you do not mean Switzerland?"

Sabrina looked at Vienna oddly. "Why would I confuse Sweden and Switzerland? I was raised in England. I assure you, I am well aware of the difference."

Now it was Henry's turn to ponder an unusual family tree. "Kim and Bob Hughes are your parents, but you grew up in England?"

"Yes."

"How did that happen?"

"Well, you see, Bob was still married to Frannie's mother, Jennifer, when Kim became pregnant. Frannie and I were born on the same day—"

"On the same day?" Henry yelped. "Are you kidding me? Saintly Dr. Bob?"

"But Kim was told that her baby was a boy, and that he was stillborn. A hospital administrator kidnapped me and placed me with an adoptive family, the Fullertons. They died when I was a little girl, and I was raised in England."

"Dr. Bob?" Henry repeated. "Doing two sisters at the same time? Two babies born on the same day?"

Frannie said, "Get over it, Henry. The rest of us did a long time ago."

Henry nodded his head and pretended to be locking his lips and throwing away the key. But all he could think was, "Dr. Bob used to be a player!"

"Where in Sweden did you send Lucy?" Vienna asked excitedly. "My family is there, not to mention many well-connected friends. Tell us where we should look, and we will get started right away."

"That's the problem," Frannie said. "We've lost track of Lucy."

Sabrina explained, "After we set up a refugee's false identity, we have to move him or her out of Montega. We can only take on their upkeep for so long before we have to make room for others who need our help. So we look for jobs in other countries that hire overseas workers. America, for instance, always needs H-1B visa candidates in the fields of computer programming, architecture, engineering, mathematics, education—"

"And fashion models," Vienna said.

"That's right," Sabrina exclaimed. "How in the world did you know H-1B visas applied to fashion models?"

"Doesn't everyone?"

Frannie said, "With Lucy's medical background, she would have made a great candidate, but she didn't want to return to America, not even under another name. There are other countries desperate for doctors that would have given her a visa in an instant, but since her degree is in the name of Lucinda Marie Montgomery, Lucy couldn't do that, either. Finally we located the perfect job for her in Sweden.

A company called Lester Keyes Enterprises. They needed a marketing person with native English language skills and a working knowledge of medical equipment and pharmaceuticals. It was tailor-made for Lucy. We put her and Johnny on a plane and we know that they arrived safely, because we checked with the airline. But Lucy never showed up for work. She never checked in at the apartment she'd rented ahead of time. It's as if she and Johnny disembarked from the plane, then fell off the face of the earth."

Sabrina turned to Sierra. "I'm sorry we didn't tell you before. But we were honoring Lucy's wishes."

"I understand. It's good that you didn't. Honestly, if I'd known, I would have been so worried. And then Craig might have picked up on my desperation and used it against me. Who knows, he might even have convinced me to work with him to find our daughter. He does know how to push all my buttons."

"Do not worry, Sierra," Vienna said. "We will find Lucy. This is a stroke of luck, Lucy's trail leading to Sweden. There, we will have a major advantage over Craig. I will mobilize my family and my friends. I will do everything I can. Henry and I will bring your Lucy home."

Their flight from Montega to Stockholm required a connection at Heathrow Airport. With six hours to kill and no desire to pursue the topic his love had been beating to death for the first leg of their journey, Henry suggested they hop in a taxi and take in the sights. Unfortunately, not even the

Tower of London with its display of crown jewels could keep Vienna from going on and on about how wonderful and serendipitous it was that their work was now taking them to Sweden, of all places. "You'll be able to see my home, Henry! You can meet my parents and see where I grew up and taste pepperkakor the way it really should be made, with fresh ginger and cloves and real butter—not that watery American substance. And we can take walks in the snow and go tobogganing, and oh, how you will love it!"

Henry smiled. He nodded his head. He oohed and aahed perfunctorily over the sparkling jewels.

But inside, all he could think of were three little words.

"Meet my parents . . ."

PART TWO

SWEDEN

9

"We still have some cash left from the ten thousand dollars advance Lucinda gave us." Henry said. "We can stay in a hotel. There's no reason for us to bunk with your folks. We'll probably just be in the way."

Vienna snuggled her shoulders into the mink-lined backseat of her parents' limousine and signaled the driver through the rearview mirror that he should pay no attention. "No one is ever in the way with family."

"Ha," Henry said.

She looked at him quizzically. "What does that mean?"

"It means, ha," he explained helpfully.

"You invited your little sister, Maddie, to live with you so she could finish high school," Vienna reminded him.

"And she was in the way."

"It will be wonderful, you will see."

"Harrumph," Henry said.

"What does that mean?"

"It means, harrumph."

"And it is most logical, too. Lester Keyes Enterprises is

located just one town over from where I grew up. We can combine business with pleasure."

"You have an interesting definition of the word pleasure." Henry stared out the window, pretending to be enchanted by the passing scenery. Though how one was supposed to be enchanted by snow, snow, more snow, and, oh, look, to break the monotony of only snow, a snow*bank*, he hadn't quite figured out yet.

"My parents are dying to meet you. I have told them everything about you."

"Everything?" Henry yelped.

"Everything," Vienna insisted. "We are very close."

"Stop the car, Sven," Henry called to the chauffeur. "I want to get out."

"You Americans. Why do you assume everyone in Sweden is named Sven? It is very ethnocentric and insulting."

"Sorry," Henry conceded. "What's your name?" he asked the driver.

"Sven," he said.

Vienna shrugged. "It is still insulting."

"All the more reason I can't be trusted around your parents. I could set off some international incident. I'll make them hate Americans. Presumably even more than they already do. Our poor, put-upon little country can't afford that right now."

"My parents love Americans."

"Well, thank God for small favors, I guess."

"It is the men in my life that they are usually not terribly fond of."

"Now you tell me?"

"They are very protective of me. I am their only daughter. They never believe that the gentlemen I date are worthy of me."

"And you've dated royalty! How the hell am I supposed to measure up?"

"Since I was a young girl blooming into womanhood, my parents have held the opinion that the men I choose to see are simply dazzled by my beauty to the exclusion of all else. That they merely wish for me to be an ornament on their arms. That they do not care for the real me, for my feelings or my desires."

"You discuss your desires with your parents?"

"We are very close," Vienna repeated.

"To be honest, your folks were on to something. Those guys you palled around with before me really were after one thing. Not that there's anything wrong with that one thing. I, personally, am a big fan of that one thing. But, periodically, it's good to have another thing, perhaps even as many as three things going on in a relationship."

"My boyfriends and I had a great many things in common."

"That's true. For instance, you and Grey Gerard both loved shiny, expensive objects. You and the prince of Leonia both loved shiny, expensive objects. Heck, you and I both love shiny, expensive objects. Only difference is those fellows could afford to give them to you. I can't."

"I do not care about such things."

"Really?"

"Well, not anymore. Not very much. Not very often."

"Ah-ha!"

"Meeting you taught me the error of my ways. Once I always chased after the money, the jewelry, the glamour, the excitement, the stimulation. But now I have you."

"Is this like Billy Joel singing, 'I don't want gorgeous, I don't want clever, I just want you'? Because I got to tell you, Vienna, you're not boosting the ol' ego, here."

"You do not understand, Henry. I grew up in the most wonderful home on earth, in the most wonderful country on earth, with the most wonderful parents on earth. But there was still great sorrow in my childhood."

"Was it the lack of a most wonderful pony?"

"Oh, no. I had several."

"A thousand pardons."

"It did not matter, you see. Because, for all of my childhood, a black cloud hung over our family's happiness. You see, I was born to be a princess. One hundred years ago, we Hyatts were cruelly cheated out of the Swedish throne."

"I thought Sweden was a constitutional monarchy. A parliament does the ruling. The king's got no power beyond grandly opening supermarkets."

"Yes. It is a constitutional monarchy. So what? It is the principle of the thing."

"I see."

"Even though it happened several generations ago, my parents still grieve the loss as if it had happened personally to them. Every day, as they go about their commonplace business, taking care of the estate, managing the servants, seeing that the boat is docked properly and the horses adequately exercised—"

"Right, your usual nine-to-five grind."

"—every day my parents face the knowledge that it could have been, should have been, different. We were ordained for more. And, as a result, each and every happiness we experience is tainted with the knowledge that it could have been even better. There is a perennial sadness in our home because of this injustice."

"True. Just having money and stuff is such a downer without a title to go with it."

"Exactly! I knew a man as sophisticated and sensitive as you would appreciate our sorrow. As soon as I grew up, I thought if I could find myself a prince, if I could turn myself into a princess, I would finally be able to make my parents truly happy."

"So that explains why you took your European tour through the Rich and the Bloodlined?"

"Precisely. Oh, Henry, you are the first man to truly understand me. I knew that we were soul mates."

"What about the rich guys you dated who didn't have royal bloodlines?"

"Oh. That," Vienna said. "That was for the shiny expensive objects. A girl can not live exclusively to make her parents happy."

"So if your parents didn't go for the royal richies, what's the idea behind bringing a pauper like me home?"

"I want to show them that I have found true happiness at last. I want to show them that you can be a perfectly ordinary, common, unexceptional, plebeian person and still lead a blissful life."

"Is that the Swedish version of a compliment?"

"Just promise me you won't take anything they say seriously. In Sweden, it is a sign of great affection if parents are dismissive and judgmental when meeting a daughter's suitor for the first time. Or the second time. Or always."

Henry couldn't be sure of it, but he thought he caught Sven smirking in the front seat.

"Tell the truth. They're going to hate me."

"They are going to hate you," Vienna agreed. "But that will be only on the surface. Deep down—"

"They'll loathe me."

"Probably yes. But it is nothing personal. Honestly." The car took a wide swoop and crunched onto the snow-covered gravel driveway of a shadowy mansion in the middle of a seemingly deserted meadow. Vienna said, "We are home."

Home.

For the second time that week, Henry found himself approaching a "home" that was, in fact, a full-fledged, honest-to-goodness mansion, this time of the genus: *Castle*. Not that he minded. Henry had been waiting several decades to commence living a life he desperately hoped to become accustomed to. He had nothing against castles. He just wished there was another word he could use to describe them, instead of the same one he applied to his own modest digs. If this was a *home* and his place was a *home*, then the English language was obviously less descriptive than he'd previously thought.

White stones taller than Henry made up the castle's base and continued up into the sky until he lost count of just how

many stories there were. The main entrance was a rounded
tunnel big enough to let two semitrucks to pass piggybacked
atop each other. The door itself was made of wood, each
plank of which appeared to be an individual oak.

Inside, they were greeted by more wood, this time polished and gleaming, as well as ornate gold mirrors, spot-
less bearskin rugs, and the requisite roaring stone fireplace.
Henry had heard of walk-in closets. A walk-in fireplace, that
was something new.

"All this and total happiness was still out of your reach,
huh?" he asked Vienna.

"There is more to life than money."

"Like a peerage."

"Exactly."

A gray-haired woman entered the room and approached
them. Vienna turned, saw her, smiled broadly, and took a
step forward. But before she could extend the proper intro-
ductions, Henry, in an attempt to appear the model guest
and suitor, rushed ahead and embraced his hostess. When
she stiffened in response, he leapt back, terrified of having
offended her. Now keeping a respectful distance, he heartily
pumped her arm up and down.

"Mrs. Hyatt," he said. "A pleasure to meet you. I can certainly see where your daughter got her striking good looks."

"Henry . . ."

"Not now, Vienna, your mother and I are getting to know
each other."

"She isn't my mother, Henry. She is Greta, our maid."

Henry stopped shaking her hand. Greta the maid appeared relieved. She also appeared to be studying Henry

with a marked lack of enthusiasm. Then again, she didn't seem that thrilled to see Vienna, either.

"Hello, Greta," Vienna said. Her stiff posture and counterfeit cheer suggested that Vienna understood perfectly well that the loyal family retainer could not be less enthused to see her young mistress home at last but noblesse oblige mandated a modicum of polite conversation. "How are you?"

"Eh," the woman shrugged. Apparently "eh" translated the same in any language.

"Your family? They are well?"

"My son is in jail. Again."

"That is very unfortunate."

"Eh. You do your best. You sacrifice everything for your children and in the end, they still make a fine mess of it all."

"Oh," Vienna said and tried desperately to steer toward a less emotionally charged topic. "And your daughter?"

"Got herself a new job."

"That is wonderful."

"Working for the city."

"That is nice. It is very secure work."

"She will make a fine mess of it, too, eventually. I have no doubt." Greta gave Henry a final look, as if to add, "And speaking of fine messes . . ." but then merely hung up their coats on a sterling silver rack in the corner and quietly exited.

"Well," Henry said. "That went well."

"Yes. Greta is more cheerful than usual." Vienna turned to face her man. She cupped Henry's face in her hands and kissed him lightly. "You are so nervous."

"I shouldn't be?"

"No," Vienna said. "I was merely making an observation."

From every direction, ancient ancestral oil portraits glared down at Henry. A disproportionate number of them seemed to be frowning, in disapproval of either his latest faux pas, or merely of his existence in general. For better or for worse, a pair of more recent ancestors—at least Henry hoped he got it right this time and these two weren't simply more hired hands—were making their way down the spiraling, cast-iron staircase.

Mrs. Hyatt possessed the same perfectly proportioned features as her daughter—facial and southward—as well as the same luxurious, a-man-would-want-to-bathe-in-it-if-he-could hair. Henry also suspected, though fervently hoped he wouldn't blurt out loud, that Mrs. Hyatt possessed a plastic surgeon so good his work effectively denied his existence. The only reason Henry presumed there was a plastic surgeon in the picture was that Vienna's mother didn't look old enough to be Vienna's mother. Which was obviously the point. Her father, on the other hand, had gone with the distinguished salt-and-pepper look, allowing gray to streak through his ebony hair and beard. He was nearly a foot taller than his wife and daughter, and dressed in a maroon smoking jacket expertly hand-sewn to look like a casual item he'd just tossed on at the last minute. It was a look Henry hoped to grow or inherit into one day.

"Henry," Vienna bobbed up and down on her toes like an excited little girl. "These are my parents, Martina and Gjord Hyatt. Mama, Papa, this is my Henry."

Henry stuck his hand forward, saying, "The pleasure is all yours."

Gjord and Martina exchanged glances. The glances did not convey a sense of "Oh, what a delightful young man."

While the Hyatts exchanged an entire silent conversation exclusively in archly raised eyebrows, Henry surreptitiously searched for the nearest emergency exit and wondered how long a walk it would be, in the dark through the snow, back to the airport. And then something unexpected happened. Vienna's parents looked back at Henry. And burst out laughing.

"Oh, Henry," Gjord smacked him heartily on the shoulder, "what a sense of humor!" Henry winced. Vienna's father had a grip like a small cookie-cutter shark. "Come," he said. "We will show you to your room."

Henry didn't know what to say. Would a hug and a kiss be appropriate? An equally hearty handshake in return? A quick Irish jig followed by a uniquely American fist pump? Unable to decide between the three, Henry settled merely for accepting their generous invitation by proceeding to make himself at home. He took off his coat.

"Oh, no," Martina said. "You had best keep that on."

Henry shot Vienna a quizzical look. She just smiled innocently and, linking her arm through Henry's, followed her parents.

"You two will be staying in the guesthouse," Gjord explained.

"Oh, Papa!" Father and daughter beamed at each other. Henry figured that when in Sweden, join in. He beamed, too. Even though no one was actually looking in his direction.

Chattering all the while about how lovely it was to have Henry visiting with them and oh, how they wished Vienna brought her friends by more often; it was ever so lonely to have their precious child living so far away, the Hyatts led Vienna and Henry through their living area, around the kitchen with its simmering pots of exotic aromas that Henry told himself he couldn't wait to try—someday—and out the back door.

The gust of frigid wind that hit Henry the moment they stepped outside was as close to a "wind" as the Hyatt castle was to a modest little "home." This was no wind. This was a semipermeable block of ice floating through space like the Plexiglas prison Superman trapped his SuperEnemies in. Henry could feel his eyeballs blistering from the cold. His lashes froze into pointy spikes. He could feel the wind whistling *through* his cheeks, for Pete's sake. This was not good.

"This is cold," Henry managed to croak out through a mostly paralyzed face.

"It is," Vienna agreed. "We are two hundred kilometers inside the Arctic Circle. The weather here is a bit more brisk than in Stockholm."

"You brought me to the Arctic?" Henry wondered how she could have left out that little detail while planning their itinerary. What had his lovely vixen been thinking?

"Lester Keyes Enterprises," Vienna reminded, as if reading his mind.

"Cold," Henry reminded back.

And now they wanted him to trudge through the snow? What was wrong with these people? Did they think toes breaking off was a natural condition? Like tarantulas shedding their skin? Did the people of Sweden regrow frostbitten extremities? Did they realize that the people of America did not?

Nevertheless, Henry did as the Hyatts commanded, learning a valuable lesson along the way. Even the nicest of Italian shoes were not made for a trudge through sludge. And Henry's shoes weren't particularly nice. Or Italian.

Fortunately, after the first few steps, he couldn't feel his inferior shoes anymore. Or his toes, for that matter. His feet were on fire. Which, considering he was knee-deep in a snowdrift, wasn't particularly likely. But the sensation still was not very pleasant.

"Here we are," Gjord said. He took out a ring of keys and proceeded to unlock a snowdrift.

Wonderful. Now the cold was making Henry hallucinate.

He had to be hallucinating. There was no other explanation for it. Now he was hallucinating that the snowdrift had a light shining inside it, and that Vienna's father was beckoning them to come in.

Sure. Why not? In for a penny, in for a phantasm.

They passed through a snow-covered tunnel that grew narrower and narrower the further they went. However, once their party reached the point where Henry and Gjord's heads were brushing the icy ceiling, the floor unexpectedly descended into a sequence of steps carved out of ice. The steps led to a slippery, sparkling floor and a series of carved columns, all made out of ice. A bed stood in the center of the room. The blankets appeared to be sleeping bags sewn out of cured reindeer pelts. The surrounding frame—headboard, legs, diamond lights twinkling at the base—was fashioned completely out of ice. Even the bar had been configured completely out of ice. Though the dozen bottles of vodka chilling invitingly atop its crystal blue surface did take the sting out of that particular desecration somewhat.

At least the igloo's walls weren't made out of ice.

They were made out of snow, with intricate mosaic patterns chiseled from floor to ceiling to break up the otherwise blue and white monotony.

"What is this?" Henry whispered. "Hell's refrigerator?"

"Is it not glorious?" Vienna asked. "Every year, my parents invite artists from all over the world to come in and create this masterpiece. It takes many weeks. They start in November, setting up the molding. Then, once the temperature dips below freezing, they spray the shapes with snow and bring in ice blocks from the Torne River to sculpt out the inside and the furniture."

"Are you kidding me? You're in the Arctic Circle and you have to *import* ice?"

"It is like living in a magical fairy tale!"

"Isn't this what they did to Hans Christian Andersen's little matchgirl?"

"You will stay here during your visit," Martina said.

"Vienna has wanted to do this since she was a little girl," Gjord explained to Henry. "She would play in here all winter, but we never allowed her to spend the night.

We always told her that we were waiting for a special occasion. Well, now that you are here, that day is finally
upon us."

Henry looked pleadingly at Vienna. Surely, she knew
how to get them out of this. Surely, she'd be uttering the
magical, polite, respectful version of "Thanks, but no—are
you kidding me?" any minute. But Vienna suddenly seemed
lost in thought. She wasn't even paying attention to Henry
anymore.

Thankfully, that was the moment when Henry remembered the Hyatts' comment about his wonderful sense of
humor and finally realized they were playing a joke on
him.

"Ha ha ha," Henry chortled. "Very funny. Have a little
goof at the foreigner's expense. Good one. You had me
going, I'll give you that. Pretty elaborate charade, building
this whole guesthouse to make me think you were actually
going to leave us here to brave the elements. What do you
say we head back inside, splash around a little bourbon, talk
about how I fell for it?"

"Papa," Vienna asked, as if Henry hadn't spoken. "Why
now?"

"Because of Henry, of course," Gjord said. "You told us
he was very special to you. That means that he is very special to us, as well. Enjoy yourselves, children. Don't let us
interrupt. Come to the main house when you are hungry.
As I am sure you sniffed when we passed through, Greta has
really outdone herself cooking for this very special occasion.
We will wait for you both there."

Gjord offered Henry another of his hearty slaps. Thankfully, Henry's shoulders, like his feet, now lacked all sensation, so it didn't hurt nearly as much the second time.

Plaintively, he watched Gjord and Martina go, still hoping for that last-minute "Gotcha." They turned at the door. Henry got his hopes up. They waved. Martina blew a kiss. They disappeared into the snow.

There was no "Gotcha." Not even a Swedish equivalent. There was just Henry, Vienna, and the silent Arctic Circle. Somehow, Henry suspected that even the dozen bottles of vodka wouldn't be enough to pull him through a night in this frozen place.

"Something is wrong," Vienna said as she walked purposefully around the ice house as if searching for something she'd lost. She tapped her finger against her cheek and peeked, curious, into every corner.

"You think?" Henry snapped. "We've been locked into an ice cube!"

"You do not understand. My parents have never done this before. Any time I have brought a boyfriend home, I begged them to let us stay in the guesthouse. They never would agree. They said that this was a special place and that I shouldn't pollute it with just anyone. They always made us sleep inside the house. So why in the world would they allow me to bring you here?"

"Just lucky, I guess."

"My parents are not acting like themselves, Henry. They did not question you. They did not demand that you disclose your intentions toward me."

"Perhaps that's because they know you've done enough of that for both of them."

"This is not right."

"I agree. They expect us to sleep in ice. We're going to wake up three thousand years from now, perfectly preserved in some giant alien life-form's martini."

"Something not right is going on. I need to find out what."

"I'm with you all the way," he said. "As long as we do it at room temperature."

Dinner at the main house, with the heat on, proved rather pleasant. Vienna's parents continued to be on their best behavior, making delightful conversation about art and literature and music without ever once demanding to know what right Henry thought he had to corrupt their precious little girl. In Henry's world, that made the dinner a rousing success. And the pea soup, cured salmon, and cabbage rolls didn't hurt either. Henry even managed to eat a few bites of reindeer with chanterelle mushrooms once he was able to banish the image of a frolicking Rudolph and a grounded Santa's sleigh from his mind.

As they were tromping back to what Henry was coming to view as their Gulag, despite his best attempts to buy Vienna's view of it being a magical icy wonderland, Vienna reiterated, "I do not understand it. Why are they being so nice to you?"

"Perhaps it's my boyish charm. My dashing good looks. Or maybe, just maybe, Vienna, they can see how much I sincerely love you and they appreciate that."

Vienna paused and looked Henry in the eye. He smiled his cracked, frozen smile. She smiled back. Henry took Vienna's hand.

And then she said, "No. That is not it."

All things considered, the night Henry spent in the Hyatts' icy Fortress of Solitude wasn't the worst of his life. Granted, its competition was the night he spent chained to a metal pipe inside a costume warehouse with only a dead-eyed ventriloquist's dummy for company, several nights held hostage in a wine cellar guarded by a sexually starved Eastern European Amazon named Olga, and an evening on a tropical island dressed in—what else?—women's clothing while fending off the advances of a nearsighted and horny hermit. In comparison, merely being cold and terrified that the roof would cave in at any moment and bury him in several tons of Arctic ice was a relative cakewalk. The insulated sleeping bags and reindeer pelts kept out most of the chill. And snuggling up to Vienna almost made Henry forget about the instances when they didn't. Plus, Vienna did look like a fairy-tale princess sleeping on a twinkling background of white, blue, and clear crystal ice, her jet black hair spread out beneath her head. Henry decided weather be damned, if this is what his love wanted, then he could be content just sitting there, shivering and sniffling, watching her sleep all day.

Unfortunately, Vienna had other plans.

No sooner had she opened her eyes, looked around, and grinned giddily at the realization that, after twenty years of dreaming about it, she'd finally gotten her little girl wish to come true, than Vienna kissed Henry good morning and promptly leapt out of bed, already making plans for the day's work ahead.

First, Vienna said, they would go one town over to Lester Keyes Enterprises and get the exact details of what had transpired with Lucy. Then they would check in with the landlord of the apartment Lucy had been planning to rent to see if he could offer them any leads.

"Come along, Henry, up, up, and away!" Vienna trilled happily.

Henry looked longingly at the vodka.

For their trip into town, Vienna borrowed an automobile from her parents' stable—a red and black, homegrown Koenigsegg supercharged sports car.

"From zero to one hundred miles per hour in three point two seconds," Vienna boasted. And then she showed him.

Her little demo made Henry very pleased he'd declined to dig into the slices of liver pate they'd been offered for breakfast.

"Eat, eat!" Vienna's father had urged. "A man needs his protein, yes?"

What Henry actually needed at the moment was some Dramamine.

He was still feeling a bit queasy when they were ushered into the private office of Nels Anderson Einar, general manager of Lester Keyes Enterprises' biotechnology division.

A pale, balding man in his sixties, Einar said he was too busy to see them, until he heard that Henry and Vienna were from Oakdale, Illinois. Suddenly the Welcome Wagon practically rolled itself over Henry's foot.

"I spent some time in Oakdale myself in the early nineteen eighties. Wonderful town, wonderful people. I would have liked to stay longer."

"What made you leave?" Vienna inquired politely.

"I was convicted of a hit-and-run in the Memorial Hospital parking lot, imprisoned, then deported."

"That would do it," Henry observed.

"I was not guilty, of course."

"Don't worry, no one in Oakdale ever is."

"But a man must do what a man must do, must he not?"

"Uhm . . . sure."

"And what may I do today for my visitors from the fine city of Oakdale?"

"We're here about an employee of yours. An almost employee, I guess you could say. Cindy Bryant? She was supposed to be coming from Montega to write English marketing copy for you?"

"Ah, yes, Miss Bryant. Most strange. My employer was very specific that we must find just the right person to fill this position. He usually does not get involved in day-to-day hiring, but in this case he did. He turned down several whom I judged to be excellent candidates before Miss Bryant came along. Then he insisted we hire her immediately. We cut through a lot of what you would call red tape to expedite her visa and bring Miss Bryant and her son to Sweden. But then she never reported for duty. Mr. Stenbeck was very—"

"Stenbeck?" Henry yelped.

"Stenbeck?" Vienna gasped.

And then they looked at each other and asked, "How do you know about Stenbeck?"

Back in the Koenigsegg, after determining that Lester Keyes Enterprises was, in fact, a James Stenbeck–owned subsidiary that he somehow managed to run from inside a Bangkok prison, and that the job description fitting Lucy Montgomery to a snug tee had been issued soon after the young doctor had left Oakdale with Johnny, Vienna, deeply distressed, quizzed Henry, "Why did you not tell me you knew the Stenbecks?"

"What's there to tell? Paul Ryan and I hardly run in the same social circles. We crossed paths a couple of times when I thought I was helping Emily Stewart cover up his murder—you know, now that I think about it, a whole lot of people want that man dead. It shouldn't be all that hard, should it? Maybe Craig and Emily could team up—"

"Why are you talking about Paul Ryan? I did not ask you about Paul Ryan. I asked you about the Stenbecks."

"Paul Ryan is a Stenbeck."

Vienna gasped again, so dramatically that Henry was almost distracted from the fact that she was simultaneously swerving across four lanes of traffic at close to seventy miles an hour. It was the third time she'd done so that morning. He figured he was getting used to it.

Swallowing hard to keep his stomach from taking up

residence between his ears, Henry explained, "Paul Ryan's father is James Stenbeck. Paul changed his name years ago. I think it was after James tried to strangle Emily and Paul shot his father to protect her. Emily said James was furious that Emily had slept with Paul. He was just a teenager then. Emily said that standing trial for James's murder was the final straw for Paul, and he decided to totally disassociate himself from the Stenbeck name and legacy."

"James's murder? But Mr. Einar said that James still runs the company from his prison. How can—"

"Like father, like son, and like Mark Twain, the reports of James's death have been greatly exaggerated. Several times. He calls himself the Falcon. Phoenix is more like it. But I hear there's another bad guy who got to the moniker first."

"I do not understand. What does James Stenbeck want with Lucy?"

"From what I hear, James's entire modus operandi for the last thirty years has been to control Paul. He knows Paul wants Johnny. James probably intends to use Lucy as a bargaining chip with Paul."

"But she escaped his clutches."

"Maybe. If you believe what Einar says about her never showing up for work. But for all we know, James might have had her snatched the minute she stepped off the plane in Stockholm. And now everybody's playing dazed and confused to cover their tracks."

"Poor Lucy! That horrible family . . ."

Henry asked, "So you know the Stenbecks, too?"

Vienna's perfect eyes filled with perfectly shaped tears.

"Do you remember what I told you? About how my family lost their throne due to the machinations of evil others?"

"The Stenbecks," Henry said, putting two and two together.

"They are the ones who plunged my family into grief. The ones who made certain that we could never experience a truly joyful moment without there being a shadow cast upon it."

"I'm so sorry, my little pepperkakor. And, please believe me, I don't wish to take away from my sincere sympathy toward the depths of your suffering. But I feel I have to ask. Why are you driving as if you're in a race with the proverbial bats out of hell?"

Vienna dried her eyes with one hand as she suddenly made a three-point turn worthy of a NASCAR driver with the other.

"Because," Vienna said with a sniffle, "there is a car that has been following us ever since we left the house this morning. And I am no longer amused by it."

After a few more stomach-tossing maneuvers, Vienna decreed that they had lost the offending vehicle. As Henry hadn't spotted it in the first place, he was in no position to disagree. He was, however, in the position to ask, "Where are we going?"

"To the main boulevard. It is where the town's hotel district is located," Vienna said. "Perhaps James Stenbeck did capture Lucy. But if he did not, if she realized that it was a trap and ran away, she could not have gone to the apartment she rented. James would have known where she was then. But, with a small child, she was not free to run too far, either. She may have stayed in a hotel, even if it was only for

the night. Someone there may remember her and give us a
clue about where she went next."

"Beautiful and brilliant," Henry exclaimed. "Vienna, you
really are a wonder."

"Yes," she agreed. "I am."

When Vienna and Henry were barely through the door of
the first hotel they visited, the concierge's face lit up and he
ran out to greet them.

"Vienna, my dear, my darling! How wonderful to see you
again. It has been much, much too long." He looked briefly
at Henry, and . . . well, it seemed to Henry as if the man
sneered for a split second before his face assumed an expression of professional obsequiousness. "Would you and the
gentleman like your regular room? Grant me a moment to
toss the pretenders currently in there out on their ears."

"Regular room?" Henry asked.

Vienna shrugged sweetly. Henry wasn't sure if the shrug
was for the concierge or for him. Vienna smiled and asked
the concierge something in Swedish. He took another look
at Henry, nodded knowingly, and held out his hand. Vienna
opened her purse, took out a photo of Lucy and Johnny, and
showed it to her old friend. Alas, the concierge hadn't seen
either of them.

At the second hotel, it was the head housekeeper who lit
up upon seeing Vienna, then waxed poetic about that lovely
fellow—a duke, was he? Or maybe a count—Vienna had
been in there with last. Would he be joining her again on

this visit? He was ever so charming. And such a generous tipper. They both were.

Vienna demurred and didn't even bother formally introducing Henry before showing the picture of Lucy. She and Johnny hadn't been seen there, either.

By their fifth stop, Henry was getting mighty tired of this stroll down Vienna's memory lane. Fortunately, the manager at the Hotel Sofitel had no delightful tales to tell of Vienna's old boyfriends.

Instead, he actually was one of Vienna's old boyfriends.

Vienna's seven-foot-tall, twenty-four-pack-buff, perfectly blond, with-way-too-many-shiny-white-teeth old boyfriend.

"It is wonderful to see you again, Ulf!" Vienna crowed as they embraced. And held on a little bit longer than Henry would have liked. "How funny it is that you are the manager here now."

"I suppose after all the time we spent here together, it seemed only reasonable. Who else had equal reason to love it so?" Ulf and Vienna laughed in delight.

Henry did his best to work up a snicker.

"Ulf, darling," Vienna said. "Has this woman stayed at your hotel in the past few months? She would have been traveling with a little boy?"

Ulf stared at the picture, then nodded. "Yes. Yes, I remember her. She seemed very nervous. Of course, when I found out what was going on, I understood why."

"What was going on?" Henry asked, willing to cut Ulf some slack for being tall, blond, and Nordic if he also proved useful. And stopped staring at Vienna's chest.

"She was here illegally," Ulf snorted. "No visa. Can you

imagine the cheek? Everyone wishes to come to Sweden, you understand, because there is no better country in the world. But if she thinks a sad story about needing to provide for her boy would compel me to give a job to an illegal . . . ridiculous!"

"Lucy asked you for a job?"

"She said she had nowhere to go. A problem for her, yes. But a bigger problem for me if I were to hire an illegal immigrant."

Henry asked, "Did Lucy say where she was going, or what she might do after she left here?"

"I did not ask." Ulf sniffed.

"Psst."

As Henry and Vienna left the hotel, a woman wrapped in a tattered fur coat and flowery head scarf beckoned to them from the shadowy corner of the snowy parking lot.

"Psst," she repeated, pointing to Henry and Vienna, then added in English, "over here. Come. Now."

They followed the sound of her voice, rounded a corner, and ended up behind the garbage Dumpster.

She said, "You looking for American girl." Henry and Vienna nodded. "I know where she go."

"You do?" Vienna asked.

All of a sudden, their fountain of knowledge dried up and got coy. "Perhaps."

Luckily, Henry knew how to deal with this kind of plumbing problem. "How much?" He reached for his wallet.

The woman, who, Henry guessed, was about forty years old, with bleached blond hair peeking out from beneath her kerchief, ignored Vienna and smiled coquettishly at him. He understood it was merely because he'd cut to the chase faster than Vienna had.

"Five hundred dollars," she said. "American."

"Naturally," Henry said. He counted out the cash, showed it to her, then kept it at arm's length. "Let's hear what you have to say first."

"Let us see friendly token of sincerity."

He handed her one hundred bucks. "The extent of my sincerity."

She counted it to make sure, then stuffed the wad past her ratty mink into what Henry could only presume was her bra.

"She was in trouble, that girl. Nowhere to go. In hotel, we always need extra hands for the cleaning. I say she should ask boss for job. He tells her no. Says it is because she is illegal."

Vienna defended, "Ulf is a man of principle. He is very loyal to the law."

"Ulf very loyal to Ulf. Hire plenty of illegals. Me, I am illegal. Russian from Latvia, across the water. He pay me less with the wages, keeps difference for himself—who should I complain to? He is not stupid."

"So why wouldn't he hire Lucy?"

"Ulf wants Lucy should to ask nicely." This time, the smile was more lecherous than coquettish. And unmistakable in meaning.

Henry asked, "Lucy didn't go for it?"

"I not let her. Enough that Ulf take my money. Does not

deserve more benefit from pretty girl. I send her here." Their informant reached into her pocket and pulled out a scrap of paper onto which she scribbled an address with the stub of an eyeliner pencil. She flashed it briefly at Vienna.

"I know where that is," Vienna said. "It is on the outskirts of the city."

The Russian woman dangled the address with one hand while holding out the other for her money. Henry looked questioningly at Vienna. "You think this is legit?"

"It is a real neighborhood, I do not recognize the precise address," Vienna said. "But it is not as if we have a choice among other clues."

"However, we do have a choice of how much we should pay." Henry told their new friend, "I'll give you another hundred."

"Five hundred! Five hundred is the price!"

"You'll get the rest of your money when the address checks out. We know where to find you. Third Dumpster on the right and straight on till morning."

She grumbled but, like Henry and Vienna, understood that she didn't have a lot of choice. She handed him the address. He handed over the money. It disappeared into her bra. Henry hoped she wouldn't be giving him change.

10

"It is not a good neighborhood," Vienna said. "The address she gave us."

"Yeah," Henry mused. "Sad how fugitives rarely hide in your better residential areas." As Vienna took another turn on two wheels, Henry glanced over his shoulder and asked, "Trying to lose the car that's following us again?"

"No," Vienna said.

When she didn't elaborate, Henry asked, "You're sure we were actually being followed before? Sweden is a small country. Maybe we all just happened to be heading to the same place at the same time."

Vienna said, "Craig threatened to follow us until we led him to Lucy."

"You think it was Craig?"

"Who else?"

"How about James Stenbeck? If he had a plan for Lucy and we got in the middle of it, he's not known for letting bygones be bygones."

"But Stenbeck does not have Lucy. She is at this address that we were given."

"Maybe," Henry said.

His skepticism was borne out when Vienna finally located the designated block. Why did Henry suspect nothing good ever happened on a street where the lights had been knocked out by rocks and half the windows had bars on the front, while the other half were simply boarded up?

"It looks deserted," Vienna said.

"Hey, better deserted than threatening—that's always been my motto."

They got out of the car and Vienna locked the door. Henry said, "You okay with leaving it on this street?"

Maybe it was Henry's imagination, but it seemed like the presence of a sports car retailing for $637,723 U.S. (Vienna had happened to mention the price in passing) worked like a thug magnet. All of a sudden, at least a dozen young men who apparently had nothing better to do bled out of the woodwork and into the street. Though, unlike Henry, Vienna seemed unconcerned by their presence. Head held high, back straight, purse not even clutched to her body all that tightly, the love of Henry's life calmly clicked her high heels down the icy cement street, searching for the designated address. Well, if she could be so calm, Henry figured it was the least that could be expected of him. He followed Vienna's lead. Sans purse or high heels. Sans the straight back and upraised head, too. Vienna might have strode down the street. Henry scurried.

Henry and Vienna were several blocks from their car before they found the house number written on their sheet of paper. If anything, this neighborhood was even worse than the one they'd parked in. No barred windows on this six-story domicile. All of the windows were covered with graffiti-defaced boards. Nevertheless, Henry and Vienna pushed the buzzer and waited.

An unexpectedly mellow female voice came over the intercom in Swedish. Vienna answered something back, and, much to Henry's surprise, they were let in.

To his even greater surprise, once they passed through the rusted steel doors, they entered a well-lit, freshly painted hallway. On their right was an open door, this one with a happy clown wearing red suspenders and a yellow hat painted on it. Over the threshold was a large, carpeted room, the walls decorated with nursery rhyme characters like Little Red Riding Hood and The Three Little Pigs, and big block letters and numbers.

In one corner, a grandmotherly-looking woman with gray hair, clad in a pink housedress, played a piano while a half dozen preschoolers sat in a semicircle and clapped along. A few feet away, another group of children was diligently squashing colorful homemade clay, using empty juice bottles in place of rolling pins. The woman who'd been doling out the molding clay stepped away from her task for a moment and approached Vienna and Henry. While Vienna pulled out Lucy and Johnny's picture and made inquiries in Swedish, Henry faked having something equally important to do by looking about the room, nodding approvingly at both Little Red Riding Hood and Piglet #3.

A little girl wearing a red sweater tucked bulkily into her

brown woolen tights, her head crowned with a big yellow hair bow, waddled over to Henry, looked up, and stuck her tongue out at him.

Henry did what any reasonable adult would do under the circumstances. He stuck his tongue out in reply.

The little girl laughed and scrunched up her face. Henry scrunched up his. She shook her head from side to side. He copied her gesture, then jerked up his lips for good measure. The little girl laughed so hard that two of her friends came over to watch.

By the time Vienna came over to him, Henry was surrounded by most of the play-dough group and half the music class. Even the grandma playing the piano was sneaking peeks in his direction as she halfheartedly urged the children to pay attention to their song. Vienna headed for the door. Then, seemingly unable to stop herself, she paused, turned, and came back to the play area. She gave the little girl playing with Henry a long hug. And then she pointed in Henry's direction and whispered something that made all of the children laugh even harder.

"What?" Henry demanded. "What did you tell them?"

"I told them I had to get you back to the circus now."

"Oh. I see. The truth."

Outside, Vienna sighed. "The teacher says she never heard of Lucy and she does not know why the hotel maid would give us this address. They are merely a school for children of Russian immigrants from Latvia."

"So maybe Lucy parked the kid here for a while?"

"She says no."

"Do you believe her?"

Vienna snapped, "It is you I do not believe, Henry."

"Excuse me?"

"I saw you with those children. You are wonderful with them. Why do you not want to have any of your own, I just do not understand."

"Vienna, my beloved, we are in a very questionable neighborhood, engaged in some very questionable activities with a very strong chance that our one ticket out of here won't be where we left it, and instead of listening for menacing footsteps, your perfect ears are tuned to the tick of your biological clock?"

"A ringing that you refuse to answer!"

"I have my reasons."

"Well, I do not understand them."

"Every great romance needs a great mystery at the heart of it. Nick and Nora Charles. *Hart to Hart. Law & Order.*" Henry snuck a sideways peek at Vienna to gauge the level of her amusement. Unfortunately, Vienna's gauge appeared stuck on Empty. Henry changed tactics. He told her, "So I'm good with kids. So what? When you're the oldest of eight and your old man takes a hike at the same time as your old lady tries to set the world record for absentee parenting, you better get damn good, damn fast. I didn't go after greatness. I had greatness thrust upon me. And you know what? First chance I got, I thrust it right back. I didn't even wait till I turned eighteen. Sixteen with a driver's license was good enough for me. Good-bye, good luck, I was out of town and out of the kid-sitting business."

"You worked as a nanny for Carly Snyder's daughter several years back."

"So?"

"That was not something thrust upon you. That was something you chose to do."

"Putting aside for the moment the issue of whether trying to avoid incipient poverty is actually a true case of making a choice rather than merely clinging desperately to the only life raft available, babysitting somebody else's kid isn't the same as having one of your own. When you're babysitting, the rules are simple: keep the kid alive until the parents get home. That's it. Still breathing by the end of the day, and you can compliment yourself on a job well done. A kid of your own you've actually got to raise. You've got to make sure they don't turn into oh, I don't know, serial killers. Or Craig Montgomery. Finally, let's say you've gotten through those tricky minefields and you can proudly say your kid is a cool person you wouldn't mind hanging out with on a regular basis, that's when they decide to flee the country and leave you wondering whether you're ever going to see them again. Yeah. Parenting. You know what, I'll pass. . . ."

At the end of his tirade, Henry expected Vienna to launch into a passionate argument explaining why Henry was mistaken in all of his assertions. At the very least, he expected a wry comment to the effect of his being a worrywart fool.

But Henry got none of those things.

Because Vienna was too busy standing frozen by the side of her car, watching nervously as three young men approached her. They all looked to be in their early twenties, though it was hard to tell through the ski masks they were wearing. Under normal circumstances, their attire would have left no doubt in Henry's mind that the mini-mob was up to no good. However, in addition to the ski masks, the youths also wore wool-lined parkas, bloated snow pants, and waterproof boots. It was very cold out. Perhaps they were merely taking a midwinter's day stroll.

Nonetheless, Henry leapt to Vienna's side, ready to protect her honor just in case.

But when he saw that each of the well-insulated young men was also packing heat—and not of the scarf and glove variety—Henry blurted out the first thing that came to his mind. In English, no less.

"Take the car!"

They stopped and just stared at him for a moment.

Though Henry noted that their obvious befuddlement in no way prompted them to lower their weapons.

Finally, in broken English, one of them replied, "We do not want car."

"You do not?" Vienna actually sounded put out by the perceived insult.

"What do you want then?"

"You. Her."

"I'd prefer you take the car," Henry urged. But then Vienna glared at him, so he shut up.

"What do you want with us?" she asked.

"We do not want you. Our employer wants you." The leader nudged his pistol in the direction Vienna and Henry had come from. "Go back," he said.

What could they do? They went. One guy crunched through the snow ahead of them, leading the way. The other two brought up the rear, making sure nobody got any clever ideas about running. Vienna looked up at Henry and whispered, "Stenbeck?"

"Got to be. Craig wouldn't have this kind of power. Not here."

"I thought Mr. Einar said Stenbeck was in prison in Bangkok."

"When Paul was a little kid, Barbara Ryan thought James Stenbeck fell out of an airplane and died. She saw it happen. Couple years later, Paul stood trial for his murder. Then James's helicopter went down in the East River. Then Paul shot him again. James, I gather, is full of surprises."

"I cannot wait to meet him," Vienna said.

"You have a heretofore unmentioned death wish?"

Vienna crossed her arms. "I cannot wait to give him a piece of my mind over what his family did to mine all those years ago."

"You know, my pepperkakor, I'd be a little bit less concerned about past history at this juncture and a little more concerned about becoming history."

They rounded the corner and entered the same building Vienna and Henry had just left, only through a different door. Unlike the other hallway with the bright colors and the happy clowns, this one matched the building's exterior. The walls were drab gray, with only uncovered lightbulbs dangling every few feet along the ceiling.

"Here," one of the thugs said, hustling Henry and Vienna into a side room and shutting the door behind them. In yet another case of stepping through the looking glass, this room also seemed to belong not only to another building but to an-

other neighborhood as well. A crystal chandelier hung from
the ceiling, illuminating a huge hand-carved wooden desk
that held a silver MacBook Air computer, a fax machine, a
pair of cell phones in their chargers, and two landlines. Sitting behind the desk in an ergonomic chair, beckoning for
them to come closer, was . . . the grandmotherly teacher in
the housedress who'd been playing the piano downstairs a
few minutes before.

She got straight to the point, albeit in accented English.
"Why are you looking for Lucy Montgomery?"

Fortunately, Henry knew how to answer a question with a
question. "Why did you have to bring us here at gunpoint?
They don't use magic words at your school?"

"You are working for her husband?"

Henry was about to ask if they were talking about the
same Lucy Montgomery and wondered if there was something Lucinda had forgotten to tell them.

Without indicating that they had no idea who the old
lady was talking about, Vienna said, "No. Of course not."

"Stenbeck, then? You are working for Stenbeck?"

"Never!"

Vienna's vehemence caught their host by surprise. "Who
are you?"

"Who are you?" Vienna snapped back.

"Lucy is not here."

"What reason do we have to believe you?"

"Because my boys outside, they carry the guns."

"If Lucy's not here, why'd you drag us back in? You
could have just let us go on our merry way," Henry pointed
out.

THE MAN FROM OAKDALE

"No. You would have continued to have asked questions of others. I do not need people asking questions that will draw attention to me."

"Neither do we. We're not really into the whole questions thing. Truth is, we're in the market for answers."

"We are working for Lucy's grandmother," Vienna said. "She hasn't heard from her in a very long time. She is very worried."

"Tell Grandmother that Lucy is fine. I have taken care of her."

"Then why did you say she wasn't here?"

"She is not here."

"But she was here?" Henry clarified.

"How did you acquire this address?"

"A chambermaid at the Hotel Sofitel. Obviously, she believed that we could be trusted," Vienna bluffed.

"That is Galina. I know Galina very well. Galina will tell anything to anyone for one hundred dollars, American."

"We gave her five hundred," Henry lied, hoping to convey how serious they were about the search.

"Then you are idiots."

Vienna asked, "How much money do you want?"

The woman in the housecoat laughed. "Do I look as if I am lacking for money?"

"Uh . . ." Henry indicated the building they were standing in. "Yeah."

"This? This is what Americans would call the front. The Swedes like to keep their immigrants poor. They are so proud of their welfare state, anybody not needing, not wanting is an insult. So we appease them. We pretend to live the

way they say we should live. We say thank you for the honor.
We are good neighbors."

"So, you're, what?" Henry guessed. "Rich in spirit?"

"I am rich in money."

"Always the better option."

"I do not understand," Vienna said. "If you are not poor,
why do you live in a building that looks this way?"

"No offense," Henry added, remembering that there were
still three fellows with guns hanging out on the other side
of the door. Who knew how Grandma would react to her
domicile being impugned?

"In Latvia," she said, "after country gains independence,
the Latvians, they no longer want Russians in their country.
Go back to Russia, they say. My mother is born in Latvia. I
have no Russia to go back to. So we come to Sweden. But
Sweden is not America. In America, the law says everyone,
even illegal must be allowed into school and hospital. In
Sweden, no school for illegals. No medical. So, in secret, we
work and we make own school, own houses, own business,
own laws."

Henry indicated the thugs who'd escorted them to the
meetings. "Own mobs."

Grandma let his comment slide. "And when we need
them, we find our own doctors, as well."

"Lucy," Vienna guessed.

"She is good doctor. She needs place for her boy to play
while she decides what she should do next. A nice girl. I
wish she stayed with us, but Sweden is not right place for
her. The ones who look for her know she is here. They keep
looking for her. So she must move on."

"Move on where?"

Grandma fixed them with a look. "You gave Galina five hundred dollars. I will take five thousand."

"I thought you weren't hurting for money," Henry reminded her.

"How do you think I have made that happen?"

Henry said, "You think I'd be stupid enough to walk into a neighborhood like this carrying five thousand dollars in cash?"

"Yes."

"Well, ha!" Henry crowed. "It just so happens that I am merely stupid enough to walk into a neighborhood like this carrying only five hundred dollars."

"I will take it." She held out her hand. Henry forked over the cash. When there were guns involved, you didn't play around. After counting the bills, Grandma said, "You will not be very much offended if, before you leave, my boys make a little tour of your pockets. Just to make certain you are not playing trick on a poor, old woman. *Ver and prover,* as we say in Russia. Trust but verify, yes?"

Henry nodded mutely. And hoped for a very short tour.

Satisfied for the moment, their hostess said, "I send Lucy back to America."

"Why should we believe you?" Henry challenged, figuring if Vienna could play the tough guy, so could he.

This time, Grandma merely pointed at the door, reminding them of her boys outside with the guns, whose presence apparently confirmed her veracity. She continued, "I have . . . business associate in Brighton Beach, New York. You have been? No? I hear is wonderful. Many Russians there. Perhaps one day, me and my family go. In America, they let you make money, yes?"

"If you play their game."

For the first time since Henry and Vienna came in, Grandma looked as if she wasn't in control of the situation. Puzzled, she asked, "What reason not want to play?"

Henry shrugged. "Not everyone is good at it."

"Then they should work harder, yes?" Back in command, Grandma brightened considerably. "My associate in Brooklyn, he is good at the American game. He makes much money. He takes care of Lucy. She is well protected. I promise to you this."

"So Lucy Montgomery is with the Russian mob in Brooklyn," Henry said, shaking his head. "I can't spell out in mere words how delighted I am with this development. I never really needed my kneecaps. They're extraneous, like the appendix."

"Something is wrong," Vienna said.

They were back in their igloo. Vienna was taking off her coat, Henry was keeping his on.

"I'd say something is wrong," he agreed. "Our next stop has to be the Russian Mafia! I'll call the airline tonight. See if I can book us on the next plane to New York. Lucky we still have some of Lucinda's expense money left."

"This room is not right. Someone has been here, Henry." Vienna looked around the glistening, sparkling beauty. "Our things have been gone through."

"Probably the maid."

"No. The maids do not clean here. They say it is too cold."

"Smart maids." Henry took Vienna in his arms. "You're just spooked. It's been a stressful day. The guns, the ex-boyfriend, the grandma. No wonder you think we're being followed and snooped on."

"And watched," Vienna said. "Someone is watching us."

"Don't be silly. We're the only ones here."

"I feel it." For the first time since they'd been banished to this outdoor refrigerator, she actually shivered.

"Okay," Henry said. "Let's say we're being watched. I vote we have some fun with it." He dipped his head and kissed the tiny strip of skin peeking out from between Vienna's layers. "Feeling exhibitionist today?"

Vienna closed her eyes and leaned in to him. "Do you not think we should find out who it is that is watching us, first?"

"And ruin the surprise?"

Vienna responded with a languid Swedish purr that Henry didn't understand a single word of, yet found amazingly arousing all the same.

"Hold that thought," Henry told Vienna.

He stepped away and ducked into a closet he'd found earlier while looking for shot glasses. In addition to the reindeer-fur-lined sleeping bags, he'd discovered that the igloo boasted several fur robes that he was most eager to see Vienna model. He rifled around until he located the perfect one—floor length (wouldn't want her to get nippy), while low-cut in the front (a few goose bumps, in the right places, couldn't hurt).

"I'm coming, my little pepperkakor," Henry cooed upon his return.

Only to find Vienna's coat and handbag right where she'd set them.

But the little pepperkakor gone.

Under normal circumstances, Henry wouldn't panic upon Vienna's leaving the room. They were not so codependent and Henry was not so desperate for female companionship that his woman's momentary departure was enough to throw him into despair.

But these were not normal circumstances. They were two hundred kilometers inside the Arctic Circle. Not exactly the ideal conditions for a spontaneous constitutional.

Henry told himself that Vienna was simply playing a kinky little game wherein he was required to search for her. But after a few minutes of looking for hiding places in a wide-open room, Henry had to admit that hadn't been her intention.

Henry then considered the possibility that Vienna had trekked out to the main house. Maybe she wanted to tell her parents about her brush with the hated Stenbeck family.

In the middle of her and Henry's amorous encounter.

Without taking either her coat or boots.

It was a ridiculous idea, yet Henry wasted no time leaping right on it. He trudged up to the house and covertly searched the premises while managing to duck and avoid Vienna's parents. His luck ran out in the kitchen, where he came face-to-face with Vienna's father.

"Henry!" he boomed. "Fortuitous timing. Vienna—"

"Isn't here," Henry blurted out.

"Yes," Gjord said.

"Because she's back at the ice house. Yes, that's exactly where she is. Safe and sound." Henry continued talking, though he'd forgotten why exactly that option was preferable to his shutting up. "I just popped in to grab us a snack." Henry's eyes settled on a still-steaming baked ham cooling on the counter. He grabbed it eagerly, squeezing it to his chest as a way to enforce the distance between him and Gjord. "You know your daughter's voracious appetites. For all sorts of things. We certainly don't want to be disturbed tonight, if you get my drift. So long, farewell, auf Wiedersehen, adieu, and doe a deer, a female deer to all!"

Henry was out the door before Vienna's father could utter another word. He ran through the snow, clutching the contraband ham and fervently praying that his babbling had at least bought him a little time before the Hyatts began wondering what he had done with their daughter.

Earlier in the day, Vienna had suspected they were being followed. And then she'd thought someone had gone through their things. She'd thought they were being watched, too. Obviously, her hunch was correct. Whoever had been following and watching them had taken advantage of Henry's leaving Vienna alone for a few minutes to snatch and abscond with her. Henry's chest puffed with pride at the thought that her kidnapper clearly considered Henry to be a virile protector and too indomitable a foe to risk snatching Vienna while Henry was around. But the question remained: Who was this heartless fiend and what did he/she want with Vienna?

Craig Montgomery had vowed to use them to locate

Lucy. He had to be at the top of any suspect list. But what good would pilfering Vienna do him? Henry couldn't see how her disappearing would fit into any plan of James Stenbeck's, either. But, then again, James just liked kidnapping women. Oakdale was awash with former victims who'd testify to that.

And then there was the old lady. She'd been mightily disappointed when Henry's predeparture strip search had produced no bonus cash. Maybe she'd kidnapped Vienna in order to hold her for ransom?

Henry was in the process of formulating a plan for storming the mob front/nursery school when he heard a knock on the door and Martina Hyatt's voice chirping, "Henry, dear, may we come in?"

"Uhm, no, sorry," Henry stuck his head out the door, reminded anew of the fact that, no matter how cold it was in the ice house, outside was much, much worse. "Still busy, I'm afraid. You know how it is, I'm young, I'm virile, I'm—"

"Alone," Gjord, who was standing right behind Martina, said. "We know that Vienna is not with you."

"Why would you say that?"

"Because we are the ones responsible."

"Come to the main house," Martina said. "We will explain."

It wasn't that far from the igloo to the Hyatts' living room. But with each snowy step, Henry was getting more and more angry, until, as soon as they were inside and Gjord and Martina had taken seats on the couch opposite Henry, before they'd even had the chance to open their mouths and begin the proffered explanation, he exploded.

"I know what this is all about," Henry shouted. "You don't think I'm good enough for your daughter. You think I drink and I gamble and I've never held a job for more than a few weeks, and then there's the minor matter of my criminal record, you think all of that makes me inferior to your precious almost royal status."

"Not at all," Gjord said.

"You are an American. We do not expect you to understand—"

"So it's because I'm an American! You don't think I'm good enough for your daughter because I'm an American so you took her away from me!"

"We did nothing of the sort."

"You mean she left me of her own accord?" Henry felt his rage deflating. Which was a shame. He needed to be filled with righteous indignation in order to keep himself from facing the obvious: Maybe nobody took Vienna. Maybe she just left. After all, when an affair went bad, women were famous for running home to their mothers. And Vienna's mother was currently only a few yards away. For all Henry knew, Vienna wasn't missing. She was merely napping in one of the many rooms upstairs.

"Vienna did not leave you," Gjord said.

"She loves you very much," Martina added. "The question is, how much do you love her?"

Henry's brow furrowed. "Is this finally the Swedish version of What Are Your Intentions Toward My Daughter?"

"In a manner of speaking."

Gjord said, "This is rather difficult to explain. You see, a few hours before you and Vienna arrived, an American man came to our door with a proposition for Martina and me. A very interesting proposition. One that we, honestly, never expected to hear in our lifetime."

"You're auctioning Vienna off to the highest bidder? This American guy is richer than me, so you're letting him have Vienna, no questions asked?"

"My goodness," Martina said. "You do enjoy jumping to conclusions. Is that something all Americans do?"

"What did this guy who showed up at your door want?"

"He said he was from Oakdale. And that he's looking for Lucy Montgomery."

Damn, Henry thought, how the hell did Craig manage to track them down so fast? Had he hijacked the plane to Buenos Aires and made it land in Sweden instead?

"What did you tell him?"

"We told him we knew nothing of any Lucy Montgomery. But he insisted that you and Vienna did. He said that you had been looking for her and he needed to learn what you knew. We told him he was welcome to stay and question you himself, but he seemed to be under the impression that you would not be forthcoming."

"Understatement. He's the guy Vienna and I are trying to protect Lucy from."

"Yes. He did explain that. He also explained that while he was certain Vienna could not be cajoled into revealing what she knew, he did believe that you might be open to his brand of persuasion."

All those chest-puffing thoughts Henry had entertained earlier? About how the kidnappers had focused on taking Vienna because they hadn't dared take on Henry? Obviously missed their mark by a mile. Craig hadn't snatched Vienna because she'd been the weaker target. He'd grabbed her because he thought Henry would be the easier nut to crack.

"Give him what he wants," Martina said, "and he will return Vienna to you."

"Or else what?" Henry demanded. "He'll kill her? I'm supposed to think you two handed your precious daughter over to a guy who threatened to kill her?"

"Do not be obscene. Of course not. Vienna is perfectly safe. We have his word."

"Then what's the threat? I don't get it. What's he supposed to be holding over my head that's going to make me spill the beans?"

"He will not hurt her. But he can also hold on to her for as long as necessary. You are his only lead to finding Johnny. On the other hand, what is Johnny to you? Nothing. If Vienna is the one you love, why not give up information that means nothing to you, in order to get her back as soon as possible?"

"How'd he get you guys to go along with this? Johnny doesn't mean anything to you two, either."

"That is not exactly true," Gjord said. He stood up. "Come. The American gentleman, he is here right now. He can explain it all. You will understand."

Henry followed Gjord into the next room, diligently working up his store of righteous indignation in an attempt to make it clear to Craig exactly what Henry thought of him.

But the man who was waiting for Henry turned out not to be Craig, after all.

The man holding Vienna hostage turned out to be Paul Ryan.

11

"What's the matter, Henry?" Paul asked in response to his befuddled expression. "Cat got your tongue?"

"No. But a bastard's got my girlfriend."

Paul smirked at Henry's reply. Then again, Paul smirked at most everything. Beneath the caramel-colored hair and hazel eyes was a broadly set mouth so expressive that it could both smirk and menace simultaneously.

And Paul proceeded to do just that. "Fortunately, it's a situation that can be rectified immediately. Tell me where Lucy and Johnny are and you and Vienna will be reunited before nightfall."

"What do you need me for? You've tracked them down this far, finish the job yourself."

"Tracked them down isn't precisely the right word. More like drew them here."

"The job offer at Stenbeck—sorry, Lester Keyes— Enterprises," Henry surmised. "That was from you, not your father."

"My father is in prison. He has more important people to torment long-distance. No, you're right, the job offer at Lester Keyes, that was all me. I figured I'd put out the perfect bait and, sooner or later, Lucy was bound to show up. It was all going according to plan, except somehow she figured it out and poof—gone again. Smart girl."

"Too smart for me," Henry agreed. "I've got no idea where Lucy and Johnny went. Vienna and I are as stymied as you are."

"I don't believe you. You and Vienna hit the local hotels, then you tore like bats out of hell, bound for someplace."

"That's Vienna's usual driving style, don't read anything into it."

"I tried retracing your steps, talked to the hotel managers myself. Didn't get a thing. I must not have your girlfriend's power of persuasion." The smirk was now gone. Paul was all menace.

"I'm telling you this morning was a bust. We didn't learn anything new."

"Oh, well. I guess I'll just have to hold on to Vienna until you do."

"Any reason why you're not doing your own dirty work?"

"Mostly because I suspect you've already done it. Make life easier for yourself, Henry. Tell me what you know and I'll let Vienna go."

Henry turned to Gjord and Martina. "What the hell is this guy offering you that you're willing to let him use your daughter as a bargaining chip?"

Paul said, "The one thing they've always wanted but could never have."

"Please. Have you seen this house? The sports car? The custom-made igloo? There isn't exactly a lot of want floating around chez Hyatt. The only thing you have that they don't . . ." Henry fought the urge to smack himself on the forehead. *It was so obvious!* "The Swedish throne."

"Vienna shared with you our family tragedy," Martina observed.

"The Stenbecks taketh away," Paul said. "The Stenbecks can giveth back."

Henry asked the Hyatts, "You trust him? Are you nuts?"

"It is a fair trade."

"Your daughter's life is a fair trade for a title that doesn't even come with the power to wage wars or host bacchanalias?"

"Please do not be so melodramatic, Henry," Gjord said. "Vienna's life is in no danger. Paul assures us she is quite comfortable. Besides, once she learns the reason for her captivity, she will understand. Vienna knows how important this is to us. The title will one day be hers, as well. She will be a princess."

"And all I have to do to make that happen is to betray Lucy and Johnny."

"I thought you didn't know where they were," Paul said sharply.

"No deal. I'm a professional. I have morals. Standards. A code of ethics."

"An all-encompassing fear of Lucinda Walsh."

"You, sir," Henry told Paul, "are no gentleman."

"And you're a coward," Paul offered. "You could get Vienna back with the snap of your finger. But you're too scared of what Lucinda will do to you. That doesn't exactly scream gentleman to me, either."

"A gentleman stands by his principles. He doesn't just whisk them away when they become inconvenient. I'm going to rescue Vienna. With no help from you," he told her parents pointedly. Turning to Paul, Henry added, "And then Vienna and I are going to find Lucy and Johnny. And we're going to live happily every after. So there."

Before anyone could stop him, Henry ran back to the igloo, grabbed the car keys out of Vienna's coat pocket, and raced to the Koenigsegg. He had to admit, he was a bit disappointed that no one tried to stop him. Paul, Gjord, and Martina merely watched him from one of the castle's front windows. What? They didn't consider him enough of a threat to be worth intercepting?

Henry's feelings of disappointment, however, were at least temporarily assuaged the moment he slipped the key into the ignition and gave it the gentlest of tugs. "My God, this thing is powerful!" he marveled. Like having a team of elephants at your command. A team of purring elephants. Who moved like the wind without jostling their passenger one iota. The only reason Henry even knew how fast he was going was that the trees were whizzing by. And suddenly he understood very well Vienna's fondness for taking two-wheel turns. How could you not?

Despite Paul and the Hyatts' decision to let Henry storm off as if he'd been harmless, Henry was most certainly not feeling harmless. He was a man on a mission, and that mission was to solve the mystery, rescue the girl, and get the money. At the moment, he was feeling the classic, archetypal hero, and he had a plan.

Unfortunately, the least thought-out part of it was Henry's realization that he would have to spend the night in the car. Why hadn't he thought ahead and timed his dramatic exit for the next morning?

Oh, well. Nothing to be done about it now. And there was a bright side. The cold—even with the heater running—ensured that Henry would have an entire night of bright-eyed and bushy-tailed alertness, during which he could take his time and think through the remainder of his game plan.

For Paul to have been able to snatch Vienna from the ice house and be back at the Hyatts an hour or so later to blackmail Henry meant he couldn't have gone too far. Vienna was obviously being held somewhere in the vicinity, and, judging by Paul's use of Lester Keyes Enterprises as the lure for Lucy, the odds were good that Vienna was being held somewhere on Stenbeck property, watched over by Stenbeck lackeys. She was probably also being force-fed Stenbeck revisionist history, such as how James hadn't once deliberately lured Paul's mother, Barbara, into a Spanish bullring and let loose a feral bull; Barbara must have wandered into the ring on her own and aggravated the sleepy animal into attacking her.

As soon as the clock struck 9:00 a.m., Henry was at the town clerk's office. His first step would be to suss out what property the Stenbecks owned in the area and proceed from there.

There were only two small problems with that plan: (1) Henry did not speak Swedish, and (2) he doubted that personal residency information would be available to a foreigner just for the asking.

For the latter problem, Henry devised a solution stemming from the one fact he'd known about Sweden prior to meeting Vienna — Swedes love long, depressing, black-and-white movies such as those directed by that guy who was not Ingrid Bergman. For the former problem, the lost-in-translation side of it, Henry merely decided to wing it.

He entered the office promptly and, dare he say, pompously made his way over to the single clerk on duty, a woman in her early fifties, with dark curly hair and huge brown eyes. When she saw Henry coming, she pushed her computer aside and smiled brightly. Henry had never had a civil service employee smile at him in America. It made him very nervous.

"Hola, bonjour!" Henry said. "By any chance, possibly, do you speak English?"

"I do!" She continued to smile at Henry. "Come right this way, sir. What may I help you with today? My name is Ariel Aldrin."

"Hello, Mrs. Aldrin—"

"It's Miss, actually."

Now Henry was feeling even more nervous.

"Miss, yes, hello. My name is Cecil B. Coleman and I'm a film director from the States. Film, you understand, not that movie nonsense the young people are so hot for these days. I'm talking lots of long tracking shots that don't go anywhere, wind-blown branches, slowly melting icicles, serious people saying very serious things."

The smile faltered just a little. "How can I help you, Mr. Coleman?"

Henry threw his nerves to the wind and assumed his most favorite position: flirting mechanism activated—full speed ahead. Because if a little suggestive flattery was what it would take to achieve his goals, then serious suggestive flattery it would be. He was doing it for Vienna, after all. Nothing was out of bounds when it came to his beloved Vienna.

"I'm scouting locations for my next film," he said. "Looking for something in the area, but very isolated. One of those 'no one can hear you scream' type of places, far away from the maddening crowds. Maybe an isolated house or cottage? A friend of mine, another very successful film producer, told me he'd seen the perfect place on his last scouting trip but ended up not using it when the money for his cinematic endeavor fell through. He remembered the place but had a little trouble summoning up directions. I thought you could take a quick mosey through your computer over there and write me up a short list of places that meet his description. Oh, and I'll also need to know the names of the folks who own them so I can call ahead and tell them that I'm planning to drop by. Don't want to pop in and be shot as a trespasser, do we?"

"Certainly not," Ariel said. "It would be such a colossal waste." She eyed him up and down, appreciatively taking inventory of the potential loss.

"I'm glad you understand. You know, in my short time here, I've found Swedish women to be particularly deep and wise. I presume it comes from peering into the recess of your soul on those long, dark nights when there's nothing better to do."

Ariel peered longingly up at Henry. "You cannot imagine the hardships, the nights that last fifteen, twenty hours . . . and no one to share them with."

As she spoke, Ariel crept closer and closer to Henry. Soon they wouldn't just be sharing the darkened hour, they'd be sharing the same clothes. Henry would have taken a step back, but that would have drawn him further away from the precious information that could lead to rescuing Vienna. So, instead, he took a deep breath and allowed Ariel's fingers to do the walking first up the back of his hand, then up his arm to his shoulder.

Ariel looked Henry in the eye. When he didn't respond, she tickled his shoulder. When he still didn't respond, she yanked her hand out and snapped, "You are not a movie producer."

"I'm not?"

"No. Our own filmmakers have to be bribed to shoot here, and over half of them don't. No one from outside of the country would come to make a movie in Sweden."

"I'm an iconoclast."

"You are a con artist."

"Hey . . ."

"And not a particularly good one."

"Hey!"

"What is it that you really want, Mr. Coleman? In my experience, I find the direct approach frequently works best. Don't you?"

He said, "You're right. I am a lousy con artist. But I'm a heck of a poker player."

"With that face?"

"Hey, hey!"

"It is a very attractive face. But not particularly deceptive."

"You'd be surprised what I can do when I'm highly motivated."

"I would very much like to be given the opportunity," Ariel said, as her hand once again found his arm.

"Think of Vienna," Henry reminded himself. "Think of Vienna."

"See, there's this guy. Name of Stenbeck. Owes me a ton of money from a poker game back in the States. He flew the coop before I had the chance to collect. I knew he was from Sweden. Thought I'd pop in and wave the collection plate around a bit, know what I mean?"

"It must be a great deal of money for you to make a trip halfway around the world."

"Oh, yeah. He's got something I really, really want."

"I understand that feeling," Ariel said.

Henry played stupid. "So you can help me out?"

"Perhaps."

"I'd be real appreciative."

"Is that a fact?"

Henry gulped and said, "Yes."

"Very well," Ariel said and turned to her computer, where she punched a few keys and told Henry, "The Stenbeck family, they own an estate a few miles outside of town. It used to be the former St. Clair orphanage."

"Stenbeck evicted a bunch of orphans so he could have himself a little country place?"

"Not precisely. The orphanage burned down over twenty years ago. Mr. Stenbeck acquired the property and, several years later, he had a castle from France rebuilt on the site."

"He relocated an entire castle?"

"Not the physical structure. According to our records, he merely had the floor plan and interiors copied down to the last details. Gossip has it he got the idea from some Scotsman he once knew, who did relocate an entire castle, brick by brick, from Europe to the American Midwest." Ariel hesitated, "But I also thought I heard that James Stenbeck was currently in prison. I don't believe you will find him on-site."

"Oh, that's all right. I'll be happy just to run into a family member and get back what I'm owed."

"No one lives on the property, as far as I know."

"I think I'll check it out anyway." Henry turned to leave. And somehow Ariel was standing in front of him.

"Did you forget your manners, Mr. Coleman?"

"Oh. Yes. Right. Thank you very much. Your help was most appreciated." He stuck out his hand, grabbed Ariel's palm firmly, and pumped it up and down. In response, Ariel raised Henry's arm, brought it to her lips, and kissed each of his knuckles.

Henry, who'd done plenty of courteous finger smooching in his day, had never been on the receiving end of said affection. Were you just supposed to stand there while the kisser finished? Where did one put one's eyes? If you looked down, you were greeted with the back of someone's head.

If you let your eyes wander to survey the room, didn't that indicate boredom? Henry supposed one could utilize the downtime to think of a proper verbal response. Alas, in his case, even after the interminable wait, once Ariel returned his hand to the proper owner, Henry could still think of no adequate reply.

He settled on, "A pleasure meeting you, too, Miss Aldrin," before turning tail and running out of the office.

12

Vienna could no longer tell day from night. And she couldn't even blame it on Sweden's dark, Arctic winters. Because she'd lost track right around the time she'd answered the door to her parents' ice house, only to discover Paul Ryan. In Sweden. And holding a cloth doused with what she presumed, in retrospect, to be chloroform.

When she'd come to (she had no idea how many hours later), she'd found herself in a room equipped with all the basic comforts—bed, table, chair, a shelf stocked with books, a vanity table propping up a large mirror and an adequate assortment of cosmetics, hairbrushes, pins, and lotions—but no windows. Or clocks. The adjoining bathroom had running water, fluffy towels, another mirror but, again, no way to see outside. A handwritten note of explanation about where she was, why she had been abducted, and how Paul was involved would have been appreciated. But Vienna had had to wait what she estimated was another few hours before Paul showed up, with a gourmet dinner and a surprisingly straightforward response to her demands that he immediately tell her what in the world was going on!

"My parents helped you to pull off this scheme?" she asked incredulously.

"They're the ones who sent me down to the ice house with instructions on how to grab you so Henry wouldn't notice. They said you'd understand that it was for the good of the family. They even seem to be under the impression that you wouldn't mind."

Vienna nodded. But whether she was agreeing with Paul or her parents' assumption wasn't clear.

Suddenly unsure of where he stood, Paul reiterated, "Your parents said it was okay."

"Am I to presume that you never kidnap without parental permission?"

"It is preferable, I must say."

"Where am I?" Vienna demanded.

"You're with me," Paul said lightly.

"Forgive me for not being comforted by the thought."

"I can assure you, you're perfectly safe. I promised your parents I'd take excellent care of you."

Vienna said, "All of my life, I knew how important regaining the throne was to my parents. I knew it, but I do not think I fully understood it." She sighed. "I understand it now."

"I'm not going to hurt you," Paul said. "This isn't one of those deals where the abductor sends a severed finger a day until the family pays up. It's a business arrangement. Henry has something I want, so I took something he wants. It's a chess game."

"It is a felony," Vienna clarified. "You wish for us to re- veal Lucy's whereabouts so that Johnny might be raised by a felon?"

"Actually, between Craig, me, and Lucy, the little tyke doesn't really have another option. Johnny is my nephew. My sister wanted him to be raised by Dusty—who, for the record, wasn't exactly squeaky clean himself. But, since he's dead, I know I'd be Jennifer's next choice. I can be a good parent. I haven't had a chance to prove it yet. There were a few times when I thought . . . It doesn't matter. Those op- portunities didn't work out. This will."

"I can just imagine the wonderful role model you will be for Johnny. With James Stenbeck as a father—"

"I am nothing like James Stenbeck."

"Ha," Vienna said.

Paul waited for her to continue. When she didn't, he pressed, "Care to elaborate on that observation?"

"No. 'Ha' is sufficient."

"Actually, with James as a father and Barbara as a mother, my success at parenting is a slam dunk."

"How so?"

"I simply do the exact opposite of everything they did and I'm guaranteed to get it right." When Vienna didn't look convinced, Paul changed his tactics. "I don't understand why you and Henry are being so stubborn about this. And don't give me that professional integrity crap. I knew Henry Coleman back when he was a weasely W-OAK station man- ager, poisoning the lead anchorwoman's sandwich so that his fluffy protégée, Katie, could step in and play "All About Eve." Henry has no professional integrity. And you . . .

everyone knows you just go where the money is. Or was it the prince of Leonia's charm, rather than his diamond jewelry, that drew you to him?"

"People are capable of changing," Vienna said.

"No, they're not. They're capable of changing their behavior. Especially when it suits their purposes. But who you are at the start is who you are for life. The only thing that might change is how you go about getting what you want."

"You are very cynical."

"I have very good reasons to be. And frankly, so do you. You're telling me it doesn't bother you even a little tiny bit that your own parents are willing to use you as a bargaining chip to reclaim a throne that doesn't even come with the ability to wage war or host bacchanalias?"

"That sounds like something Henry would say."

Paul ignored her. "You're changing the subject. We were discussing your bold assertion that your parents allowing me to hold you for ransom doesn't bother you in the slightest. I don't buy it."

"I suppose I am a touch . . . surprised. But I have already told you, I know how important reclaiming the throne is to them. I have always known. When I was a little girl, I thought it was my fault that, no matter what I did, or how good I tried to be, there was always this unhappiness in the house. I tried to fix it. It was foolish, I realize now. But back then, I was constantly fluttering around, trying to be charming, trying to make them smile. I thought if I could only figure out what it was I was missing, I could learn to do it and finally make them happy." Paul didn't reply. He just stared at Vienna for so long that she grew self-conscious under his gaze and conceded, "I said that I realize now how foolish I was."

Paul said, "My parents weren't married when I was born. My father didn't even know about me. Barbara had me in secret and gave me up for adoption to a friend of hers. Sometimes I think I even remember that other woman a little bit. But, then again, Barbara is such a force of nature, I doubt any competing maternal presence would register. I was about three when James Stenbeck found out I existed and decided he had to get me back at all costs. He bribed my adoptive parents into giving me up, and then he pursued my mother with, let's say, typically Stenbeck-ian zeal, until she agreed to marry him and make me legitimate. The legitimate part was key, because it was the only way I could qualify to inherit the Stenbeck fortune and the only way James would be able to control it." He'd been staring at Vienna so hard that it surprised her when Paul suddenly sprung up and turned away, as if he couldn't bear telling her the next part of the story while making eye contact. Paul stood with his back to her, addressing not so much her as the past itself when he continued, "I think my parents were married for a grand total of six minutes before James started cheating. With Margo Hughes, as a matter of fact. It was before she married Tom and became a cop. Back when the bad boy still appealed to her, I guess. Anyway, James started cheating, and my mother became more and more miserable. She tried to divorce him. Which is when he drugged her and hired people to make her think she was going crazy, all in the interest of having her committed and getting custody of me." Paul turned back to Vienna. And, for a moment, he wasn't the man holding her hostage. He was a little boy who winced when he said, "I remember those days. I remember how unhappy my mother was. And I remember thinking that it was all my fault." The wince turned into a rueful smile. Vienna didn't smile back. But she did nod her head ever so slightly. "I tried to be a very good boy, too. My mother hired a Stenbeck cousin, Gunnar St. Clair, to give me guitar lessons. I thought if I learned to play the guitar very, very well, I could make her happy. She did seem so invested in those lessons."

"Did it work?" Vienna asked.

"In a way. I didn't become Jimi Hendrix, but my mother fell in love with Gunnar. He helped her leave James. She married him, and for a few years there she was actually happy. But then he died, and we were right back where we started. Barbara miserable, me thinking it was my job to save her."

"It is not fair," Vienna said. "It is not right for a parent to make their child feel responsible for their happiness."

"Agreed," Paul said. And then, softly, almost as an afterthought, he added, "You could show your parents you're done playing that game."

"How?"

"You could nullify my bargain with them. Tell me where Lucy is yourself."

"I do not understand."

"The deal I made with your parents states that when Henry reveals where Lucy is, I give them back the throne. Technically, if you, rather than Henry, give me that information, our deal is null and void. No throne for them. This is your chance to hurt your parents the way they've hurt you."

"You bastard!" Vienna exploded. "You are just trying to manipulate me."

"Doesn't make it any less of a good plan."

"I have no interest in hurting my parents. I love my parents. You truly have no shame. Your sad story . . . was it even true? Any of it?"

Paul studied her closely. And then he said, "No. Not a word. You're right, I was just trying to manipulate you. Stupid me thinking you'd believe it."

"You are no better than your father," Vienna said. "You do not deserve to raise a child. I will never tell you what I know about Lucy and Johnny. Not even if you keep me locked up for a thousand years."

Paul stood up. He unlocked the door. "Suit yourself."

And then locked it soundly behind him.

After Vienna had eaten all the dinner Paul had brought her and experimented with every combination of available makeup and hairstyles to relieve her boredom, she heard footsteps outside her door again. This time, Vienna vowed to be prepared when Paul approached. She looked around the room for something to strike him with when he entered. If she disabled him even for a moment, Vienna might be able to turn the tables, lock Paul up, and escape. Granted, Vienna had no idea where exactly she was or whether she was being guarded, but common sense insisted she had to try something.

Unfortunately, everything in the room large enough to

serve as a weapon was nailed down. And she doubted Paul would endure much trauma from her hair-dryer or a stab with a mascara brush. Vienna finally settled on a heavy book, which she took off the shelf. Vienna saw that the tome was a comprehensive collection of short stories by O. Henry. She smiled and took it as a good omen.

She assumed her position by the door and waited.

And waited.

She could still hear the footsteps, but Paul wasn't coming in.

Instead, ever so faintly—so faintly that she couldn't be sure if her ears were playing tricks on her—she heard, "Psst . . . Vienna . . . Psst . . . Are you in here? It's Henry."

"Henry!" Vienna shouted with all her might, not even caring if it was Paul trying to trick her.

"Vienna!"

"Henry!"

"Vienna!"

"Henry!"

Both simultaneously realized they'd reached the extent of that particular exchange's usefulness.

"Hold on," he said. "I'm coming for you!"

Vienna heard a thump outside her door. It vibrated on the inside. And then she heard a subdued, "Okay, not that way."

In a few moments, she heard some scratching. The doorknob jiggled. The tip of what Vienna presumed was a credit card briefly peeked in through the crack in the door, bounced up and down, then disappeared again, but nothing happened.

"Damn it," Henry cursed. "Stupid Fashions credit card. I expected a store owned by Barbara Ryan to produce tougher stock. This is too flimsy. American Express is what's called for under the circumstances. Never should have left home without it." When Vienna failed to respond appropriately, he said, "That's a joke. Pop cultural reference. Work with me."

"Ha, ha, ha," Vienna said and tugged on the door with all her might. As Henry was doing the same on the other side, neither made much progress.

"I'd pick the lock if I had a torque wrench or even an Allen. Heck, I'd be willing to settle for a paper clip at this point, just something to pop the cylinders with."

"Will this do?" Vienna asked. She plucked a bobby pin from out of her new hairdo and slid it under the door to Henry.

"How do I love thee, Vienna Hyatt, let me count the ways! What have we got here, boys and girls? Five measly cylinders? Come to Papa, you flimsy little things. This should only take a minute."

Thirty-two of them later, Henry triumphantly flung open the door and said, "See? I told you. Piece of cake."

"Oh, Henry," Vienna flung herself into his arms. "How did you ever find me?"

"A gentleman never sleuths and tells."

"But how did you get past Paul's guards?"

"No guards. Place is deserted as far as I can tell. No gate, no Keep Out signs. I walked right in the front door."

Vienna withdrew from his embrace and poked her head out to peer down the hallway they were standing in. Hers seemed to be just one of a series of nondescript doors. And there wasn't a window to be found.

"This is very peculiar," Vienna said.

"Hey, if Paul Ryan doesn't know how to protect what he's rightfully stolen—not my job to teach him the ABCs. Come on, let's get out of here. I looked around when I drove up, there wasn't another car anyplace on the property far as I could see. But that doesn't mean Paul isn't lurking somewhere. Those Stenbecks, they're known for their lurking."

Henry took Vienna's hand and confidently led her down the hall. Vienna followed, wishing she could believe his conviction that everything was exactly as it appeared. She couldn't help wondering why Paul would go to all the trouble of stashing her away and locking her in an impeccably prepared room and then literally leave the front door unlocked?

"Come on, it's this way," Henry said, beckoning Vienna toward the door at the end of the hall. He stepped through first, leading her by the hand.

But they both plunged straight down into a pitch-black pit.

13

Even since they'd gotten back from Montega, Tom and Margo Hughes had been sleeping in separate rooms. By accident.

Sure, the flight back from South America had been a touch tense. The memory of Tom's recent shenanigans with Vienna had hung over them like a dark storm cloud following a beleaguered cartoon character. Conversation had devolved to a periodic exchange of grunts interspersed with overly polite formality.

"Would you be so kind as to pass me the blanket from the overhead compartment?"

"I don't believe I would care to do so at this time."

"Thank you anyway for your consideration."

But Margo had figured that just as vacation romances tended to dissipate once they were brought down to the terra firma of everyday life, so would vacation squabbles. Margo had had every intention of putting away her grudge—no matter how reasonable it was—and getting back to normal once they were home. Except that their first night back in

Oakdale, Margo had gone into her son Adam's old room, looking for a pair of socks she could borrow to make up for being too tired to do her own laundry. While digging around in his dresser, she was distracted by an old photo of her, Tom, Adam, and Casey when the boys were little. Usually, the sight of twenty-year-old pictures just reminded Margo of how young she and Tom had once been and how cute he'd looked with a beard and wouldn't it be fun for him to try growing one again? But this time, what had caught her attention was how in love she and Tom looked. There they were, with a pair of squirming preschoolers on their laps, a photographer waving his arm trying to get everyone to peer in the same direction at the same time, and still, Tom and Margo only had eyes for each other. Judging from the photo, Tom had just said something to make Margo laugh. He had that twinkle in his eye that dared her to be the first to crack up while he innocently kept a straight face. And she'd fallen for it, because she looked as if she was about to burst out laughing. That's why, despite having several other, traditionally posed family portraits, they'd ended up enlarging and framing that one. Everyone looked so real in that shot. So alive. So . . . them. Somewhere along the line, Margo and Tom had stopped being themselves. She wasn't sure when or why. And she wasn't sure how to reverse the process.

As Margo sat staring at the long-ago photo, exhausted and jet-lagged, she fell asleep on Adam's bed.

By accident.

Only Tom didn't see it that way. The next morning, he assumed she'd done it as a way to punish him or to make a point. At first, Margo wanted to correct him. But, somehow, she never got around to it. She didn't know why.

She didn't correct him that evening, either, when Tom made it clear that he expected her to continue with her sulking. Because by then, Margo had decided that correcting his misperception would be tantamount to giving in and agreeing that he was the one who had the right to be angry, not her. So for close to a week, Tom and Margo slept in separate rooms, even though neither one wanted it that way. Because each was trying to prove a point to the other.

Margo told herself she liked sleeping alone. It was especially nice since Tom had claimed the master bedroom, and she didn't have to worry about being woken up by the phone in the middle of the night. Between Tom's and Margo's jobs, plus four kids ranging in age from preteen to adult, phone calls in the middle of the night were a Hughes family staple.

That night, Margo was planning to ignore every call that came in. Except that, even with a pillow over her head, it was hard to ignore the loud, insistent ringing of the phone at a little after 3:00 a.m. standard time, especially once she heard Tom instructing, "Okay, first thing, if you see large chess pieces lying around, stay away from the Cheshire cat."

Either her husband was having an intimate chat with the Mad Hatter or . . . no. It couldn't be. Not after all these years!

Margo ran into Tom's room.

"Is that . . . ?" she demanded.

He nodded. "Henry and Vienna. Seems they've stumbled into our old haunt."

"They're in France?"

"Sweden."

"Mr. Big's castle is in France."

"Seems James had it copied and reconstructed in Sweden; lock, stock, and booby traps. I shudder to guess what for. Paul used it to hide Vienna from Henry. Henry had no trouble getting in to rescue her. Because, as I'm sure you remember, the challenge is in getting out."

"How did Henry know to call us?"

"He remembered what you said on the plane to Montega, about our last vacation being in a booby-trapped castle in Europe. Henry thought we might be able to advise him and Vienna on how to get out alive."

"Which room are they in?"

"They're not sure. It's dark. I warned them about the Cheshire cat in the Wonderland room. Grabbing it makes the floor collapse."

Margo took the phone from Tom. "Henry? Avoid the hearts painted on the floor. Stepping on one triggers an arrow."

A pause on the other end. Some static. And then Henry's: "You're kidding me."

"No. If you and Vienna are in Mr. Big's old castle, I assure you, we are not kidding. Those booby traps are deadly. If you're in the room with the hearts, that's the one he called The Room of Love. The trick to getting out of there is Elizabeth Barrett Browning's 'How Do I Love Thee' poem. You count the number of—"

"All I see is some ropes, swords, a pirate's chest—"

"Pirate's chest?" Tom and Margo exchanged looks and, in unison, blurted out, "The *Treasure Island* room."

"Henry," Margo said. "Tell me exactly what you're doing right now."

"Making a booty call."

"Say what?" Margo asked, while Tom advised, "Not a good time, man."

"Pirate's booty," Henry patiently explained. "Wonder what's in the trunk—"

"Duck, Henry!" Margo screamed.

"Why?" The last vowel of his query was drowned out by the sound of several cannons going off. "Oh," Henry said after a moment. "That's why."

"Was I not clear about the booby traps?" Tom asked.

"Okay." Henry sounded winded and not nearly as eager for adventure as he'd been a moment before. "I've had enough fun. How do we get out of here?"

"The room you're in resembles the hull of a ship, right?" Tom asked. "It's in the shape of a U, with rounded walls and ropes and barrels on the sides? Listen carefully. You're standing by the treasure trunk. There's nothing in there to help you. Turn around and you'll see a door at the farthest end. It's hard to make out in the dark, but if you're in Mr. Big's old castle, trust me, it's there."

"At the end of the plank?"

"But don't step on it. It's rigged to set off more cannons."

"How are we supposed to reach the door without stepping on the plank?" Vienna asked. "There is no other path."

"Grab one of the ropes hanging from the ceiling. Swing your way across."

"Me, Tarzan, her, Jane?"

"Wrong work of classic literature. But, yes, that's the general idea."

"Listen up," Margo said. "You're not out of the woods yet. When you get to the door, make sure you don't trigger the—"

"Ceiling full of descending spears?" The familiar creaking that still sometimes invaded her nightmares crackled through the phone lines as, raising his voice to be heard over the din, Henry remarked, "You know, Margo, that might have been a useful piece of information for us to have prior to swinging over."

"I was about to tell you. Would you just shut up for a minute and listen?" No response from the other end. Just the determined clanging of foot-long, sharpened nails making their way South, right on top of Henry and Vienna. "Henry? Henry, can you hear me? Damn it! Vienna, somebody, answer me!" Margo looked helplessly at Tom. "He can't hear me. It's too loud in there. Henry!"

"It'll be okay," Tom reassured her. "We figured out how to escape. They will, too."

"Are you kidding? In just the first year of our knowing each other, we managed to survive a hungry cougar, a pit of snakes, a raging African river, and landing a plane in the middle of a field while it leaked the last of our fuel. Henry passed out walking from the air-conditioned car to Sierra's mansion."

"You have a point."

"There's got to be something we can do. Someone we can call. Henry! Vienna! Answer me!"

Tom crossed the room to where he'd dropped his sports coat across the back of a chair. He fumbled in the front pocket for his own cell phone while Margo still clung to the landline. "I'll see if I can reach the local authorities."

"No, it'll be too late!"

"Don't you remember? Two hours and thirty-two minutes. That's how long we had to find our way out of the room."

"How long have Henry and Vienna been in there?"

"I don't know."

"Then they might have run out of time!"

"Margo, come on." Seeing how upset she was, Tom returned to where she was sitting on the bed, clutching the receiver desperately in both hands and shaking it slightly, as if that could somehow will Henry and Vienna to hear them. Tom wrapped his arms around Margo and urged, "Have some faith. Each of the rooms had a clue that hinted at how to escape. Henry's a well-read guy. He's smart. He'll figure it out."

"We're out!" the phone crackled.

"See?" Tom said.

"Oh, thank God!" Margo cried.

Tom shot her a smug look, then cheered Henry. "I knew you could do it. Which clue finally got you through? Was it the black spot? The talking parrot? The one-legged—"

"I picked the lock," Henry said.

Tom looked at Margo. "You know, the entire time we were in there, why did we never think of that?"

"Have bobby pin, will travel," Henry crowed. "Listen, thanks for all your help. Hope we didn't scare you too badly when the phone cut out. I just needed to focus on Ye Ole

Lock Picking. The descending spikes—excellent motivation. I think I beat my own personal best time back there."

"I'm glad you're okay," Margo said.

"Sorry to bring back bad memories."

"Actually, I . . . it's all right. They weren't all bad." She
smiled at Tom. He smiled back. They hung up the phone.

And turned if off for the rest of the night.

Most of the following day, too.

Back at Chez Hyatt, Henry all but thrust Vienna into the
faces of her parents and Paul. "See her and weep, people."

Although Henry couldn't help noticing that Vienna didn't
look particularly happy about having just been gallantly rescued from a fate worse than . . . some nonspecifically bad
fate. She hadn't looked happy since Henry had come stumbling through the door of her luxury prison.

The least Henry expected Vienna to do was blast her parents for the illegal and immoral stunt they'd condoned. But
she declined to do even that. Instead, Vienna merely looked
from her parents to Paul and back to Henry, her face utterly
inscrutable. To compensate for her ambivalence, Henry
ramped up his own rambunctious glee. "Yes, that's right,
you heard me: See her and weep. Or pucker up and smell
the smorgasbord. Or whatever winning poker expression
you've got here. Vienna's back. I've got her. And that means
your little plan is up the creek without an ice floe."

"Vienna." Martina touched her daughter's arm lightly.
"Are you well?"

"I am fine. Henry is right. He saved me."

Well, at least she was acknowledging him in word, if not exactly grateful deed. Maybe the grateful deed would come later that night? Henry could only hope.

"If it weren't for Henry," Vienna cautioned, "I might have been killed by a cannon or by a ceiling full of descending spikes."

"What?" Gjord roared and turned to Paul. "You promised she would not be hurt!"

"Okay, two points of order, here. One, as you can see, she wasn't hurt. So I kept my part of the bargain. And two, I promised she wouldn't be hurt as long as she was with me. I didn't put her in the room with the spikes. Henry did."

"Is that true?" Gjord demanded.

"Yes," Henry said meekly, before recalling that he was the one who had a right to be indignant this time around and he wasn't about to be bullied into giving it up. "You trusted a Stenbeck to keep his word? How do you know that even if I had spilled what I know about Lucy, he'd have given you what he promised?"

"We'll never know now, will we?" Paul told Gjord and Martina, "because our deal is off."

"No!" Martina shouted. "No, no, wait. Our bargain was for the return of the throne in exchange for information. Does it matter whom the information comes from? What if it were to come from Vienna?"

"I suppose we could amend the terms," Paul conceded magnanimously.

Martina told Vienna, "My darling, did you hear what Mr. Ryan said? You can still help us. If you tell him what you know about his nephew's whereabouts, we can still get our birthright back. Please, Vienna." Martina gripped both of her daughter's hands. "You know how much this means to us. We have been waiting our entire lives for such a miraculous opportunity. And now, you are the one who can make our dreams come true."

"Surely you jest!" Henry made a lunge to free both of Vienna's hands from the grips of maternal manipulation but only managed to acquire one. "After what you two just put her through? You expect Vienna to do you any favors? Don't make her laugh!"

"This is none of your business," Gjord said. "It is a family matter."

"Some family. You let your kid nearly become shish kebob, and then you expect her to turn around and betray her professional ethics, not to mention the love of her life, so you two can ride around in parades a couple times a year?"

"It is a bit more than that," Martina said, ever so subtly pulling her daughter closer. "Vienna understands. Don't you, darling?"

"What Vienna understands," Henry pulled her back in his direction, less subtly, "is that her precious Mama and Papa care more about some meaningless title than they do about her. Well, you know what Vienna has to say to that? Take your precious crowns and shove them, right, Vienna? Come on. Tell them it's absurd. Tell them you have no intention of going along with this."

Vienna looked at Henry. And then she looked at her mother.

The clock ticked loudly.

But still, Vienna did not say no.

"I can't believe you didn't say no!"

For a conversation this important, Henry had refused to retire to the ice house. He'd insisted that he and Vienna needed privacy—and, frankly, warmth. So the two of them had retired to her childhood bedroom on the second floor, complete with framed pictures of various European royalty on the walls and photos of Vienna and her doting Mama and Papa over the years. All three of them were always holding hands, hugging, or looking at each other adoringly. Their mutually doting gazes implicitly promised, "I would do anything, anything at all to make you happy. Just ask."

Under the circumstances, Henry did his best to ignore the décor, just like he did his best to ignore the fact that the closet was stuffed with silk gowns fit for a princess, not a fry cook at Al's Diner. Instead, he focused on unambiguously expressing his displeasure at Vienna's refusal to tell her parents what they could do with their much-coveted, promised scepters.

"I need to think," Vienna said. She sat down on the bed and instinctively reached for a child's sparkly toy tiara hooked onto the bedpost. She rolled it around her fingers, brushing off the glitter that rained off onto her lap, and refused to meet Henry's eyes.

"What's there to think about?" he asked.

"They are my parents. I have a responsibility to them."

"Wrong tense. Maybe you once *had* a responsibility to them, but I'm willing to bet that, from a legal standpoint, all familial obligations were rendered null and void the minute they sold you down the river—literally—for a couple pieces of gold."

"You do not understand."

"Obviously."

"We are family. We do things for each other."

"They had you kidnapped! And you know the best part? They told me—and this is with a straight face, both of them—they told me they didn't think you'd mind."

"I do not," Vienna said.

Henry opened his mouth. He closed it again. Perhaps, in the annals of witty rejoinders, there existed an adequate one for this particular occasion, but Henry simply could not think of it at the moment.

"Huh?"

"They were correct, I do not mind. They did it for the good of the family. For the good of us all. You do not understand. You and your family, you barely speak."

"I doubt Mom could find the phone through all the empty bottles and cigarette smoke. And you know Eve, she only gets one call a day up at maximum security."

"You love Maddie," Vienna reminded him. "Would you not do anything for her?"

"I wouldn't kidnap and lock her up Rapunzel-style!"

"Even if it was for the good of the whole family?"

"Are you out of your mind?"

Vienna sighed. "I knew you would not understand. You

just do not care about your family in the same way that I care for mine."

"You know what, sweetheart? I think you spent a little too much time poolside with Craig Montgomery. He kidnapped Lucy a while back to prove what a caring dad he is. Now you're saying the fact that I never stuffed my kid sister in the trunk of a car proves that I don't understand familial devotion. It's nuts."

"It is family."

"Well, then I don't want any part of it."

"Yes," Vienna said softly. "You have made that abundantly clear."

"Oh, no." Henry held up his hands. "Oh, no, no, no, no. Don't you turn this around on me. I'm not the crazy one here. This isn't another example of big, bad commitment-phobic Henry refusing to get married and sire babies and live happily ever after because he's selfish and immature."

"You are being selfish," Vienna said. "You are refusing to understand what this could mean for my family. And for me."

"Ah-ha!" Henry cried. "Ah-ha! Ah-ha! Ah-ha! Now we get to the real gist of it. This isn't about Mama and Papa wanting to play King and Queen. This is about Princess Vienna! All this talk about your parents and their boo-hoo lifelong melancholy—"

"This is not some generalized malaise. My parents truly are suffering. Your belief that the cause of their pain is trivial and irrelevant does not make it any less real. For them or for me. Every child has dreams of playing the hero for their parents. Do not tell me that, no matter how angry you may have been with her, you did not fantasize of rescuing your mother from her unhappiness?"

"Luckily, a bottle of gin got the job done much quicker."

"Be serious. For once in your life, please try to be serious. Try to understand. I am saying that this is my chance. Not merely to fulfill my parents' dreams, but mine, as well."

Henry tried to do what Vienna asked. He tried to be serious and to take her seriously. But there was something people didn't publicize too much about being serious. Being serious required thinking and soul-searching and coming to conclusions that were much better off left unconcluded. Being serious was scary.

Whereas being flip handily shoved all that discomfort into the deep recesses of his psyche, from where he hoped it would never spring forth again.

Faced with the choice, there really was no choice.

"Whatever you say, Your Highness." Henry bowed at the waist. Ironically, of course. "And I'm sure that your getting a fancy title of your own to flaunt around and show off to your old friends has nothing to do with this."

She kicked him. With Henry's smirking face so close to her crossed legs, it was understandably tempting. But it still hurt when her toe met his nose.

"Stop it!" Vienna cried. "Why are you behaving like this?"

"Because I thought you were on my side," Henry, still clutching his throbbing nose, whinnied. "I thought we were in this together. We were on a mission, we were a team."

"We are still a team."

"Sure, until someone richer waves a shiny bauble in your face, and then you're off! Like the Kentucky Derby."

"This is not about money, Henry."

"Everything is about money with you."

Vienna gasped. Considering the fact that Henry heard what he'd said at the exact same time that she had, he might well have gasped too. But gasping in shock at your own statement suggested that you didn't mean it. It also cast doubt over everything that came before. And Henry still stood by everything he'd said before. So while Henry was sorry for having blurted out his remark about Vienna and money, he stubbornly refused to apologize or change course.

"It's nothing to be ashamed of, Vienna. I'm a gold digger myself. That's why we fit so well together. I don't blame you for going to the highest bidder. Heck, I'd be disappointed if you didn't. I like to pride myself on being a good judge of character, and I always knew it was just a matter of time before you threw me over. I just expected it to be for another prince of Leonia type. But I see your point, becoming a princess yourself is truly much better. Cuts out the pesky middleman."

Who said that? Even as the words were sailing most eloquently—if he did say so himself—out of his mouth, there was a part of Henry standing off to the side, wondering, "Who said that?" And, more importantly, what the hell was that damn fool thinking?

"Please go now," Vienna said.

Another woman might have screamed obscenities, clawed his eyes out, burst into tears. But Vienna simply stood up and with no hysteria, no rancor, with barely so much as an excess movement, indicated the door and repeated, "I would like you to go."

Henry did as he was told.

His last thought as the door was shut—politely—behind him was, "She really does deserve to be a princess, after all."

14

It proved fortunate—for Henry, if not the Hyatt family's insurance premiums—that he still had the keys to their Koenigsegg sports car in his pocket. After being unceremoniously dismissed by Vienna, Henry blew past Gjord, Martina, and Paul, grabbed his coat, and, for the second day in a row, peeled away from the ostentatious estate with no one seeming to care where he went.

He drove into town and promptly pulled up in front of the first bar he saw. Inside, black-and-white checkered tablecloths laid out horizontally battled with the vertical, metallic stairs for visual dominance. After a few belts of Absolut failed to improve his spirits, not to mention his vertigo, Henry moved on to another inebriation emporium, where the bartender proved to be way too chatty for Henry's liking. Even if Henry couldn't understand a word he said.

Deciding that perhaps the Swedish bar scene wasn't for him, Henry hit the street again, figuring to score an entire bottle of Absolut and continue drinking in the privacy of his very expensive car.

He struck out in the first three grocery stores he visited. In a torrent of Swedish and international sign language, the message was conveyed that stores did not carry alcohol. Henry would need "Systembolaget." But whether that mysterious noun was animal, vegetable, or mineral proved elusive.

At that moment a guardian angel appeared through the combination of snow and Henry's alcohol-infused fog to whisper sweet nothings about Systembolaget being Sweden's government alcohol monopoly, blah, blah, blah, it existed to curb alcoholism and forcibly improve public health, blah, blah, blah, by making sure that alcohol could never be sold for profit and limiting the number of stores and the hours those stores could be open and refusing to sell to minors and the visibly inebriated and . . . wait! That last part! Henry suspected that last part might apply to him.

Fortunately, his guardian angel was prepared for just such an emergency, and, as Henry waited outside, the angel disappeared into the Systembolaget premises and exited moments later carrying enough golden elixir to turn the visibly inebriated into the fall-down drunk without permission from the government. Which was, as far as Henry could piece together the next day, precisely what happened.

Hangovers, Henry had decided long before turning twenty-one, were something that happened to other people. Which is why he actually awakened fresh as a daisy the next morning. Well, fresh as a daisy with a pounding headache and a stomach lodged somewhere in the neighborhood of his spleen. But as long as Henry refused to perceive it as a hangover and assumed he'd developed a noncontagious case of the flu, his youthful pledge still stood. On the other hand, waking up in odd circumstances with just a touch of temporary amnesia was something that did happen to Henry. Probably a smidge more often than it did to other people. But, then again, he was the sensitive type.

So it was with all these caveats in mind that Henry rolled over, opened his eyes, and found himself in bed with that devoted, hand-kissing public servant, Ariel Aldrin—aka, he now realized, his Angel of Mercy!

"Good," she said. "You're finally awake. We can get down to business."

Henry sat up slowly. He gingerly lifted the blanket tucked beneath his chin and peered down long enough to ascertain that he was still fully clothed. Which either meant that nothing had happened, or that something had happened, except Henry had proven so deficient at it that he'd been ordered to put on his clothes and go home but had passed out instead.

"Oh, get over yourself," Ariel snapped. "I've got more important things on my mind than ravaging your skinny body."

"But . . ." How exactly had Henry tripped into the position of having to defend himself? And what exactly was he defending himself from? "Back at the office, you—"

"That was before I figured out what you were really after. And how I could be of help to you. I thought you were just a fresh face passing through. We don't get a lot of fresh faces around here."

"Are you speaking Swedish? It sounds like English, except I have no idea what you're talking about."

"You're here as an agent for Lucinda Walsh."

"How do you know Lucinda Walsh?"

"She and I have an ex-husband in common. And a stepson."

"Come again? Is everyone in this town from Oakdale?"

"Just the people you need to concern yourself with. And I'm not from Oakdale. I just happened to settle down there for a few years. A few very bad years. But, now that you're here, I may finally get that payoff I was owed two decades ago."

"Yup," Henry said. "Definitely still speaking Swedish."

"Listen closely, I'm about to do you a big favor."

"That's great. I'm all for it. But first, I've got to know: Who was the husband you and Lucinda shared?"

"John Dixon."

"And the mutual stepson?"

"Dusty Donovan."

"Dusty? Johnny's father?"

"Dusty has a kid?"

"A very popular kid."

"Well, I haven't seen Dusty since he was fourteen years old. We didn't exactly keep in touch. He hated me, and the feeling was mutual."

"He's dead now."

"May he rest in peace. Now, do you want to hear what I've got for you or not?"

"You have the floor."

Ariel got out of bed. She too was fully clothed, which meant Ariel had been telling the truth—she wasn't after his body. Henry breathed a sigh of relief, then realized he was also a tiny bit offended.

"I know why you're here," she said. "You and the little Hyatt twit are working for Lucinda Walsh, trying to track down her granddaughter. Paul Ryan promised to give up the Stenbecks' claim to the throne in exchange for you two coughing up what you know."

"I told you all this last night?"

"Of course not. Last night, you were a babbling, drunken idiot."

"Some people find that charming."

"My mother filled me in about what you were after. She works for the Hyatts."

As Henry had only met one domestic so far, he took a wild guess. "Greta the maid is your mother?"

"Yes."

"So you're the daughter with the new job working for the city?"

"Yes." Ariel dismissed Henry's sterling detective work with a wave of the hand. "After you came into the office with your ridiculous cover story about looking for the Stenbeck estate, I called her and we put two and two together. I can help you."

"No need. I've already rescued Vienna."

"Your Rapunzel doesn't interest me. I'm offering proof that Paul has no legal right to the Stenbeck throne. Which means he also has no legal right to offer it to the Hyatts."

If Ariel thought she'd had Henry's attention before, it was
nothing compared to how alert he was now. "Which means
Vienna doesn't have to choose between me and her parents!"
He sprang up in bed. Hangover—er, flu—be damned.

"You're a bright boy. Now let's see you do some arithme-
tic. How much is Lucinda paying you to find Lucy?"

"A gentleman never tells."

"This gentleman spent half the night sobbing onto my
shoulder about how much he loves Vienna Hyatt and how
crushed he'll be to lose her. I'm offering you a way out. So
let's try it again. How much is Lucinda paying you?"

"Fifty thousand dollars."

"I'll take it."

"You'll take what?"

"Fifty thousand dollars. I'll take it in exchange for spilling
what I know about Paul and the Swedish throne."

"I don't have fifty thousand dollars on me. That's money
Lucinda promised us, not money I already have."

"I'll take a personal check and cash it after you track down
Lucy and her grandmamma pays out what she owes."

"What if I stop payment on the check?"

"What if I tell Vienna we slept together?" Ariel picked up
her cell phone and displayed one of thirty-two photos on its
screen. "What if I show her some pictures?"

"You've really thought this through."

"Credit cards are also accepted."

"If you cash the check before Lucinda pays us, I'll be
wiped out. Actually, if you cash it after she pays us, I'll
be wiped out, too. I'm not exactly solvent at the moment.
Lucinda's fee was supposed to cover debts I've already got."

Ariel reminded, "I'm not the one who's afraid of losing Vienna. How much is she worth to you?"

"Vienna means everything to me."

"Prove it." Ariel reached over and plucked Henry's wallet off the end table, where she'd laid it conveniently out of his reach. "Going once, going twice—"

"Fine!" He lunged across the bed, scribbled a check, signed it with a flourish, and flung it at Ariel with his trademark dramatic flair.

She said, "This is only half."

"I want to hear what you have to say first."

"You're not as dumb as you seem."

"It's my dashing good looks. They cloud the issue."

Ariel didn't smile.

He said, "This better be worth it."

"Oh, it is." *Now* Ariel smiled. She smoothed down the bedspread and sat down next to Henry. She told him, "Paul can't make any decisions about surrendering the Stenbeck throne because Paul isn't a Stenbeck."

"Give me my money back," Henry said.

"I'm telling you the truth."

"Paul hates his father. Paul's mother, Barbara, hates James even more. If Paul weren't really James's son, that little tidbit would have come out years ago. Paul would give anything not to be related to that man."

"Shut up and listen. I didn't say Paul wasn't James's son. I said that Paul wasn't a Stenbeck. Neither is James."

Henry shut up. Henry listened.

Ariel said, "Fifty years ago, the Stenbeck nanny wanted to give her own son a better life. So she switched newborn baby boys. Her son was raised as the Stenbeck heir, and the real one was dumped in an orphanage."

Henry might have been slow on the uptake where some things were concerned, but when it came to lying and cheating to advance one's own interests, he could keep up real well. "An orphanage that then mysteriously burned down?"

"Coincidentally, the same one, yes."

"Did the real Stenbeck heir die in the fire?"

"No. This was years after he'd grown up and gone."

"How do you know all this? It can hardly be public knowledge, since James is still running around the world using the Stenbeck name. And Paul may have dropped the name, but he doesn't seem to have any qualms about dipping into the money now and then, or utilizing the family property for his own nefarious purposes."

"It may not be public knowledge, but Paul knows, and so does Barbara. Also John Dixon."

"He told you?"

"Actually, I told him. In a manner of speaking. He overheard James and me talking about it. And then he blackmailed James and there may have been a few murder attempts on both sides. All water under the bridge now."

"And you knew about it because before your mother was the Hyatts' housekeeper, she was the Stenbeck nanny." Henry, once again, went with the obvious deduction.

"My mother raised James."

"She did a sterling job." Henry wondered aloud. "The Hyatts hired someone who used to work for the Stenbecks?"

"Oh, they loved it. Any chance they get to take something from the Stenbecks, they leap at the opportunity."

"You know what this means?"

Ariel tossed Henry's checkbook back into his lap. "It means you and Vienna can be blissfully reunited away from the machinations of her evil family. And you owe me another twenty-five thousand dollars."

"Just a second." Henry had already given in a mite too easily to the extortion attempts of a Russian hotel maid and an elderly Mafia mama. He was determined to get a fair deal on this transaction. "I'm going to need some proof."

"How about James's original birth certificate, complete with teeny tiny footprint?" Ariel waved the photocopied sheet of paper in Henry's face.

When Ariel said she'd thought this all through, she obviously wasn't kidding.

Henry sighed. And for the third time in as many days, paid up.

As the keys to the sports car didn't also include ones to the Hyatts' front entrance, Henry was reduced to peeling up the driveway, loudly slamming the driver's side door, heroically storming up to the house . . . and knocking politely. When his well-bred taps were ignored, he considered parking himself below the second-floor windows and shouting, "Vieeeeena," Marlon Brando–style. But then Henry realized that to do the homage justice he would need to rip off his clothes in a fit of passion.

And it was way too cold for that.

So instead, Henry channeled his otherwise always game passions into merely knocking louder. Eventually, his banging brought Greta to the door. Now that he knew that she shared a bloodline with James Stenbeck, Henry treated her with the same respect as before, but supplemented with a healthy dose of wholesome fear. Greta told him that Mr. and Mrs. Hyatt were out, and that Vienna had retired to the ice house. Over Greta's shoulder, Henry could see Paul approaching to find out what was going on.

"Have a nice visit with Grandma," Henry blurted, then quickly shut the door and hightailed it back to the igloo.

Once he got there, however, Vienna refused to let him in. She wasn't subtle about it, either.

"No," Vienna said. "I refuse to let you in, you horrible, rotten, terrible man."

"But I have good news."

"You have contracted an incurable illness?"

"Better!"

She opened the door a crack. "What could be better?"

"I've found the solution to all our problems!"

"And it involves your reeking of a woman's perfume?" Vienna sniffed the air delicately, then added, "A cheap woman's perfume?"

"Vienna, I am shocked and insulted that you would think such things of me. Why, I will have you know that I spent the entire night soberly and chastely pondering all of our options, and, I'm happy to say, I have come up with a solution."

"You spent the night drinking and hitting on random

non-English-speaking women. It is a small town, Henry. Everyone knows everyone else's business."

"So I may have indulged in a bit of wine, women, and song. Which reminds me, how did your old man manage to stock up on every vodka known to humanity if you can only buy alcohol through those smorgasbord or whatever-you-call-it watchdogs?"

"If you know the right people, you can import anything you want from overseas. The rules are only there to protect others from themselves."

"Wow. How condescending and hypocritical of you. Finally, something about this country I can understand. In any case, my drinking and carousing—it was all for a good cause. I was doing it for us, my little pepperkakor."

"There is still an us? I did not realize."

"Please tell me you haven't divulged Lucy's whereabouts to Paul yet."

"Why? Will that change how you feel about me? Will that convince you that I am nothing but a spoiled gold digger with no morals, ethics, or concern for your stance on the matter?"

Henry winced. "Is that the impression I gave you?"

"It is merely the conclusion I drew after you called me a spoiled gold digger with no morals, ethics, or concern for your stance on the matter." Vienna tapped her fingernails on the doorframe. "Say what you came to say, Henry, then go. Please. I have no interest in our rehashing the same conversation over and over again."

"So did you or did you not tell Paul about Lucy and Johnny going to New York?"

"No, I have not."

"That's great."

"It does not mean that I will not. I just felt I needed some more time to think it through. No good can come of flying off half-cocked and doing something I might regret."

"Really? I may have to reconsider every one of my life choices. But another time." Henry grabbed Vienna by the hands. "My great news is that Paul is not a legitimate Stenbeck heir. He couldn't reinstate your parents to the throne if he wanted to, which means you're off the hook. You don't have to decide whether or not to tell Paul anything, because it would be pointless either way."

Henry laid out Ariel's story for Vienna. As he spoke, he kept expecting to see the light of comprehension dawn in her eyes, followed by glee and delight at his cleverness. But Vienna just looked more and more perplexed as he relayed the convoluted saga. Finally, she pulled away from Henry and said, "But very few people know that James is not a real Stenbeck. Officially, Paul is the legitimate heir, which means if he relinquishes his claim to the throne, my parents can still regain it."

Henry said, "Well, technically, yes—"

"So your discovery is irrelevant."

"Well, technically, yes—"

"Although," Vienna mused out loud, "I suppose it will do my parents no good to reclaim their birthright in an illegitimate way, since that would only leave it open for a challenge and potentially more heartbreak down the road."

"Right, that's exactly what I was just going to say," agreed Henry, who, in fact, had been desperately rifling through his brain, hoping to come up with an argument even half as good.

"But, Henry, there is one more thing."

"The part where you throw your arms around me and call me a genius? I'd say that part can commence right now." He opened his arms, preparing for the throwing and the genius calling.

"No. Not that."

Henry lowered his arms.

Vienna said, "Our argument earlier."

"Is a moot point now," Henry finished for her.

"The specifics may be moot, but not the generalities."

"Okay," Henry said. "I get it. You're right. I owe you an apology. Looking back, I can see how you might have taken me calling you a gold digger the wrong way. But it's not an insult in my book. It's an accolade."

"Not that," Vienna said.

"Then what? What's the problem?"

"You and I, Henry. We are the problem. We fought because my feelings about what it means to belong to a family do not synchronize with yours."

"So what, we also disagree on how much chili powder to put in the meat loaf."

"It should not be powder. We should use fresh chilies."

"Exactly. Our relationship is strong enough to overcome any obstacle."

"Paul's offer left me in the position of having to choose between my parents and you."

"Now you don't have to do that anymore. Problem solved."

"But does it not upset you, the not knowing whom I was planning to choose? Will you not be racked with angst, always wondering where you stand with me?"

"No."

"I find that hard to believe."

"You know what I find hard to believe? I find it hard to believe that a woman as gorgeous and as cultured and as clever and—how to put this in family-friendly terms?—as sensually inventive as yourself would have anything to do with a guy like me. You've got to understand, my pride went into free fall a long time ago. I'm the guy who married Katie knowing that she planned the entire ceremony as a wacky scheme to get her ex to admit he still loved her. I'm the guy who stayed married to her, even though I knew that the only reason she'd blurted out 'I do' was that the ex hadn't stepped up and said, 'You don't.' Finally, I'm the one who nobly let her go so she could pursue the guy she really loved. In case you haven't noticed—I'm a patsy. I'm the best friend, the man of honor. Yes, Vienna, I've actually been a man of honor. Several times. I've lived in Oakdale for a decade. Do you know how many couples got married and divorced during that time, while I wasn't getting any action whatsoever? I'm just grateful you gave me a second look. You love your parents more than me? Fine. You love your country more than me? Okey-dokey. Heck, you love this overgrown ice-cube more than me? I'll take it. I don't care if I haven't made your Top Ten. I don't care if I haven't made your Top One Hundred. As long as I'm on the list, I'm the luckiest guy on earth."

"I did not realize you felt that way," Vienna said, actually blushing for, as far as Henry knew, the first time ever. "Henry, I am sorry."

"Don't be. It's cool. We're cool. Come on." Henry grabbed the love of his life and kissed her in a way he was pretty sure her precious Sweden never could. Once they'd both caught their breath, he said, "Now, let's go ruin Paul Ryan's day."

15

Henry and Vienna joined Martina, Gjord, and Paul up at the main house, catching all three in the parlor. With his trademark flair for the dramatic, Henry explained why Paul could no longer blackmail the Hyatts and why he wouldn't be getting any information about Lucy and Johnny, either.

When Henry was finished, Paul folded his palms in front of him, pointed both at Henry, and said, "I'm sorry to ruin your day."

"That's supposed to be my line," Henry corrected.

"Not when you hear what I've got to say."

For a moment, Henry feared he'd been royally and definitively had by Ariel. She'd swindled him out of his money by spinning a tale without a germ of truth to it, backed up by a phony birth certificate whipped up in Photoshop. Probably because Henry had rejected her advances back at the office. A woman scorned, Ariel had obviously done it to express her extreme frustration with his not wanting her. Henry felt horribly guilty. But he also stood up a little straighter.

"Unfortunately," Paul said, "Ariel didn't tell you the whole story."

"But it is true," Vienna insisted. "James is not a lawful Stenbeck."

"It's true," Paul shrugged.

"So you lied," Gjord raged. "You are in no position to return our peerage to us."

"I will be," Paul said. "If your daughter tells me where I can find Johnny."

"Nonsense," Vienna huffed. "I just told you, Papa, he is not the true heir, he can do nothing for us."

"You're right, I'm not the real heir," Paul agreed. "But Johnny is."

"Johnny?" Henry scoffed. "How exactly does the son of your sister and Craig Montgomery qualify to be the king of Sweden?"

"That would be the part Ariel left out. What did she tell you Greta did with the real Stenbeck heir?"

"Dumped him in an orphanage. By the way," Henry informed Martina and Gjord, "lovely woman you've got working for you. Next time, I'd suggest a slightly more thorough background check."

Paul said, "The real heir grew up as Gunnar St. Clair."

Henry couldn't be sure of it, but he thought he saw Vienna react to the out-of-the-blue name. Paul caught her eye and winked. Vienna, for reasons Henry didn't understand, looked away and appeared strangely chastened.

"When I was a little boy," Paul continued, "Gunnar came to Oakdale under the misconception that he was a distant Stenbeck cousin. That's the cover story Greta gave at the orphanage to disguise the truth. Turned out he was the real thing. Gunnar didn't want the money that came with being a Stenbeck, but he did want my mother, Barbara. Got her, too. So I guess he did end up taking something away from James, after all."

"So this Gunnar St. Clair is the man we should be dealing with?" Martina asked.

"Can't. He's dead."

"Then what is the point of this story?" Gjord demanded.

"Gunnar had a son."

"The true heir!"

"Indeed. Like Gunnar, his illegitimate son was raised in some rather humble surroundings. Would you believe the true Stenbeck heir spent the first decade of his life traveling with a rodeo? His stepfather was some sort of horse person. When they first came to Oakdale, the duo practically lived at Lucinda Walsh's stables. I believe it's how he met Lily."

"Dusty?" Henry and Vienna guessed at the same time.

"Bingo! Dusty Donovan, the biological son of Gunnar St. Clair. A true Stenbeck. I suppose I should have known it back when we were kids. Dusty inspired me to commit my first criminal act, you know. It's true. I was six or seven, an adorable, towheaded, painfully sheltered little fellow. Dusty was a couple years older, and, boy, did I think he was cool. He talked me into shoplifting a bracelet from my own mother's boutique."

"But Dusty is dead, too," Vienna pointed out.

"He is. Fortunately, he left behind a legally adopted heir—John Dustin Donovan. Current location: Unknown."

Paul turned to Gjord and Martina. "So you see, all I need to do is locate Johnny, bring him home, and be declared his legal guardian. Once that's done, as regent, I can still return you to the throne. Perfectly legally, this time. Of course, the whole process would be made much easier if your daughter would be kind enough to fill me in on what she knows about Lucy's whereabouts. If I find Johnny on my own, I'd hardly have a reason to be so generous."

"We're back where we started," Vienna lamented.

Up in her old room, she allowed Henry to take her in his arms and soothingly pat her hair while she fretted.

"Not exactly," Henry pointed out.

"You have another plan?" She looked up at him, her face eager and full of hope. Henry was so not looking forward to watching it all shatter.

"Not exactly," he repeated.

"What do you mean? Once again, I have to make a decision: Do I honor your wishes or those of my parents? Do I make you happy or them? It is exactly the same situation as we were in before."

"Not quite." Henry wondered if changing the wording would make what he had to say next more palatable. "Yes, we're faced with the same dilemma, and yes, we're no closer to finding Lucy than we were yesterday."

"That is not true. At least we know that she is in New York City. In Brooklyn."

"Being sheltered by the Russian mob. In a borough with a

population of two and a half million, she isn't just a needle in a haystack. She is a very well-guarded pirogi."

"But it is still possible for us to go to New York and try to find her. We could still get to her ahead of Paul."

"You mean it would be possible. If I hadn't signed away all of our money."

16

Overall, Vienna took the news of their ruin quite well. At first she tried to be sensible about the whole thing, insisting that as Ariel's information proved to be useless, they should be entitled to get back the checks Henry had written her. Which was an excellent suggestion, except for the fact that, in the past several hours, Ms. Aldrin seemed to have flown the coop for parts unknown. It was at this point that Vienna burst into tears and started keening in Swedish, which, at least to Henry's inexpert ears, sounded more sad than furious. Then again, thanks to the many Ingmar Bergman movies he'd seen, all Swedish sounded melancholy and cheerless to him. For all he knew, Vienna was crying tears of joy and singing his praises, though somehow he doubted it.

Although he was literally on top of the geographic world, Henry thought this was the lowest he'd ever felt. But then Martina swept into the room, took one look at her weeping daughter, and brushed by Henry to murmur some equally melancholy-sounding consolation to Vienna. Gjord stood in the doorway, arms crossed, surveying the scene and glaring menacingly. That's when Henry realized that he was capable of feeling even lower, thank you very much.

An unintelligible but spirited Swedish conversation flew above Henry's head as Vienna, Gjord, and Martina proceeded to discuss his selfishness, cluelessness, general worthlessness, and utter lack of weather resistance. Then again, they could merely have been discussing which reindeer to butcher for dinner.

Though would the latter really require quite so many nasty glares in his direction?

Finally, Martina turned to Henry and thrust a finger into his chest. "My daughter is in love with you!"

"I'm thinking 'is' might not be the accurate verb tense."

"This is ridiculous," Martina fumed.

"Unheard of," Gjord agreed.

"Unbelievable," she added.

"It changes everything," Gjord concurred.

"Hey, hey," Henry said. "Look, I know I'm no prize, okay? I've got no money, no job, no prospects, and then there's the whole leaving her at the altar thing."

"You did what?"

Over her parents' shoulders, Vienna frantically shook her head to indicate that perhaps Mama and Papa were not exactly aware of his latter offense, and that now was probably not a good time to share it with them. Apparently, despite her earlier assertion to the contrary, Vienna didn't exactly share *everything* with her folks.

Henry cleared his throat. "But, my point is: I'm not all bad, okay? I love your daughter. She makes me smile. You know how rare that is? Sure, the world is full of people who can make you laugh. That's why there's a comedy club on every corner. But smiling is something different. Smiling is when you see her walk into a room, and your heart and your guts and a few other organs a gentleman doesn't mention in mixed company rise up and practically float away. I see Vienna, and she makes me smile. I like to think I do the same for her."

"You are a horrible man," Martina said.

"Mama!"

"It is true. Every other man that Vienna has brought home in the past had nothing. No honor, no grace, certainly no comportment. Only money. Money, money, money."

"It does make the world go round," Henry conceded.

"It was easy to ignore and belittle those men, because we knew Vienna did not truly care one bit for any of them."

"It was rather a jolly sport," Gjord chimed in. "Martina and I so enjoyed placing little wagers to see how quickly we could offend one and send them on their way."

"I am shocked," Vienna said. "Truly shocked."

"My darling." Gjord sighed. "We are two hundred kilometers inside the Arctic Circle. Our nearest neighbors are forty-five minutes away by car. We have night for twenty hours at a stretch. We need ways to entertain ourselves."

"And it was entertaining," Martina sulked. "Until your Henry came along."

"We thought he was just another nothing," Gjord lamented. "Another prince of Leonia."

"Or duke of Moldavia."

"That baron."

"The earl!" Martina explained to Vienna, "That is why

we agreed with Mr. Ryan's proposal. We never anticipated you would actually have a problem acting against Henry's wishes. We never dreamed you would care how he felt about anything you did, much less that you would hesitate to help us because of him!"

"I do love Henry," Vienna pledged. Then burst into a fresh torrent of tears. "He makes me so happy," she whimpered in between sobs.

"We understand," Gjord said.

Henry was glad one of them did.

"And we wish to apologize for how we have treated you."

Vienna sniffed at them expectantly. "How?"

Martina and Gjord exchanged looks. She sighed. Then he sighed.

"We have talked it over," Martina said, "and we have decided that if you truly would rather not cooperate with Mr. Ryan, we will understand."

"What does 'understand' mean?" Vienna's tears instantly dried up as she all but pulled out a legal pad on which to draft terms. Based on her parents' lack of surprise, Henry guessed they'd witnessed many such abrupt transformations before.

"It means," Gjord said, "that we will not pressure you to make a decision in our favor, nor will we blame you if you choose to support Henry's cause."

"I choose to support Henry's cause," Vienna said.

Martina and Gjord exchanged looks again.

"Very well," Gjord said. And then, to Henry, he added, "I hope you will accept this as our apology for the way we treated you."

These people had banished him to sleeping in the Arctic Circle, collaborated in the kidnapping of the love of his life, then almost gotten him killed in a room full of spikes, cannons, and obscure literary references. Was a pithy "sorry" supposed to erase all that?

"We accept," Vienna said and gleefully hugged both of her parents.

"Oh," Henry realized. "Guess it does." (As Oscar Wilde said, "Always forgive your enemies—nothing annoys them so much.")

He asked, "Can I be the one to tell Paul?"

"You're making a mistake," Paul seethed.

"We do not think so." Gjord slipped one arm around his wife's shoulders and another around Vienna's. Henry stood off to the side, happy the man only had two arms.

Martina said, "Our daughter's happiness is more important to us than any title."

"Oh, I didn't mean you two," Paul said dismissively. "You two are making the right call. This heir business is nothing but trouble. And paperwork. God, so much paperwork . . ." Paul turned to Henry and Vienna. "You're the ones making a mistake. I am going to hound every step you two take. You'll slip up and lead me to Lucy eventually. You might as well have earned something for your trouble."

"Save it," Henry said. "We already heard this speech last week from Craig Montgomery." He turned to Vienna and asked, "Darling, did you pack your pink Chanel suit?"

In the end, they didn't need the suit to lose Paul at the airport. They did need to sell both Vienna's suit and the one that Henry had worn—Grandma Mafia bought them—so they could raise enough money for their trip home. The Hyatts offered to help, but Henry was too proud to accept their charity. Or so Vienna told him.

He and Vienna considered stopping over in New York to see what they could suss out about Lucy, but with Paul on their tail and no money left from Lucinda's advance, they decided to go home to Oakdale. They could manage to live broke there. They wouldn't have been able to afford to leave the airport in New York without a trust fund.

"I feel certain that Lucinda will give us more money," Vienna reassured Henry as they boarded their flight home. "After all, we have brought her so much new information."

"You have brought me nothing!" Lucinda roared.

Henry and Vienna had been avoiding that roar for the past ten days. They'd returned to Oakdale almost two weeks earlier, fully prepared to do the responsible thing and deliver to Lucinda the news of their failures. They'd awoken every morning convinced that today would be the day they'd drive out to her estate and face the music. And yet, when evening had come around, both had been sincerely stunned to discover they hadn't yet done so for some reason.

Ultimately, it was Lucinda who'd summoned them. She'd

heard from Lily that Al's was open again, which meant Henry and Vienna were back in town.

So they'd arrived on her doorstep. When the butler had announced their inauspicious arrival, Henry had almost expected to hear him call out, "Dead man walking!"

Lucinda had greeted the weary travelers in her living room. She was dressed in a crimson, Asian-style dressing gown with a flock of golden dragons intertwined along the sleeves. The dragons appeared not to be of the fire-breathing variety. Lucinda, on the other hand . . .

Henry and Vienna had begun by telling her about their success outwitting Craig in Montega and neutralizing his blackmail attempt. They'd told her about Paul's attempt to lure Lucy to Sweden and about Lucy and Johnny's flight to Brooklyn under the auspices of the Russian Mafia.

And still Lucinda roared, "New York? Lucy is somewhere in New York?" She did not tell Henry and Vienna to take a seat on the sofa. But the sheer force of her displeasure buckled their knees and made them fall back into a sitting position nonetheless. "That's the best you can do? Are you aware of how many people live in New York?"

"There are eight million stories in the naked city?" Henry channeled *Dragnet*.

"There are nine million people in the entire country of Sweden, yet you couldn't find my Lucy there!"

"Of course not," Vienna said slowly, puzzled. "Because she was not there. She is in New York."

But Lucinda was on a roll. "I should have known. I should have listened to my instincts that howled this was a bad idea. I shouldn't have let you talk me into this."

"We did not exactly—," Vienna began, not realizing that, in Lucinda's world, all failures were the fault of absolutely everyone except Lucinda.

"A con artist you were, Henry, and a con artist you will always be."

He insisted, "All we need to locate Lucy and Johnny is just a little more money—"

" 'A little more money'—the battle cry of the incompetent."

"We'll go to New York and we'll—"

"You'll go nowhere. Nowhere, *comprende*? You're not getting another red cent out of me. This fiasco is officially over. You're fired. Now get off my couch."

Home sweet home, aka Al's Diner, didn't look nearly as sweet now that Henry saw it as it really was—peeling Formica, ready-to-bust red imitation leather seats, stained menus—instead of through the rosy-green-colored glasses of fifty-thousand-dollars' worth of capital improvement with which he'd been viewing it during the ten days they'd spent avoiding Lucinda in the hope that she might still pay them something for their trouble.

Vienna hung up her coat, set her purse down on the counter, and told Henry, "We cannot go on like this."

"No kidding," Henry agreed.

"We simply must talk about what has happened. I did not wish to bring it up until after we closed the chapter on our failure to find Lucy, but during our entire journey from

Stockholm, I could not stop thinking about it. How can you and I possibly hope to preserve our relationship when it has become distressingly obvious how different we are on so many fundamental and vital issues?"

For the bulk of their journey from Stockholm, Henry had been thinking about his overdrawn bank account and wondering how, without the money they'd expected to earn from Lucinda, they'd be paying for their flights once the credit card bill came due. Fortunately, after a few drinks, that had ceased to be a concern. At no point had he ruminated over his and Vienna's relationship, which, he now had been informed, was ripe with fundamental and vital differences.

Nevertheless, Henry said, "Right. I couldn't think of anything else, either."

"It is awful," Vienna sighed. "Your ideas about family and mine are diametrically opposed."

"That's probably because your family and mine are diametrically opposed. Oil and water. Cheese and chalk. Pasta and anti-pasta."

"Family and anti-family," she concurred sadly.

"Hey! I'm a progressive, liberal, twenty-first-century kind of guy. If two consenting adults in the privacy of their own home want to engage in the unnatural act of procreation, that's their prerogative. Just don't ask—and don't tell—me to join you."

"You simply do not understand how wonderful having a family can be. It is like having a safety net. It is knowing that no matter how big a mistake you make or how wrong a path you might end up on, there are people who will still love you no matter what. The world is such a difficult, awful place. A family is an oasis in the middle of it all. Your own personal hiding spot from trouble."

"Vienna."

"What?"

"Your parents just had you abducted."

"Oh, but they did not mean any harm."

"I'm sure my mother didn't mean any harm either. For all I know, she thought leaving eight kids alone for days at a time, or teaching us how to scam social services for extra food stamps which she then gave away to her boyfriends was a way to build character and life skills. Guess what? It produced at least one serial killer. That we know of. My sister, Eve. And it produced *me*."

"So maybe both of our parents made some mistakes. You and I, we will do better with our children. Just imagine it, Henry, a baby that is a mixture of both of us."

"It better have your looks," Henry said. Then, after he thought about it some more, he added, "And your brains. Maybe a touch of my joie de vivre wouldn't be amiss—"

"He will be wonderful. A baby of our very own. We can dress him up and show him off and teach him to do all sorts of adorable tricks."

"That's a puppy, Vienna, not a baby. We already have one of those."

"We will travel the world together, and we will teach him about art and music and which wine to order with which main course. We will send him to the best schools, and we will attend his Christmas pageants. Oh, you should see how adorable the children back home are on Santa Lucia day. The girls wear white dresses and crowns with candles on them, and the boys are in white shirts and trousers and pointed white hats."

"They sound like little Klansmen. Little pyromaniac Klansmen."

"All of the parents look so proud watching them."

"Is that before or after some kid trips the one in front of him while another sets a little girl's pigtails on fire with his candle? And are you sure the parents are proud, or are they glassy-eyed from having stayed up all night sewing the adorable costumes? Maybe they're just delirious due to running one-hundred-and-four-degree fevers from the latest infection little Lars or Sven brought home from that petri dish of bacteria otherwise known as school? I'm sorry, Vienna, but your idyllic fantasy life doesn't exactly mesh with the reality of child rearing. You're forgetting something: I've done this before. I've scoured the dregs of the refrigerator looking for an old bagel and a packet of mustard that I could pack and pass off as a kid's lunch. I've yanked bubble gum out of kids' hair, and I've been puked on—and worse—more times than a college resident assistant. I went to my first parent-teacher conference when I was eleven, and I've been called a jerk and a son of a bitch and a dictator—that would be Maddie, she was our brightest Coleman—in the same breath as I was asked for money or for a ride someplace."

"This would be different. You were a little boy forced into something you were not ready for. Your sisters did not respect your authority, and they took the anger they felt toward your mother and father out on you."

"So what? Fact remains: I've done the parenting thing. It

sucks. I don't want to do it again. You know why? Because it's hard. It's too hard. And me, I'm lazy!"

"What if I do?" she asked. "What if I do want to do it someday? Then what?"

Henry shrugged. "Your life. Remember what I said about consenting adults."

"I would like your consent, as well."

"Not going to happen," Henry said.

"So where does that leave the two of us?"

"Living life in 3-D. Diner, dog, and enough debt to smother us all."

Vienna crossed her arms and pursed her lips, a sure sign that she was about to most emphatically dispute his conclusions. Fortunately, Henry's cell phone rang at the exact same instant. "Ah, saved by the ring tone."

From the electronic beep of "Oops, I Did It Again," Henry knew it was Maddie on the line. He'd picked the song himself. He'd felt it was appropriate.

"Madeline!" Henry trilled, as delighted to hear from his baby sister as he was to put the discussion with Vienna on permanent hold. "What wonderful news do you bring me today from the world of academia? Shall we deconstruct something?"

"Hi, Henry." Maddie's greeting lacked the enthusiasm of his salutation.

"Uh-oh. What's wrong, kiddo?"

"It's kind of complicated," Maddie began. At which point, from the background, Henry heard the distinctive and unmistakable sound of a young child launching into a scream that would rival fire-engine sirens.

"Maddie . . . ," Henry hedged. "Is there something you need to tell me?"

"Yes."

"Is this something I'm going to want to hear?"

"That depends."

"On what?"

"Well, Henry, see, the thing is . . . I've kind of got Johnny Donovan."

PART THREE
NEW YORK CITY

17

Twelve hours later, after Henry had hung up, grabbed Vienna and his already maxed-out credit card, driven like a madman to the airport, making very little sense along the way as to where they were going and why, made even less sense on the plane despite Vienna's sincere attempt to coax a coherent sentence out of him, Henry finally got the chance to articulate the questions that had been eating at his brain not unlike a tapeworm in the lower intestine. "Why? Who? How?"

Twelve hours later, he, Vienna, and Maddie were seated at a corner window table in the cafeteria of Wesleyan University in Connecticut. Maddie was pouring syrup on her waffles, Vienna was adding just a touch of pepper to her egg-whites-only omelet, and Henry was ignoring his plate of hash browns and sausages in favor of nervously jiggling an unopened sugar packet. Next to them sat John Dustin Donovan, aka Craig Montgomery Jr., age three and a half. The boy had his late mother's red hair, and the mischievous eyes of both his deceased adoptive father and his living biological one. Currently, the little fugitive who was the object of, at last count, a three-continent manhunt, was messily experimenting with the effects of overabundant ketchup on the common French fry.

"How in the world did you end up with Johnny?" Henry demanded.

Maddie sighed, "Gwen called me a couple of days ago."

"Gwen?" Vienna said. "The wife of Jennifer and Paul's brother, Will?"

"Right. Gwen called me from Chicago. She said she and Will were taking care of Johnny. Lucy got in touch with them at the beginning of the week saying that she was in New York and that she was going to meet with Craig to see if they could end this thing once and for all."

"How did Craig find Lucy in New York?"

"I don't know. She didn't say. All she said was she couldn't risk meeting him with Johnny. Lucy wouldn't put it past her dad to snatch her little brother and run off."

"Probably exactly what Craig had in mind," Henry said.

"That's why she needed to hide Johnny somewhere. So she asked Gwen and Will to do it. They're Johnny's family, and they don't want Johnny to end up with Craig, either."

"That still doesn't tell me how Johnny ended up with you."

"I'm getting to it. It's kind of messed up." Maddie looked over at Johnny, who was now trying to pry the top off Vienna's pepper shaker. Maddie ignored it. In response, Johnny poured the pepper into his water glass. She ignored that, too. Henry hated to say it, but his sister had a bit of a glassy-eyed hostage look about her, as if the initial incarceration had been so brutal that she was too beaten down to resist, or even react, to any subsequent assaults. "Lucy told Gwen and

Will she'd be back in Chicago for Johnny in a couple days, but she never showed. Never even called them to explain what's going on. It's like she just disappeared."

"Sounds like Craig is up to his old tricks."

"That's what Will and Gwen are afraid of. Except it gets worse. Paul somehow figured out that Johnny was with Gwen and Will."

Henry turned to Vienna. "How the hell did this happen? We're the ones who were supposed to find the kid, and now we're the last ones to know anything!"

"Well, technically," Vienna said, gesturing to the boy, "we did find him. You do not see Craig or Paul around here anywhere, do you?"

Maddie said, "Paul called Gwen and Will and tried to talk them into handing Johnny over to him. To protect him from Craig, is how Paul put it. But Lucy kidnapped Johnny specifically so he wouldn't end up as a pawn in Craig and Paul's tug-of-war. So before Paul could get to Gwen and Will's house, Will jumped on a plane in Chicago and brought Johnny to me here."

"When was this?"

"Two days ago." Maddie watched impassively as Johnny proceeded to knock the pepper-flavored water onto his lap. She pulled a wad of napkins out of the dispenser and offered them to Johnny. He stared uncomprehendingly for a moment, then slapped both hands against his sopping wet pants, laughing uproariously. "Two days too many."

It was Henry who wiped the boy down, then shook him side to side like a puppy to get rid of the excess water. Johnny chortled with glee. "Again! Do it again!"

"No." Henry plopped the boy on his knee, handed him a whole sausage, and indicated the raging river of ketchup. "Go crazy." To Maddie, Henry said, "So Gwen and Will haven't heard from Lucy since she dropped off Johnny?"

"And I haven't heard from them either. Last time I saw Will, he said Paul was really pressuring them over the phone to spill where they've stashed the kid. Will figured Paul was on his way to see them in Chicago in person. Maybe they're afraid to call me now and explain what's going on because Paul's watching them."

"What should we do?" Vienna asked Henry. "Take Johnny to Lucinda?"

"No. No, that won't work. Lucinda has no legal claim to Johnny. It's Lucy she was concerned about. If we turn Johnny over to Lucinda, both Craig and Paul will just fling their lawyers at her. And they'll be in the right, too."

"I don't care what you do with him," Maddie said. "But you've got to take this kid off my hands! I haven't been to class in two days, everything I own is sticky, even the stuff he hasn't touched, and my roommates are about ready to mutiny. This kid" — Maddie lowered her voice and then, for good measure, switched to French — "is evil."

"Or he's a kid," Henry mumbled. "Tough to differentiate between the two sometimes."

"Do not be silly." Vienna, fluent in several languages, including French, waved Maddie's words away. Speaking French did so lend itself to waving things away. "He is adorable."

"So were Leopold and Loeb," Maddie snapped back in English. Speaking English did so lend itself to snapping back.

"Define evil," Henry prodded.

"He won't do anything I say. It's like he's permanently stuck on 'no.' I tell him not to touch something, he touches it. I tell him not to do something, he does it. He won't go to sleep, then he won't wake up. And he shrieks every time he doesn't get his way. Every. Single. Time."

"Poor baby," Vienna cooed. "Poor Johnny."

"Poor Johnny? How about poor me?"

"You don't understand, Maddie. Think of it from his perspective. He is in a strange place, with strange people. His mother is nowhere to be found and he doesn't understand what is happening to him. He must be terrified. You must be sympathetic, not punishing."

"You be sympathetic," Maddie said. "You be anything you want, just leave me out of it. You two are still on the hunt for Lucy, right? Henry told me Lucinda paid you a boatload of money to play detective. So you two take Johnny, find Lucy, give him back to her, and then everybody will get to live happily ever after, okay?"

"Actually, Mad—" Henry began.

"Of course," Vienna said in a tone that suggested Henry wouldn't be getting a vote in the matter.

"You know," Henry told Vienna, "Lucinda fired us. We're not looking for Lucy anymore. We've got no responsibility to this kid whatsoever."

They were walking across the Wesleyan quad, Johnny dragging his feet toward what the adults could only hope would be an available taxi.

"Then why did you leap on the first available plane to come here if you do not still feel involved in the search?"

"Because I was scared my sister was in over her head. As long as Maddie had Johnny, she was a target for both Paul and Craig. No way am I putting her in those crosshairs."

"All right then, why did you not tell Maddie before now that we were no longer on the case and that she should call someone else, maybe Margo or Barbara, to come fetch Johnny? They are not Lucinda. They are Johnny's family. They could have made a legal claim to the boy without either of us getting involved."

"Because," Henry said.

"I see."

"Good."

"Because why?"

"Because," Henry replied as he hefted Johnny onto his hip to speed up the interminable process of walking a few feet without stopping every eighth centimeter to ponder a dirt-encrusted rock, pick up a discarded gum wrapper, or lick a metallic pole. "I didn't want to tell Maddie how badly I blew it, okay? There happens to be one person left in the entire world who still thinks I'm a cool and awesome dude, and I'd like to keep it that way."

"Only one—Henry. I do not think you—"

Their taxi pulled up and nipped the discussion in the bud.

Jennifer's brother, Will, his wife, Gwen, and their own toddler daughter, Hallie Jennifer, were currently living in

Chicago, a few hours' drive away from Oakdale. Henry got himself, Vienna, and Johnny tickets on the next flight there.

"How are we affording this?" Vienna asked.

"Credit cards," Henry said. "Many, many credit cards."

"But how will we pay it all back?"

"If we track down Lucy, Lucinda is bound to reward us handsomely. Even if she did fire us." Henry whistled in the dark.

"How will we accomplish this? Maddie said even Gwen and Will do not know exactly where Lucy is."

"No worries, my little pepperkakor. As long as we've got Johnny, Lucy is bound to come to us sooner or later. The only trick now is to let the right people know that we have Johnny without tipping off the wrong people."

"And figuring out who is who."

"Precisely."

From his days of flying as a grown-up person, Henry seemed to vividly recall that parents with children were accorded early boarding status, similar to that of the filthy rich and the tragically handicapped. But it seemed that particular privilege was no longer available to those traveling with the ankle-biting set. Henry, Vienna, and Johnny had to wait to board until their coach seat numbers were called along with everyone else's. Which meant they got to walk through first class with Vienna half-leading/half-dragging Johnny by the hand while Henry brought up the rear, pulling the wheelie-suitcase Will had told Maddie contained everything necessary to keep Johnny entertained on long flights.

Once in aisle thirty-one, Henry proceeded to try and
buckle Johnny into the window seat. Didn't all kids love the
window seat?

"No!" Johnny kicked his feet and shook his head. "Too
sunny!"

Henry reached over and pulled down the shade.

"I want the window open!"

"But you said it was too sunny."

"I want the window!"

"Open his window, Henry. Please. We are blocking other
people from getting to their seats." Vienna smiled apologetically over her shoulder. No one smiled back.

Henry opened the window.

"Too sunny!"

"Make up your mind, kid."

"Open it!"

"It's open."

"No! Open it right!"

"What does that mean?"

"I want to sit there." Johnny pointed to the seat in front
of them.

"We can't. That's not our seat."

"It's all right." The woman in front of them popped her
head up and bent over to gather her things. "We can switch.
The three of us"—she indicated the couple sitting next
to her—"we're together. We can switch with the three of
you."

Henry and Vienna exchanged looks of surprise.

"Thank you," Henry said. He picked up Johnny, carried him out of their assigned seats, and moved to the ones in front.

Vienna beamed. Well, she hurried to collect all of their traveling accoutrements and toss them over the seats while beaming. And lecturing Henry, "You see, people are so considerate of traveling families. They understand that children are our future, and those who selflessly choose to bring them into the world and raise the next generation are doing it for the benefit of everyone."

"Uh-huh," Henry said to Vienna. To their accidental savior, he said, "You're very kind."

"Kindness had nothing to do with it," the woman assured Henry and Vienna as she buckled herself into her new seat.

"Then why . . . ," Vienna began.

Happily ensconced into what according to him was clearly the superior position, Johnny had already begun rhythmically kicking the seat in front of him.

"That's why," the woman said. She told Henry and Vienna, "I raised four kids of my own. All boys. Believe me, I've seen it all."

"But it gets easier, yes?" Vienna pleaded. "With experience, you know better what to do."

"Of course it does, honey," the woman soothed as she patted Vienna's hand. "You never make the same mistake twice."

"That is good to know."

"But you'd be amazed how many new ones there are to keep making."

"I'm hungry," Johnny said.

"We have to wait until the plane is up in the air before we can ask for food," Vienna explained.

Henry frantically riffled around in what had been promised as the magic suitcase. He found a pad of paper and a box of crayons. "Care to draw?"

"Give me!"

"I'll take that as a 'Yes, please.' " Henry handed Johnny the art supplies. Johnny stuck both hands into the crayon box's window, bypassing the pesky lid because that would clearly be too simple and conformist, and tugged. A rainbow of wax flew every which way. The majority hit the floor and proceeded to roll under the feet of the passengers in front of them. Thus ended Johnny's stab at self-expression.

"How about some juice?" Vienna asked as she dove into the suitcase and emerged with a rectangular box featuring smiling and dancing fruit.

"Mine!" Johnny shouted.

Vienna handed him the juice box. Johnny screamed and threw it on the floor.

"Open it," he ordered.

"And how am I supposed to do that," Henry snapped, "after you threw it on the floor?"

He expected another milk-curdling shriek in reply. But Johnny merely turned both palms up toward the ceiling, crinkled his lips, and shrugged innocently.

Henry groaned, reached under the seat, and felt around with his fingers until he'd recovered the juice box. He looked for a pull-tag, like on a beer can or, failing that, at least a spout like on a milk carton. He found nothing.

What—was the kid supposed to gnaw his way through the cardboard?

Vienna pointed out, "The straw. You take it off the side and put it through the hole on the top."

"How do you know that?"

"There is a little picture on the back. The happy fruit is drinking the fruit juice."

"Doesn't that seem a little cannibalistic to you?"

"Please just give it to him, Henry."

Easier said than done. He wrestled the straw out of its plastic wrapping and off the box with a minimum of damage, but actually getting the straw into the box proved to be an even bigger challenge. Using too little strength only got Henry as far as denting the foil covering. It took one more I-really-mean-it-this-time jab before Henry was able to splinter the straw all the way through to the juice-flavored water inside. And get a slosh full of overflow to the crotch for his trouble.

At least it made Johnny laugh.

And, in the tot's defense, it made Vienna laugh, too.

"I am sorry, Henry," she sputtered as she did her best to stifle her giggles.

"No, no, it's okay. If you can't laugh at my pain, whose pain can you laugh at?"

Johnny pulled the juice box out of Henry's hands, managing to spill even more when he clutched and squeezed the middle of the box. The sugary elixir bought them a modicum of peace and quiet during liftoff. But once the plane reached cruising altitude, so did Johnny.

Their redheaded terror opened the food tray on the seat in front of him. It flopped into his lap. Johnny gave it a tap with both fists, like a very small quality-control inspector, then slammed it shut.

He opened the food tray. Everything still under control.

He slammed it shut.

One more time.

They could see the head of the passenger in front of them being jostled repeatedly. The man leaned over and confided to his seatmate—while projecting as if midperformance in Carnegie Hall without a mic to a house full of hard-of-hearing senior citizens—"Some people should just be Constitutionally forbidden from becoming parents."

The observation might have visibly upset Vienna, but, truth be told, Henry couldn't have agreed more. Especially when, for the duration of their flight from Connecticut to Chicago, Henry and Vienna were repeatedly informed by their pint-sized traveling companion that the pair's attempts at scientific explanation regarding the nature of clouds and stars was woefully lacking. Also reportedly lacking was their span of knowledge regarding the color of trees, the sound a horsy makes, how long a sandwich could remain flung to the ground before it was classified irrevocably inedible, and the exact number of pigs tormented by The Big Bad Wolf.

When they disembarked, the businessman who'd been sitting in front of them handed Vienna and Henry a card and told them they should give him a call the next time they intended to fly. He would happily contribute for them to rent a private jet, simply to keep from sharing the friendly skies with their like again.

Vienna looked ready to burst into tears.

Henry told her never to look a private jet in the mouth.

In response, Vienna looked as if she yearned to smack Henry in his.

They arrived at the hotel after a mere three arguments with Johnny, covering the topics of yes, you must absolutely wear your seat belt in the cab; no, you may not play with the automatic backseat window in the wintertime in the Midwest; and shh, we know the driver has hair in his ears but it's not polite to broadcast this fact at the top of your lungs or to ask if he's a monkey and does he want a banana?

Up in their room, Henry and Vienna didn't blink an eye when Johnny climbed onto the luggage rack and proceeded to jump from it to the bed and back again. He was jumping onto inanimate objects, not people Henry and Vienna would need to apologize to or compensate. Ergo, they didn't see any harm in the activity.

Henry said, "I got Gwen and Will's home address from Maddie. I'm going to drop in on them, see what they can tell us about where we should start looking for Lucy."

"You are leaving me alone?" Vienna gasped. "With . . . him?"

"We can't take him with us. Maddie said Paul's been calling Gwen and Will, trying to get them to tell him where Johnny is. What if Paul is also having their place watched or something? He sets eyes on Johnny, the gig is up. He'll snatch the kid right out from under our noses."

"He will?" Vienna asked hopefully.

"Eyes on the prize," Henry reminded her. "Johnny will lead us to Lucy. She's got to come back for him sometime. And finding Lucy will lead us to Lucinda's money."

"How much money?" Vienna asked.

Henry looked at Johnny, now doing somersaults across the bed and off the side. "Lots."

If one could draw conclusions from the strollers, scooters, and bikes lined up in the hallways, Gwen and Will Munson lived on the fourth floor of a very family-friendly apartment building near the University of Chicago. As Henry did his best Dick Van Dyke imitation, stepping nimbly aside to avoid being smacked in the shins by a miniature NASCAR racer on a trike, he wondered what the hell was wrong with people these days. Why this rush to reproduce? Whatever had happened to careerism or—even better—hedonism? Where, he asked himself, had all the lovely "me, me, me-ism" of the baby boomer generation gone?

Henry knocked on Gwen and Will's door, half-expecting to see them emerge as if from hibernation, dripping sticky, squalling children from every limb. But Gwen arrived merely leading her toddling daughter, Hallie, by the hand. Henry was relieved, and he had to admit they looked adorable together, the blond mother dressed in jeans and a maroon U of Chicago sweatshirt with white lettering, the dark-haired tot in a matching white T-shirt with maroon lettering.

"Henry?" Gwen stared at him, puzzled. "What are you doing here?"

"Who is it?" Will called from the other room.

"Henry Coleman," Gwen called back.

"What's he doing here?"

Ah. Henry guessed this was what was meant by being a perfectly matched couple. You even asked the same banal questions in the same banal way. Domestic bliss, and neither of them barely old enough to drink. Was this really what Vienna wanted for the two of them? Premature geezerhood?

"It's about Lucy," Henry said.

"Hold on a second." Gwen gestured for Henry to keep his voice down.

"What? I know she was here."

"This isn't a good time, Henry."

"Am I interrupting the bambina's schedule? A thousand pardons. Just give me a couple of minutes to put our heads together and see if we can figure out where she went after she left you guys, and I'll be on my merry way."

"You know what they say, Henry . . ."

Henry heard the voice of Barbara Ryan's son coming from the other room.

"Four heads are better than three."

Unfortunately, it was his least favorite of Barbara Ryan's sons.

Paul stepped into the hallway, followed by an anxious-looking Will.

"We need to stop meeting like this," Henry said.

"We also need to come up with better bon mot material."

Will bent over to sweep Hallie into his arms, then stepped between Henry and Paul. "You know, guys, we don't need this. Gwen and I left Oakdale specifically so we could raise our daughter away from all this drama."

"What are you doing here?" Henry asked Paul.

"Same as you, looking for Lucy and Johnny."

"What makes you think Gwen and Will know any-thing?"

"Well, you're here, so I figure they must."

"Cut. It. Out," Gwen said sharply. "Better yet—get out. Both of you."

"Excellent suggestion." This time, the mystery voice came from behind Henry. And, once again, it was not one of his favorites.

Henry turned and saw Craig smiling at Gwen and bearing a stuffed crocodile for Hallie. "Why don't you two poseurs heed your hostess's directive and get out. She and I need to have a little chat about the location of my son."

18

"How the hell do you two keep doing this? How do you keep showing up wherever Vienna and I are?" Henry demanded. "Are you both spending all your time just following us from place to place? The little pepperkakor and I *are* a pretty entertaining pair. Maybe we should start charging for tickets."

Even as he said it, Henry realized that couldn't be the case. If Craig and Paul had indeed been keeping such close tabs on them, they'd have known where Johnny was by now and wouldn't be bothering Gwen and Will. It was a piece of information Henry could use to his advantage. If he could just figure out how.

"Are you two working together?" Henry asked Craig and Paul.

"Don't be an idiot," Paul said.

"No need to be insulting," Craig agreed. "The fact is, the trail you and Vienna left was so obvious, only an utter dullard could fail to follow it. That said, I am a bit surprised Paul managed to find his way here all on his own."

"It's because he followed us," Henry accused.

"Please," Paul snorted. "Why would I be following you? You couldn't find an infant in a playpen."

"Then how do we all keep ending up in the same places?"

"Valentina Valentinovna sends her regards."

"Who?"

"The Granny Godmother."

Oh, crap, Henry thought. "How did you find her?"

"I didn't," Paul said. "She found me."

"Me, too," Craig chimed in.

Paul looked at him in surprise. Craig just smiled innocently and asked, "What, Paul? Did you think it was your boyish charm that did the trick?"

Paul sighed. "If you can't trust a criminal octogenarian, who can you trust?"

Henry asked, "What are you two talking about?"

Paul explained to Henry, "It seems that when Lucy took refuge with the Latvians, she spun them a story about being on the run from an abusive ex-husband."

That explained the old woman's question about whether Henry and Vienna were working for Lucy's husband.

"A very poor, abusive ex-husband," Craig interjected. "If you're going to tell this, Ryan, do it right."

"The Latvians let Lucy play doctor for them, and when she'd put in her time, they helped her sneak back into the United States. Valentina figured that was the extent of Lucy's usefulness to them. Until you and Vienna showed up. The way you clowns threw money around tipped Val off that there might be more to the story than Lucy first told them. So she did a little research—apparently the old gal is pretty computer savvy—and realized that instead of a poor ex-husband, Lucy and Johnny actually had a rich Daddy and that Johnny had an even richer—"

"For the moment," Craig interjected.

"—uncle, who would pay handsomely for information about his whereabouts."

"Valentina played us one against the other," Craig said. "Made us bid back and forth until she'd settled on her best price."

"And then tipped you both off anyway?" Henry noted.

At least both Paul and Craig had the decency to look equally sheepish at the realization that they'd been had by an Eastern Bloc grandma.

"That's irrelevant," Craig said.

"Exactly," Paul agreed. "What matters is that you and Vienna are useless to us now. We know as much as you do. We know Lucy and Johnny are traveling on Montegan passports and we have the fake names they're using."

Gwen piped up. "If you guys aren't getting out of our apartment, the least you can do is get out of our hallway." Gwen reached behind Henry and Craig and shut the door behind them. "I don't want the neighbors knowing what kind of nuts we're related to."

"Hey," Paul said. "I'm the only real relative here. Those two are interlopers. Get them out of here and we can have a nice little family chat."

"No, thanks," Will replied. "The two of them will be back sniffing around the minute you're out the door. The three of you need to settle this, and you need to settle this now. Gwen and I are not getting in the middle of it."

"But you already are," Craig pointed out. "Lucy came to you."

"She came and then she went," Gwen asserted, avoiding both Craig's and Paul's eyes. "We have no idea where she and Johnny are." Henry hoped neither man would notice the lack of eye contact.

Of course they noticed.

"You're lying," Craig said.

Gwen threw her arms up in the air, turned around, and walked into the living room, Will and Hallie following her. Paul, Craig, and Henry made up the rear.

The living room, Henry couldn't help noticing even amongst the drama, mirrored the décor in the apartment building's hallway. The grown-ups might have brought in a couch, two love seats, a TV, a bookshelf and a carpet, but all of it was mere background for the baby paraphernalia. Hallie's portable swing, playpen, dollhouse, and menagerie of stuffed animals took over the entire space, not unlike talcum-powder-smelling kudzu.

Will set Hallie down, and she toddled straight over to Henry. Her dark brown curls were pulled into a single, pink-ribboned ponytail on top of her head, like a chubby-cheeked onion. Her mouth boasted four teeth, two top and two bottom. In addition to the University of Chicago tee, she wore miniature denim jeans with butterflies embroidered on the back pocket and socks designed to look like sneakers, complete with faux laces. She was the dictionary definition of adorable. Henry wondered if Vienna had called ahead and told the Munsons to make Hallie particularly presentable, if only to wash the taste of flying the fiendish skies with Johnny out of Henry's mouth.

No matter. When Hallie flashed Henry her irresistible, four-tooth grin, Henry resisted and more or less shoved the kid aside to ask Craig and Paul, "I still don't get how you went from knowing that Lucy's in New York to thinking she's with Gwen and Will."

"Easy," Paul said.

"Trivial," Craig agreed.

"Once I had the names they were traveling under, all I had to do was check airline records. Cindy and Dustin Bryant flew out of LaGuardia Airport and into O'Hare. Only Cindy Bryant flew back to New York."

"What he said," Craig echoed.

"People just gave you this confidential information? Homeland Security isn't in the security business anymore? They're now in the spilling-guts business?"

"If you know the right people, they are," Craig and Paul said almost in unison.

"I feel very secure."

"So Lucy may have gone back to New York, but Johnny is still somewhere in Chicago," Craig mused. "And who better to leave him with than the girl who played Mommy to my little boy for months?"

"Because of you," Gwen spat. "You're the one who switched my baby with Jennifer's. You're the one who let Jennifer think her son was dead, when it was actually my baby that died. You let me think that Johnny was mine. Because of you, I had to live through losing my baby twice."

"My depravity is well established, Gwen," Craig acknowledged. "Especially among this group. It is also, at the moment, irrelevant. If Jennifer had allowed me access to my son in the first place, none of what you described would have happened. Which actually serves as an excellent illustration for why you should stop stalling and just allow me to reunite with Craig Jr. ASAP."

"Did your impromptu trip to Argentina pop your eardrums, Craig?" Henry asked. "Did you not hear Gwen and Will the first time? They've got no idea where Lucy and Johnny went."

"If you believe that, Henry," Paul inquired, "what are you still doing here?"

"It'd be rude to cross-examine and run."

"Be our guest," Will said. "The door's that way."

"You know, what I don't understand," Craig mused to no one in particular, "is you, Gwen."

"Yeah, I'm a regular enigma, all right."

"I don't understand how you—someone who knows what it feels like to have your biological child ripped away from you and given up to be raised by someone else—can stand there and morally defend keeping me from my flesh and blood?"

"Fortunately, Craig," Gwen seethed, "all moral dilemmas become crystal clear when you're part of the equation. You aren't fit to raise a child."

"But isn't that what they said about you? Trailer trash Gwen Norbeck, knocked up while still in high school, living in a dirty room above a diner, no money, no education, no couth."

"Because couth," Will snapped sarcastically, "that's the most important criteria for being a parent."

Craig ignored him, zeroing in on Gwen, who, despite her best efforts to appear indifferent, was clearly listening to Craig's every word. "They said you weren't fit to raise your boy, and they gave him to Jack and Carly. They said you couldn't provide a good home for him. But you knew differently. You knew you loved him, and that was all that mattered. You knew no one—no one!—could love that lad as much as you could. Because he was a part of you."

No one spoke. Gwen looked down at the floor. She took a deep breath.

Craig had gotten to her, and everyone in the room knew it.

When she finally looked up again, everyone also had a pretty good idea of what she'd say. She was going to spill about Maddie. And that would lead to Henry. And to Johnny wreaking havoc on a hotel room less than a mile away.

Gwen said, "I loved my son. When they took him away from me, they might as well have ripped my arm out of its socket, because it couldn't have hurt any more. I still think about Billy every day. And I love him every day, even though he's not here."

"Then you know how I feel," Craig said.

"No. I don't." For the first time since Craig had made his surprise appearance, Gwen looked him straight in the eye, unafraid. "I don't know how you feel. Because when you say that no one could love a child more than its biological parent, I think of Hallie. Hallie's dad, my brother, Cole, he just turned his back on her and walked away. Didn't give a damn, except for the brief time he thought he could make some money out of this. All that mattered to him about Hallie was what she could do for him. Sound familiar? My brother didn't love his daughter. But Will and I do. Just as much as I loved Billy. So don't try to tell me you and I are the same, Craig. Because when you talk about loving a child, I don't know what you're talking about. And when I talk about loving a child, I'm certain you haven't got any idea what I'm talking about."

It was a historic moment. Craig Montgomery had been struck speechless. It would be over soon, Henry thought, but boy was it fun while it lasted.

Will said, "You heard my wife, Craig. Go ply your snake oil somewhere else. Because you've hit a dead end here."

Craig stood up. Hallie looked curiously at him, then made a face and dove back into her dollhouse.

"I got this far without your help," Craig snarled. "I'll find my son whether you brats help me or not. Though making an enemy of me . . . that's not smart. Ask your dear mother about it, William."

"Gonna set us all on fire, Craig? Once, you can still claim it was an accident. Twice, people will start to talk."

"Tough words, little man. But here's something for you to ponder: Me, I've got nothing to lose." He patted Hallie on the head. "You do."

"Get out!" Gwen shouted.

Will was way ahead of her. Despite standing more than a head shorter than Craig, he was able to use a combination element of surprise, fury, and being thirty years younger—

little man, indeed!—to grab Craig by the shoulders and shove him out the door, then slam it shut.

"Bravo!" Paul stood and applauded.

Will spun around, breathing heavily from the exertion and adrenaline. "One wrong move, and you're next, big brother."

"Wouldn't dream of it," Paul swore.

Gwen went over to Will and wrapped her arms around him. He buried his face in the crook of her neck, struggling to calm himself.

Paul said, "But you know, Craig did sort of have a point."

"That's it," Will said, indicating the door. "You, too."

"Just hear me out. Craig is a sociopath and a criminal, and his taste in hairstyles leaves much to be desired. But he is right about one thing: family. It's important. Sure, Cole didn't want his daughter. But, look, you and Gwen did. You gave her a home. Because she's family."

"Because we love her," Gwen hissed.

"I love Johnny, too. Come on, Will, be honest. You know how much I loved Jennifer."

"Was that before or after you found out Craig had switched babies on her, but you decided to let Jen keep believing Johnny was dead?"

"I had my reasons for what I did."

"Hating Craig Montgomery. 'Fess up, Paul, have you done anything in the last few years that wasn't motivated by your hatred of Craig Montgomery?"

"None of your business," Paul said.

"You want Johnny, but it's not because you loved Jen. You want him because you hate Craig. That's no life for a kid."

"All right, here's a riddle," Paul said. "Since you're an expert in all things Jennifer: Who would our sister have preferred to raise Johnny, me or Craig?"

"She wanted Dusty to raise him."

"Well, a nutcase with a poisoned syringe took care of that,
so it's time to see who's behind door number two."

"Under the circumstances, I think she'd have been okay
with Lucy raising her son."

"Jen wouldn't even let Lucy be Johnny's pediatrician."

"That was in the beginning," Will pointed out. "If Jen
knew how far you and Craig had gone in your vendetta,
she'd have accepted Lucy as being the best choice."

"So where is she then? This paragon of selfless motherhood, or sisterhood, or whatever Lucy's got you two believing she is? Where is she? I know she left Chicago without
Johnny. She abandoned him. For what? A spa weekend? A
new boyfriend? Just what the hell was more important to her
than protecting Johnny?" Paul asked furiously.

"Lucy was protecting Johnny," Henry thought.

No. Wait. Everyone was turning to look at him.

Apparently, he'd also said it out loud.

If looks could kill, both Gwen and Will would have been
facing felony charges.

"Was I not supposed to say that?" Henry inquired, hoping that a sheen of charm would take the edge off his over-
whelming stupidity.

"On the contrary," Paul beckoned. "Tell me more."

Obviously convinced that if Henry was allowed to speak
further he would only make a bad situation unimaginably
worse, Gwen cut him off and took personal control of the

unfolding disaster. She told Paul, "Lucy went back to New York alone because she was meeting Craig."

"Say what?"

"Craig emailed her—"

"How?"

"I don't know. Maybe his Russian Mafia bribe came with the free bonus gift of Lucy's email address. Craig asked to meet Lucy. He said he wanted to call a truce, settle things once and for all between them. That sounded really tempting to Lucy. These last two years have been hard on her. She's been living on the run, always looking over her shoulder, never being able to let her guard down or make friends. Plus, she's been both mother and father to Johnny twenty-four-seven."

"Oh, God," Henry exclaimed. "That sounds awful . . . or so I would imagine."

Luckily, since everyone was ignoring him, no one seemed to have noted his slipup.

Will offered, "Lucy figured she'd hear what Craig had to say. She was, you know, cautiously optimistic. But she was also wary enough to first take Johnny someplace where Craig wouldn't be able to find him."

"Here in Chicago?"

"Nice try, Paul."

"So what happened at the big summit? What did Craig say?"

Gwen and Will exchanged looks.

"We don't know," Gwen admitted.

"What do you mean, you don't know?"

"That was over a week ago. We haven't heard from Lucy since."

"I knew it," Paul snarled. "Craig snatched her again."

"That's what we're afraid of, too," Will admitted.

"That son of a bitch. He's probably holding her hostage, threatening not to let her go until she tells him where Johnny is."

"But as long as he has no intention of hurting her, it's cool. Right, Paul?" Henry asked sardonically.

"What's Henry talking about?" Will asked his brother.

"Who cares?" Paul said dismissively. "What's important is that Craig has Lucy, and that means he's close to finding Johnny."

"Your concern for Lucy is touching," Will observed.

But Paul was already flying down the hall toward the front door, hollering, "Damn it, Montgomery!" and intent on chasing Craig into the night.

That proved to be unnecessary, as Craig was standing in the hallway right outside Gwen and Will's apartment, lounging casually against the doorframe, scrolling through Google headlines on his BlackBerry.

In response to their surprise at seeing him still there, Craig said, "You said I had to leave the domicile, not the city limits."

"I was hoping you'd at least clear the building," Will noted.

"Yes, well, much harder to eavesdrop that way. Besides, I still wanted to have a personal chat with Paul. Away from the domesticity."

"What have you done with Lucy?" Paul demanded.

"I beg your pardon?"

"You lured her to New York, and now she's missing."

"Actually, according to my records, my Lullaby has been missing for almost two years now. Why the newfound histrionics?"

Henry explained, "Gwen and Will said you sent Lucy an email, asking her to meet you in New York so you two could work out some kind of arrangement."

"I did no such thing. Craig Montgomery does not negotiate with emotional terrorists. I will accept nothing short of total surrender. And an apology."

"You're full of crap," Paul said. "Where are you holding Lucy?"

"Oh, use your head. Just this once. If I had Lucy in my clutches, why would I come here to play Twenty Questions with Barbara's remaining dim-witted offspring?"

"To throw us off the scent."

"That makes no sense. Until I came here, you had no idea I knew where Lucy was or that I knew she'd been in touch with Gwen and Will. Why would I show my cards like that?"

"To mess with us?" Henry wondered.

"Get a life," Craig sniffed.

"So Lucy isn't with you?" Gwen clarified.

"Not only is she not with me but I absolutely and unequivocally deny any charges of having lured her anywhere under any pretenses for any purpose."

"So where is she?" Paul repeated.

"For all we know, you've got her," Craig accused. "Maybe you're the one who's holding Lucy. Maybe the reason you're here is because she won't tell you where Johnny is. And Lucy is no good to you without that."

"Craig has a point," Henry said, visions of a kidnapped Vienna dancing in his head.

"Shut up, Henry," Paul said.

"You shut up, Paul."

"How about you both shut up," Will barked.

He, Gwen, and Hallie were standing beneath the archway separating the living room from the entry hall to their apartment corridor. Gwen was balancing a sleepy, thumb-sucking Hallie on her hip, the little girl's chubby legs wrapped around Gwen's waist, her head on Gwen's shoulder. Will put his arm protectively around his wife. They looked so sweet and wholesome that Henry had to look away lest he go into sugar-shock.

Will said, "This is pointless. You all seem to know that Lucy went back to New York, so you don't need Gwen and me for that. As for where Johnny is, we're not giving that up no matter what anybody says or does. The three of you are on your own. So get lost. It's Hallie's bedtime."

The three men trooped out of the apartment. Henry had been on a lot of awkward elevator rides in his life—though, unlike Craig, he'd never delivered a baby in one. Henry had, however, once come upon his ex-wife, Katie, and her latest fling, Brad, attempting to have sex between floors, which had been cringe-inducing in its own way. Nevertheless, the four-level descent wedged in between Craig and Paul quickly made it into Henry's top five most uncomfortable elevator rides ever.

"What are you doing back in the States?" Paul demanded of his rival. "Shouldn't there be a warrant out for your attempt to murder me?"

"Ask Henry," Craig said with a smirk, then changed the subject. "How did you manage to get Valentina to spill her guts to you? She told me I was the highest bidder."

"I appealed to her in person."

"Don't you think I tried that, too? Woman's got herself buried so deep underground . . . How the hell did you find her?"

"Ask Henry," Paul said.

Without asking him anything, both men just glared in Henry's direction for the remaining two floors.

With Paul and Craig continuing their bickering on the front steps of Gwen and Will's building, Henry took the opportunity to slink away—not that either of them cared. Which was ironic, actually, considering the fact that neither would have been able to get a bead on Lucy if it hadn't been for various stupid decisions on Henry's part. Didn't Craig or Paul consider him worth stalking anymore? Just in case he screwed up again?

Making sure he wasn't being followed, Henry snuck back to his hotel. He found the lights off, except for a small bedside lamp and Vienna sitting cross-legged on the bed, leafing through magazines. The television was on. Johnny lay on the floor in front of it, his feet on a pillow, the remnants of what looked like several room-service dinners scattered all around him. Henry looked at Vienna questioningly.

She said, "First he said he wanted a hamburger. But when it came, he said there were too many seeds on the bun."

"Did you try to take them off?"

Vienna held up her hands, displaying the sesame seeds stuck beneath her nails. "He asked for a hot dog, so I got him that. He said it was not the right kind. I got him a pizza, but the cheese was too hot, and then it was too cold. The chicken nuggets were too crumbly, the fish sticks did not have enough crumbs, and the cereal was too soggy. Plus, the hotel only had regular and chocolate milk, no strawberry."

"Did he finally eat anything?"

"Your filet mignon." Vienna indicated the one empty plate that also happened to be on a table, not the floor. "Johnny loves filet mignon."

"How does he feel about lobster?"

Vienna pointed to another plate. "He said this one was overcooked."

A host of responses went through Henry's mind, but he was too tired to actually utter any of them. Instead, Henry flopped down on the bed. He'd been aiming to land face-first in Vienna's cleavage. He often found that landing face-first in Vienna's cleavage solved many a pressing problem. Alas the cleavage in question was draped in a chastity belt of glossy-paged parenting magazines.

"I have been reading," Vienna explained. "And I know now what is wrong with Johnny."

"Demonic possession?"

Vienna frowned. "His behavior is all our fault."

"For ever agreeing to watch him in the first place, yes, I agree."

"No. We neglected to set any limits for him. You see, right here, it says that children want limits. They crave them, in fact. We have been too solicitous of Johnny. We thought we were being kind to him, indulging his whims. We thought how scared he must feel, being separated from his mother, and so we spoiled him to compensate."

"We did, did we?" Henry mused.

"The kindest thing we can do for Johnny is to offer him stability in this time of frightening change. Stability comes from consistency. A child needs to be able to anticipate what comes next. He will try to test how far he can push us, but we must remain firm and hold our ground. He will thank us for it later."

"I'd prefer that Lucinda thank us later. In cold hard cash, preferably, but stocks, bonds, and even gift certificates to Target would be acceptable."

Vienna set the magazines aside. "Oh, yes, that is right. We are in Chicago for a reason. I am sorry, Henry, it was such a challenging evening that I forgot. What did Will and Gwen have to say?"

"Mostly 'Shut up, Henry.' Though I think they did get in a 'Shut up, Paul,' and a 'Shut up, Craig' or two."

"Paul and Craig were there, also? Oh, no! Does that mean they know we have Johnny?"

"No. All they know is that Lucy left Johnny with Gwen and Will while she went back to New York, but Gwen and Will didn't spill a word about Maddie, which means the Gruesome Twosome haven't traced Johnny back to us. Yet.

Paul accused Craig of holding Lucy hostage, and Craig accused Paul right back."

"Who do you think is telling the truth?"

"Who knows? The only thing I figured out tonight is that we've got to get on the next plane to New York and see if we can find Lucy ourselves. Before Paul or Craig do."

19

Henry awoke the next morning snuggled in his favorite position—spooned around Vienna, his face in her hair, his left arm around her waist, his legs intertwined with hers. Vienna opened her eyes, smiled sleepily, and whispered, "Good morning, dear." Henry cuddled up even closer to her, wriggling like a happy puppy as Vienna stretched her arms forward—and toward Johnny, who was crouching by the side of the bed, chin on his fists, frowning curiously at them both.

"I'm awake," Johnny announced.

"I can see that. How very clever of you," Vienna said.

Henry was about to point out that he was awake too but Vienna hadn't seen fit to compliment him on the achievement, had she? Then he decided that might sound a wee bit petulant.

"I have a very exciting surprise for you, Johnny." Vienna sat up in bed, pushing Henry off of her. "Henry, you and I are going on another airplane ride this morning!"

"Yay!" Johnny shouted.

"Yes, it is very wonderful. So how about we eat some breakfast, change our clothes, and then be on our way?"

"No," Johnny said.

The denial actually appeared to make Vienna happy. She took a quick peek at the magazines stacked on their bedside table, then beamed at Henry, as if she'd had some sort of plan, which had just fallen into place. Henry was sure that she did think she had a plan. He just wasn't equally confident about the falling into place part. Nevertheless, as his opinion was not being sought, he decided to keep it to himself. For now.

"First clothes, then breakfast," Johnny insisted.

"Now, Johnny, that is not a good idea. Your clothes are dirty from last night's dinner."

"Dinners," Henry mumbled to himself.

"There is no point in your putting on clean clothes first. What if you spill food on them? It is much more efficient to eat first."

"Clothes first."

"No, Johnny. You may either eat your breakfast and then put on your clothes, or you may put on your clothes first, but then there will be no breakfast." Vienna turned her head and whispered to Henry, "Giving a child a choice makes him feel in control of the situation."

"Oh, I'm sure he feels very in control of the situation already," Henry assured her.

"First clothes, then breakfast," Johnny whined.

"That is not one of the choices, darling."

"Give me my clothes!"

"So you are saying that you would like to put on your clothes, but then you would not like to have breakfast?"

"I want breakfast!"

"Then eat your breakfast before putting on your clothes."

"I want my clothes!"

Henry wanted a martini. But he settled for a shower.

When he came back out, freshly dressed to face the day, he saw Johnny standing on the bed, wearing new clothes, but with a towel draped over him as he chowed down on his French toast.

"We compromised!" Vienna offered brightly. Though the pedagogical zeal in her eyes appeared rather dim compared to what it had been thirty minutes earlier.

While Johnny slurped, swilled and otherwise Jackson Pollacked his plate and towel, Henry and Vienna finished packing and got dressed themselves.

"Come along, Johnny," Vienna said. "Time to put on your shoes."

"No, thank you." Johnny chose to remain as he was.

Vienna whispered to Henry, "We should just ignore him. He will get bored, and then he will put on his shoes and go." Vienna deliberately turned away, intending to coerce Johnny into complying by denying him what the magazine article she'd made Henry listen to her read out loud last night described as "the most precious gift you can give your child—your attention."

To Vienna's credit, Henry did have to admit that Johnny immediately noticed the snub. He called, "Vienna! Hey, Vienna!"

She paid him no mind.

"Look at me!"

"I am afraid I cannot, Johnny. Not until you put on your shoes."

"Oh," Johnny said.

Vienna shot Henry a triumphant look.

Henry responded with, "He's balancing his breakfast plate on his head."

A loud crash.

"Well, not anymore he's not."

"I broke it," Johnny announced.

"I am sorry to hear that," Vienna replied, still refusing to look.

Johnny got up from the table.

"Are you ready to put your shoes on?" Vienna asked.

"No, thank you." Johnny walked over to the bedside table, where the ever-so-helpful magazines still lay, and commenced contemplating the lamp. If Henry had to pick an adjective, he would describe Johnny as contemplating it in a predatory manner.

Henry even got a chance to use the adjective a few minutes later when Vienna surreptitiously asked, "What is he doing now?"

"He is eyeing the lamp in a predatory manner. What are we supposed to do now?"

"The article said to keep ignoring him. Otherwise, you are creating a positive feedback cycle wherein the child learns that escalating bad behavior will grant him the attention he craves."

"So you're just supposed to ignore bad behavior?"

"Correct. Ignore the bad, praise the good. That way the child learns that there is no reward for misbehaving."

"How about the satisfying crunch of a lightbulb shattering into a million pieces?"

This time, Henry's painfully precise words coincided with the exact sound he was so aptly describing.

Vienna winced. And then she admitted, "I do not know. It was all logical when I was reading about it."

"If you keep this up, we'll miss our plane. And we're not exactly so flush that we can afford to keep buying ticket after ticket in the hope that Johnny will eventually deign to leave the room."

"But we cannot give in to him. It will shake his sense of security."

"Tragically, that's not the part of him I'm itching to shake." Henry grabbed the still-shoeless kid under his arm, picked up their suitcase, and marched out the door.

Surprisingly, their second airplane ride in as many days with Johnny proved miraculously hassle-free. The secret, they learned from an elderly woman who took pity on them as they wrestled toward the departure gate, was a stick of licorice. It kept Johnny busy, trying to wrench free the sticky goodness with his teeth, for the duration of the entire flight.

As they were disembarking, Vienna confidently told Henry, "I think he is finally starting to bond with us."

If "bond" meant fuse his candy-covered hand to Henry's freshly pressed pants, then yes, most definitely, he was.

Back in Chicago, Henry had been able to put the hotel bill on his credit card with reasonable certainty that his limit wouldn't immediately be exceeded. In New York City, Henry was afraid to charge a stick of gum for fear of being declined.

"What are we supposed to do?" Vienna asked as they waited in line at the taxi stand at JFK airport. In order to blend in with the natives, she'd donned traditional New York black—a cashmere turtleneck sweater and a pencil-straight suede skirt beneath a fitted macintosh trench coat with matching hat. "We cannot afford a hotel."

"How about a hostel?"

"That is for those who do not shower! It is for young people!"

Henry indicated Johnny. "You calling him a senior citizen?"

"We have nowhere to stay," Vienna lamented.

"You know, that's the problem with you rich people. You figure it's a hotel or bust. How about some creativity, my pepperkakor?"

"For instance?"

"For instance, we could bunk down right here at the airport. The way flights get delayed and canceled, there's always somebody sleeping on the floor or washing up in one of the bathrooms. No one would notice us taking up residence. And it worked for Tom Hanks, didn't it?"

"Tom Hanks also chose to grow gills and reside at the bottom of the sea. That option does not appeal to me, either."

"Okay. Well, there's a famous children's book about a couple of kids who run away from home and live at the Metropolitan Museum of Art."

"Perfect! Johnny's room can be the one with all of the precious Ming vases!"

Henry pondered Vienna sideways. "Impending homelessness makes you a touch cranky."

"Think harder, Henry."

"Well, my personal favorite refuge has always been the hospital."

"You mean faking an illness so you will be admitted?"

"No! No, no, no. One doesn't seek shelter in a hospital by pretending to be a patient. One does so by pretending to be a relative or friend of the less fortunate." In response to Vienna's puzzled look, Henry clarified, "Outside of ICU works best. They've usually got comfy couches, maybe even a coffee machine, plenty of pillows and blankets. If someone dares question your reason for being there, just squeeze out a few tears about poor Grandpa getting a pacemaker and how he needs his closest kin nearby."

"And this works?" Vienna asked, incredulous.

"Oh, yeah, all the time. Way I see it, if you're homeless in a city with an airport or a hospital, you're just not trying very hard."

"You Americans are a very peculiar people."

"At least we don't need a permission slip to buy our liquor."

Their cab finally pulled up, and Henry, Vienna, and

Johnny gratefully piled in. Johnny snatched the yellow ticket the attendant was in the process of handing to Henry and happily tossed it out the window, into the February breeze.

"Don't you have a car seat for the kid?" the driver asked.

"It's against our religion," Henry snapped.

"Suit yourselves." He then mumbled something in his native language. Henry suspected it was not a compliment.

Henry told the driver to take them to Times Square. Henry figured it was as good a spot as any from which to launch their manhunt for Lucy. After all, Times Square advertised itself as the crossroads of the world. If nothing else, Henry, Vienna, and Johnny could just camp out there and wait for Lucy to eventually walk by.

"So which hospital will we be crashing today, Henry?" Vienna inquired. "I will need time to come up with a plausible story. How about, my boyfriend is afraid he has prostate polyps."

"Okay. You're mad. I get that."

"I am not mad, Henry. I was up half the night with Johnny and I am exhausted, that is what I am."

"I did mention this to you, did I not? Taking care of children is as physically taxing as digging ditches and as mentally trying as splitting the atom. Or vice versa. You know what you need?"

"Live-in help?"

"To have some fun. Forget sleuthing for a bit. We can hit Brooklyn tomorrow. Let's take the day off, grab a pizza, and have a picnic. It's a gorgeous day . . . for the middle of February. Johnny can run around in Central Park, work off some of that inexhaustible energy he seems to possess, and we can get some romantic canoodling time in, all snuggled up on a bench. It'll be iconic. *Love Story 2: This Time Without the Leukemia.*"

"No."

"Okay, forget the pizza. And the leukemia. But I warn you, I'm not budging on the iconic canoodling."

"No pizza. I want a proper luncheon served in a proper restaurant with waiters in starched white shirts, polished—not plastic—silverware, linen napkins, and menus printed on heavy stock paper and a wine list. A two-page wine list, at least. That is what I need to lift my bad mood."

"You deserve all that and more, my pepperkakor. But do you really think Johnny is ready for a six-course sit-down? Does Gerber make My First Caviar?"

"I do not care. Are you are saying that people with children can never go out on the town and have fun again? That is what you're saying? You are saying that once you have a child you must bid farewell to your former life and, overnight, turn into a completely different person? No more evenings at the opera, it is all Wiggles, all the time. No more sailing on the Riviera, only little plastic boats in the bathtub. You are saying: Good-bye lobster thermidor, hello fish sticks."

"Seems I don't really need to say it. You're doing all the work for me."

"You are wrong, Henry. What is more, you know that you are wrong, and you are just trying to paint a particularly negative picture for me. You are trying to—what do they call it with taking children to prison?—'scare me straight' about having a baby."

"My goodness, I'm clever," Henry said. "Here I thought I was merely pointing out to you that finger paints and foie gras don't mix."

"You said you wished to cheer me up. I am explaining to you how to get the job done."

"And how do you propose we pay for all this good cheer? I can swing a pizza, maybe, but after this cab ride even extra cheese would be a stretch."

"I have some money," Vienna said. "My parents gave me a few traveler's checks before we left. Just in case of an emergency."

"I thought you told me we were too proud to take their money."

"I said that *you* were too proud to accept their money. It is not an issue with me."

"So your parents don't think I'm capable of supporting you?"

"No, they do not."

"Well, thank God for that. How many shiny euros have we got?"

"Enough," Vienna said. "Trust me."

"I do love it when you boss me around," Henry said, then tapped the driver on the shoulder. He told him, "Take us to your best restaurant, my good man. Take us to Mona Lisa New York."

Henry didn't know much about MLNY, beyond the fact that the Upper East Side hot spot was a franchise of Oakdale's own Lisa Grimaldi's restaurant of the same name, and that its success kept Lisa so busy that people sometimes couldn't find her for weeks at a time as she jetted back and forth between the two locations. All Henry knew the day that he, Vienna, and Johnny dropped by for lunch was that a great miracle happened there — somehow, after they got out of the cab and before they walked into the restaurant, John Dustin Donovan morphed into the miracle child.

He hopped into his booster seat without a peep. He asked the waiter for "Filet mignon with fries and ketchup on the side, please," and didn't even shriek to send it back to the kitchen when it arrived with a baked potato instead. He used the linen napkins to wipe the milk mustache from his lips, and managed to keep the crystal goblet it was served in from tipping over by holding on tightly with both hands.

"You see?" Vienna beamed. "I told you. Having a child does not mean your life comes to an end. You simply take him by the hand and bring him with you wherever you may need to go."

"Like a clutch purse?" Henry wondered aloud.

"Must you be so cynical?"

"Oh, trust me, I must."

Johnny's exemplary — if somewhat mystifying — behavior continued through dessert and coffee. It was only after Vienna had taken care of the bill (thank you, Mr. and Mrs. Hyatt; that kidnapping business? — all forgiven) and Henry said it was time to go that the old familiar Johnny resurfaced.

"No," he said, clutching both sides of the booster seat with his hands. "No go."

"Oh, geez, what is it now? Your juice isn't in a box, your lobster's not from Maine, you haven't taken a swing at the lightbulbs yet? What?"

"No," Johnny said, and then he did the last thing Henry expected. He didn't scream, he didn't pitch a fit, he didn't hurl the bread rolls at their heads. He simply began to cry. Silently. First Johnny's eyes blinked furiously, then he took two loud, deep gulps through his nostrils. His upper lip trembled, then his lower one joined in. His shoulders started to shake, his head dipped, and tears ran down his cheeks, all without his making a sound. Which, in light of the multiple sounds he'd been making for the past few days, proved not only disconcerting but also genuinely frightening.

"What is wrong?" Vienna cooed as she knelt down beside him. "Are you sick? Was the food too rich for you? Does something hurt?"

Johnny shook his head and took one of those halting, serial, gulping breaths that always made a kid sound like he was choking on his own agony.

"Then why are you crying?" Vienna asked.

More gulps, more tears, and then Johnny managed to croak, "Mama."

20

Vienna looked guiltily at Henry, who shrugged helplessly. She asked Johnny, "You miss your mama?"

"You said . . . you said . . ." Johnny struggled to form a sentence. "You said we are going to see Mama."

"I did? No, Johnny, I never said that," Henry replied. "We are looking for your mama, and we hope we will find her soon, but I did not say we were going to see her right now."

"Right now," Johnny insisted. "In New York. You said Mama Lucy is in New York."

"I didn't say Mama Lucy," Henry desperately tried to explain. "I said Mona Lisa. That's the name of this restaurant."

"You said Mama Lucy. I want my mama right now!"

Hoping to distract Johnny and to get away from the fellow diners glaring in their direction, Henry and Vienna high-tailed it out the door and ducked into the first playground they saw on the east side of Central Park, figuring that here they could blend in among the other caregivers dealing with screaming tots.

On that score, they were wrong.

Henry and Vienna had barely calmed Johnny down and encouraged him to go play on the slide, giving up the fight about his wearing a hat in the February weather in an attempt to prevent another meltdown, when a woman in a full-length fox coat came over to them and, without benefit of introduction, lectured, "You really shouldn't be letting your little boy go without a hat. It's cold out."

Vienna looked up at her in surprise. "Thank you," she said. "We know that it is cold out. But he does not like to wear hats."

"He'll get an ear infection," the woman said. "And you know your doctor will insist on antibiotics, which, of course, are horribly overprescribed. Too much, and it could make him drug-resistant to that entire category of medication."

"Thanks for sharing," Henry said, hoping the combination of dismissive tone and him all but turning his back on their unsolicited Furry Godmother would send the message that this was really not a conversation either of them wished to pursue at the moment.

"Don't get me wrong. I understand: Let an ear infection go untreated, and you risk developing serious long-term hearing problems. Which, of course, affect language development and auditory processing. It's a tough call. If I were you"—she smiled and patted Henry on the shoulder before leaving—"I would make him wear the hat."

Henry and Vienna watched her return to her seat, smiling the superior, contented smile of the self-righteous.

Vienna turned to look at Johnny. He was not so much skimming down the slide as sitting at the top of it, sadly banging the heels of his shoes against the metallic surface and still periodically sniffling.

"That poor little boy. How could we have been so insensitive? All of his horrid behavior over the past days—he was just missing his mother."

"Look, I feel as bad for the kid as anyone, but let's not get carried away. Some of his bratty performance art didn't exactly look virginal. I have the feeling he's experimented with that particular bag of tricks before."

"Oh, no," Vienna swore. "I do not believe that. No child would act like that on purpose. Children want to be good, they want to please. No child wishes to upset their parents."

"Vienna . . . you and you alone does not a sample set make. Believe me. Some children yearn for, nay, they thrive on, bringing their parents as much grief as possible."

"It makes no sense, Henry. Think about it. Children are utterly dependent on their parents. For food, for shelter, for protection, for love. Why would evolution make children to deliberately defy those who nurture them? And in reverse, if every child misbehaved with his parents the way that Johnny did with us, it would inevitably lead to parents producing less and less offspring until the human race ceased to exist altogether. No one would continue to breed under such circumstances. It would be like voluntarily entering a daily war zone."

"Exactly. That's exactly what I've been trying to tell you. Having kids is exactly like drowning in a daily war zone.

And you don't so much as get a medal at the end. Not even for simply staying alive."

"A child of ours would never be like Johnny. Our child would be ours. He would know that we loved him and wanted to take care of him. So he would have no need to act—"

"Don't you care about that boy at all?" a female voice interrupted Vienna. They'd attracted another lecturer. This one was wearing a knee-length mink. She pointed at Johnny on the slide and said, "He's just sitting there."

"We are sorry," Vienna said. "Is he in the way? Does your child wish to go down the slide?"

"Oh, no, I never let my daughter go down the slide. Once we finished the unit on kinetic friction, there was no educational value left in the activity. Slides are fine for pre-K and below, but we've moved on to working with angular velocity on the swings." The woman indicated her daughter, pumping furiously with her legs while attempting to write something down on a notepad balanced between her knees. The mom in mink then returned to the topic of Johnny. "I don't think you have him stimulated enough. Have you considered altering his diet? I find that a no-sugar, no-dairy, no-gluten blend does wonders for increasing positive neural activity."

"Johnny's got his own diet. All filet mignon, all the time."

"Well, there you go! Red meat, with all those hormones, it's like poison to children. No wonder he looks sad."

"He looks sad because he is sad."

"But it's such an unproducti.., emotion!"

"He's pondering his next serial killing," Henry said. "Is that adequately productive for you?"

The mom in mink started to smile. She thought Henry was kidding. Then she stopped and considered the possibility that he wasn't kidding. Without waiting for clarification, she ran to the swings, grabbed her daughter by the arm, and pulled her away from the playground. Someone was going to miss her daily lesson on angular velocity.

Vienna looked at Henry in horror. "Why did you say that?"

"Because I wanted her to go away. And, look, she did."

"She was just trying to be helpful. I did not realize there was so much we did not know about being parents!"

Henry stood up and beckoned to Johnny. He shouted across the playground, "Come on, we're leaving. I've got an idea."

The Montegan consulate occupied five floors of a historic Upper East Side town house. It boasted a view of the Central Park reservoir from one corner of windows and several blocks of Museum Mile from another. Two marble columns, a bronze plaque, and a huge Montegan flag flanked the mammoth brass-door entryway. An armed soldier stood at attention right over the threshold, checking bags and asking what business visitors had with the consul.

"Let me handle this," Henry told Vienna, who was holding Johnny by one hand and trying to present her purse for inspection with the other. "We are here to investigate poten-

tial investment opportunities in Montega. Please direct us
to your highest-ranking official. We have no time to waste
with riffraff."

The soldier did not look particularly convinced, but, after
a moment, he picked up a phone. He whispered something
into the receiver that neither Henry nor Vienna could make
out. Then he returned their belongings and gestured for
them to step through the metal detector and down the hall.

"First elevator on your left," he said. "Second floor. Mr.
Fazendiero will meet with you."

"Just follow my lead," Henry urged Vienna, trying to get a
word in edgewise between her warning Johnny not to touch
that, not to lean there, to please, please let go of that. "I've
got a plan."

Mr. Fazendiero turned out to be a swarthy, curly-haired
young man, closer in age, by Henry's estimates, to Johnny
than he was to Henry.

"I asked to meet with someone capable of making business decisions in the name of the Montegan government,"
Henry said. "Not their highest-ranked Eagle Scout."

"I assure you, sir, I am qualified to address all such que-
ries. You said you wished to make investments in our heroic
nation of Montega?"

"That depends." Henry took a seat without being invited
and magnanimously gestured for young Fazendiero to do
the same. "What can you offer me?"

The boy reached for a binder behind his desk, opened it
to the first page, and was about to launch into what Henry
assumed was the standard sales pitch when Henry slammed
shut the offering and announced, "You insult me!"

"I beg your pardon?"

"This is the best you can do for a man of my stature? Don't you know who I am?"

"Well, as a matter of fact—"

"This is peanuts. Penny ante stuff. A million here, a million there, how am I supposed to keep track of that kind of pocket change? Why, I pay my business manager twice that amount just to file the paperwork for me. Don't you have anything to offer bona fide investors?"

"I'm afraid I do not understand. Considering you have no previous relationship with us, why would you be interested in investing a disproportionately large—"

"We are Swedish," Vienna blurted out.

Fazendiero turned to look curiously in her direction. As did Henry. He distinctively recalled instructing Vienna to follow his lead, not go traipsing merrily off on her own.

"You're Swedish," Fazendiero repeated.

Vienna leaned forward conspiratorially. She also offered a bit of cleavage, which, Henry knew from his own experience, could be very persuasive in its own right. "I do not know if you are aware of it, sir, but in Sweden, the tax rate is a bit prohibitive. It is one thing to turn 50, maybe even 60 percent of one's earnings over to the government. But, when you start to enter the arena of 80, 90 percent—"

"And they don't let you drink as much as you want," Henry interrupted. "An evil people, that's what they are."

Vienna managed to shoot Henry a nasty look while continuing to point her most important assets in Fazendiero's direction. "Not evil. Perhaps a bit . . . misguided. It is my opinion that we can teach my countrymen the error of their ways by setting a good example and investing in a nation with a less confiscatory tax policy."

"Like the lovely Montega," Henry gratefully leapt in. "You know, Miss Hyatt and I have just come back from visiting your beautiful country, and, I must say, we were very impressed with what we saw."

"Thank you. Montegans take great pride in the strides we've been able to make since the damage of the revolution."

"In fact, Vienna and I were even thinking of making our permanent home there, maybe even taking Montegan citizenship."

"Montega is a very welcoming nation. But, you understand, we do have rules and regulations regarding our naturalization process."

"Of course, of course," Henry said. "But tell me something, if we were to prove our worth to the beneficent state of Montega through, say, generous investment in your infrastructure and other such noble things, and if we then were lucky enough to acquire citizenship, what sort of, oh, what could one call it? Protection? Yes, that's an excellent word. What sort of protection could a citizen of Montega expect from his government?"

"Protection? I'm afraid I don't understand."

"Let's say a Montegan passport holder somehow, through no fault of his or her own, managed to get into a spot of trouble with another government? Even a government friendly to Montega. Say the United States, for instance. Let's say a citizen of Montega were wanted for, I don't know, a felony in the United States. Would the government of Montega offer assistance in the form of shelter or asylum or even physical relocation—"

"How dare you!" Young Fazendiero leapt from his chair, startling both Henry and Vienna into sinking deeper into theirs. "I understand now. I understand everything!"

"You do?" Henry wondered.

"You disgust me."

"Really?" Henry propped both elbows on the desk, chin in his hands. "How so?"

"I don't know what you've heard, but Montega's integrity is not for sale. Very well, maybe a decade or so ago, it's possible that a few less-than-desirable individuals were granted citizenship as a ploy to escape prosecution for crimes they committed in other countries, but that was due to a bit of nefarious dealing close to the president. It wasn't official policy, and it has since been completely rectified."

"Yes," Henry said. "We're familiar with the nefarious dealer himself."

"So you admit it," Fazendiero accused. "That is why you're here. You know about Craig Montgomery's selling citizenship to the highest, most crooked bidder, and you believe Montega is some Third World banana republic you can use to bamboozle the American and Swedish governments. You believe we are so desperate for your precious investment dollars and euros that we will sell our souls and thank you for the privilege! Let me tell you something, my good sir—Montega is a nation of honor. We have not turned a blind eye to Craig Montgomery's dealings. In this consulate alone, there is a dossier filled with enough incriminating information to send him away for a long time."

"Works for me," Henry said.

"Unfortunately, the scoundrel has been under the protection of our former president, Sierra Esteban, so our hands are presently tied."

"Actually—" Vienna began, but Henry caught her eye and shook his head. He had no desire to open that proverbial can of worms. Not only would he and Vienna be put in the position of having to explain how and why they were so up on the current happenings at the Esteban estate but there was also a humanitarian issue involved. The young man was turning quite red. Henry worried about his health.

After all, he'd only come here to see if they could get any leads on where a wanted fugitive traveling on a Montegan passport might have turned for sanctuary. He hadn't meant to cause an international incident.

But it was apparently too late to dodge that bullet as, in lieu of smacking Henry about the face with his glove and demanding pistols at dawn, the consul was now furiously listing all of Montega's many virtues for Henry's benefit.

"Montega has the highest gross national product in the region. Our human rights record has been praised by no less an authority than Amnesty International. We have the greatest number of high-school graduates in the region. Our tech sector is booming, and our unemployment is at 10 percent. That's only twice that of the United States!"

"Terrific, fantastic," Henry said, rising from his seat. "Go get 'em, Tiger. I'm sorry we've upset you. We'll just show ourselves out."

"And that's not all!"

"I'm sure it's not."

"Montega doesn't only think about itself. We are a haven for the world's refugees."

"That," Henry said, "I am very well aware of."

"We participate in multiple multinational humanitarian missions. We are members of the Red Cross, we provide troops for the United Nations, we send Montegan volunteers all over the world as part of Physicians Without Politics. It's a program very dear to our former president, Sierra Esteban's, heart. Her own sister, Bianca Walsh, runs it under the auspices of the UN!"

The consul might have gone on, but neither Henry nor Vienna was listening any longer. As soon as the words had come out of Fazendiero's mouth, the pair had turned to look at each other, their eyes lighting up with excitement.

United Nations.

Physicians Without Politics.

Bianca Walsh.

Jackpot!

They detached themselves from the fuming consul as quickly as possible, fervently apologizing for their bad judgment in having come to him with such a proposition, and promising to never again take the name of Montega in vain.

Then, as soon as they were out in the hall and out of his hearing, Henry and Vienna all but tripped over each other to blurt out, "Lucy is a doctor."

"She needs to get out of the country in secret."

"Bianca Walsh is her aunt."

"The UN sends doctors all over the world."

"Under diplomatic cover."

"We've got to get to the UN," Henry said, already turning toward the elevator.

"No," Vienna said.

Henry halted in his tracks. "No? Why no?"

"Because first"—she indicated the empty hallway—"we need to find Johnny."

21

"Okay, let's not panic," Henry said. "He's got to be some-where."

"I realize that. But where?"

"Back in the office? Maybe we left him back in the office."

Henry knocked on Fazendiero's door. He popped his head in before he heard a "Come in," managing to duck back out before the inevitable "Get out."

"He's not in there."

"So where is he?"

"Let's think. Did we walk out of the office with him?"

Vienna looked panic-stricken. "I do not remember."

"Me neither."

"We walked in with him, of that I am certain."

"Right. I remember that, too. So maybe, while we were talking, he got bored and decided to blow this Popsicle stand."

"To go where?" Vienna wailed.

"He couldn't have gone far. Kid's got tiny legs. Though, admittedly, a great deal of motivation and energy."

"We should check the other offices on this floor." Vienna moved ahead of Henry and began throwing open doors, desperately asking if anyone had seen a three-and-a-half-year-old boy dressed in brown corduroy pants, a turtleneck sweater with a red fire truck embroidered on the front, and a blue winter coat. Or had he taken off the coat when they'd gone inside? Vienna couldn't remember that, either.

"No, sorry."

"Sorry, no."

"I haven't seen your boy. You really should keep a closer eye on him. Children require a great deal of attention, you know."

Vienna slammed the door shut and turned back to Henry. "Now what?"

"The elevator. Maybe he went in and pushed some buttons. Didn't that happen back in Oakdale? He got himself stuck and Paul had to rescue him?"

"That was Ethan Snyder, not Johnny."

"Really? Damn, those ankle-biters all look alike to me."

"Johnny is too small to reach the buttons." Vienna had a horrible thought. "But what if the doors opened on their own and he stepped inside? And what if there was someone already in there? What if Craig was lying in wait for us?"

"Craig wouldn't voluntarily venture inside a Montegan consulate. That would be like a vampire stepping out into bright sunlight. They hate him here. Calm down, Vienna. Johnny has got to be somewhere. Let's just look."

Their subsequent in-depth search of the entire floor, however, failed to produce so much as a sticky-fingerprint trace of the redheaded tyrant.

"Holy crap," Henry exclaimed. "He's really missing."

"Did I not say so before?"

"No. You don't understand. Before, the kid was simply misplaced. Gone astray. But now he's really gone. Damn it, Vienna, how can you be so calm?"

"I thought you just said—"

"What kind of idiot listens to me? Johnny is lost. He could be anywhere. He could be hurt. He could be kidnapped. For Pete's sake, don't just stand there, woman, call out the Marines!"

"The stairs," Vienna said. "Maybe he went down the stairs."

Henry didn't wait to see if she was following. He tore off, leaping down steps two at a time until he reached the third floor, where they reenacted their door flinging and closet rifling from above, this time to even more shouted protestations, insults, and threats to unleash the wrath of Montegan security.

By the time Henry and Vienna arrived at the ground level, they could hear walkie-talkies going off in various parts of the building, advising the honor guard to be on the lookout for crazy interlopers. But Henry didn't care about any of that, because in the same instance as he spotted the armed security guard from the front entrance heading their way, Henry also spotted the top of Johnny's auburn head—barely peeking out from inside the lobby's marble fountain.

Shoving irrelevant onlookers out of his way, Henry dove into the fountain himself, only to discover that it had apparently been drained for the winter season. As Henry's forehead made painful contact with the bottom of the three-foot-high foundation bowl, he realized that the structure was empty and, rather than drowning, Johnny was merely happily stomping around in a two-inch puddle, the biggest water damage being to his shoes and pant cuffs, not, like Henry had feared, his mouth, nose, and lungs.

"Henry!" Vienna shrieked, knocking the security guard aside to lean over the rim. She offered Henry her hand so that he might, if not precisely climb out with his dignity intact, at least turn around so that he wasn't stuck in a head-stand position, his knees practically wedged into his ears.

Henry rolled over, clicking his teeth and shaking his head to make sure nothing was permanently broken as, at the same time, he felt the bulk of his joie de vivre and bon vivant and any and all other French phrases that usually described how Henry liked to envision himself fade away. In that instant, he reverted to the Henry who'd spent high school doing preschool pickups and nagging third graders to eat their dinner and wear their coats and who sounded like a beaten-down, cranky octogenarian at sixteen.

"What the hell did you think you were doing?" Henry grabbed Johnny under the arms, set him firmly down on the ground, and proceeded to climb out of the dry foun-tain himself. "Where do you get off just wandering away like that? Do you have any idea how scared Vienna and I were?" He dragged Johnny to a nearby bench, plopped him down, and peeled off the boy's wet shoes and socks. "You do not, under any circumstances, walk away from an adult without telling them where you're going. Do you understand me?" Much to Vienna's and the security guard's surprise, as well as that of the consul, who'd come down to see what all the commotion was about, Henry then went on to remove his own shoes and socks. As well as his coat. He used the latter to dry off and warm up Johnny's feet. Then he slid his own socks over the tiny ankles, pulling them way up past Johnny's knees before replacing the shoes. Realizing that he was being stared at, Henry stopped the tirade long enough to look up and ask, "What? Kid's feet were wet. We take him outside soaking in this weather, he gets pneumonia before we hit the curb. Jeez, don't any of you know anything?"

The consul, now recovered from the sight of his pristine lobby being turned into a day-care center, pointed toward the door and blustered, "Get out! You are not welcome on Montegan soil now, nor ever again in the future. I shall see to it that you are both placed on our Terrorist Watch list."

"Oh, yeah," Henry snarked. "That's the ticket. That and the chatty folks at Homeland Security will keep you safe and sound." He plopped Johnny onto one hip, grabbed Vienna with his free hand, and walked with as much dignity as a sock-free man in a wet trench coat with a burgeoning goose egg on his forehead could muster.

It wasn't until they got out on the street and Henry was marching to the corner, arm raised in a fruitless attempt to hail a cab, that Vienna had a moment to observe, "You are trembling."

"It's February. My coat just played the role of towel, and I'm not wearing any socks. I'm *cold*."

"No. This is not cold. You are scared." Vienna gently touched his elbow. "I have never seen you scared before."

"Try again. Remember back in *Treasure Island* Land? I don't know what sniveling and whimpering means in Swedish, but in English, it's subtle code for lily-livered coward on the premises."

"No. This is different."

"That's because it's cold, not fear. Keep up, Vienna."

"You were terrified that we had lost Johnny. You were, admit it."

"Okay. Fine. The little brat scared the bejesus out of me. There. Are you happy? Are you enjoying your little dry run at parenthood? Because this is what it's really like. Not the cute outfits and the fancy restaurants and the Mommy and Me spa days. It's not even the tantrums or the battles of will or even the bills that come due before you've charged them. It's the screwups. The screwups, Vienna. That's what parenting is all about. Making mistake after mistake after mistake and then dealing with the consequences. We didn't know the fountain was empty for the winter. We were just lucky. Johnny could have drowned while we were tossing around the cleavage and listening to Fazendiero sing 'Oh, Montega' upstairs."

"But it did not happen. He is all right."

"Today. How about tomorrow? Or how about in the next minute? You can't watch them all the time. And even when you do, you still end up missing the obvious. I brought Maddie to live with me so I could take care of her. There she was, right in front of my nose every day. And still, I somehow failed to notice that she was living in fear because the son of a bitch who'd raped her in Chicago was back, looking to do it again, and threatening to kill her if she said a word."

"That was not your fault."

"Then whose fault was it? Whose fault was my failing to realize that my other sister, Eve, was slicing up local teens with a butcher knife to avenge Maddie's 'affair' with Eve's rapist husband? I screwed up, Vienna. Not just with Maddie, but with Eve, too. So fine, so my old man and the old lady both skipped out on the child-raising thing. I stepped up, which means I'm responsible. I was all those girls had, and, as of right now, the score stands: one rape victim, one whack-job serial killer. Hell of a record. Great job, Hank. Father of the Year trophies all around."

"You were not Maddie's father. Or Eve's."

"But I'm still the one who screwed them up. And you want to know the kicker? This wasn't one of my patented half-ass jobs. I tried, Vienna. I really tried. I did the best I could with Maddie and with Eve, and still I let them down. It's what I do. I screw up and I let people down. Everyone I've ever given a damn about, I've harmed."

"That is not true, Henry."

"Oh, no? Did I misread the subtle signs? Were those tears of joy you cried upon being left at the altar?"

"I have come to terms with it."

"No, you haven't. You've tried ignoring it in the hopes it will go away. Like maybe I'll forget that you still want to get married and I don't. You still want to have kids, I don't. Tell me you've come to terms with that."

"This is neither the time nor the place to discuss this, Henry."

"You're right." A yellow cab pulled up and Henry gratefully yanked open the door. He tossed Johnny in, then stood aside to let Vienna enter and sit next to the drying boy. Only then did Henry take the last seat and, without looking at either of the other two passengers, told the driver, "Take us to the UN."

They entered alongside a multiethnic tour group and followed the program for a few yards. Ten minutes in, however, Henry, Vienna, and Johnny took a surreptitious left at the third outsized monument erected by the UN to champion its own greatness, and proceeded to wander about looking purposeful yet nonthreatening while searching covertly for the office of Bianca Walsh. Whenever security approached and demanded to know why they weren't with their group, Henry would smile apologetically, point at Johnny, and explain that they were desperately hunting for a bathroom. Sometimes it was darn convenient to have a child in tow. Especially one as naturally fidgety as Johnny. Every guard they encountered believed their story. And left Henry and Vienna alone to tend to their potentially leaky boy.

In this manner, the trio managed to poke around undisturbed for close to a half hour, when, out of the blue, Vienna told Henry, "You are right."

Unused to hearing those words, Henry initially didn't even register Vienna's observation. He naturally assumed she was talking to someone else. It was only when Vienna added, "You and I would make terrible parents," that Henry surmised the comment had been addressed to him.

He turned to look at Vienna questioningly, unsure of how

to respond. "By George, I think you've got it," seemed rather crass under the circumstances.

"We have done a criminally unacceptable job taking care of Johnny. We could not discipline him, we could not get him to eat, we lost him and then did not even notice he was gone. Worst of all, when he was so unhappy and missing Lucy, what did we do? Nothing. We did not do one single thing to make him feel better."

"Should we have cut out gluten?"

"Stop it, Henry. Be serious. You know I am right. We are woefully unprepared to be parents."

"No argument here. I've been the Zero Population Growth guy from the start."

"I am sorry I did not believe you. I should have listened."

Henry was about to agree with Vienna that yes, she should have, when Johnny interrupted what might have been the turning point in their relationship by pointing in Vienna's direction and announcing, clear and unmistakable as day, "Mama!"

Vienna gasped. She bent her knees and knelt at Johnny's eye level. "Mama?"

"Mama," he nodded.

Vienna glanced over her shoulder at Henry, eyes glistening. "Did you hear that? He called me Mama! He must have finally understood why I was being so strict with him. It worked. He finally feels secure with us. We have bonded."

Henry watched Vienna. She appeared so happy that she was practically glowing. He couldn't remember the last time he'd seen her like that. Henry admitted, "You do look hot rocking the mom look."

"We can do it, Henry," she insisted. "We can be good parents. This is the sign we needed. It is proof that we do not have to make the same mistakes again."

"True," he agreed. "We can make new and improved mistakes. Longer lasting. More psychologically crippling."

But even Vienna could tell he didn't mean it. Not this time.

"Mama," Johnny repeated.

Vienna smiled at him beatifically and took the child into her arms.

But Johnny wriggled out of her grasp and, without so much as a look back, took off in the opposite direction—straight into Lucy's arms.

She swept the little boy into a hug, spinning him around and, in the process, shooting an apologetic glance at Henry and Vienna.

Henry understood that the situation called for a momentous utterance along the lines of "Dr. Livingston, I presume," or at least a "Eureka! I have found it!" (Surely, Oscar Wilde would have offered something appropriate.) But, under the circumstances, with Vienna looking crushed on his one side and Lucy contrite on the other, all Henry could manage to summon up was, "You!"

"Me," Lucy admitted guiltily.

Johnny still clinging to her with a death grip, Lucy led Henry and Vienna into Bianca's office. Which, for the record, Henry and Vienna had been merely minutes away from locating on their own.

Lucy closed the door behind them and gave Johnny one more hug. "I missed you so much!"

"I had filet mignon," he boasted.

"Is that a fact?"

"Two times!"

Lucy apologized to Vienna and Henry. "I rarely let him have it. Red meat makes him hyper."

"Now you tell us."

Lucy asked, "How in the world did the two of you end up with Johnny?"

"Gwen and Will passed him on to Maddie. Maddie gave him to us because she knew your grandmother Lucinda had hired us to find you," Vienna explained.

"Oh, no. I was afraid Grandmother would not be able to stay out of this."

"Craig and Paul tracked you to Chicago, so Gwen and Will decided Johnny was not safe staying with them. Gwen and Will are very worried about you. They expected you to contact them. You said you would."

"I'm sorry. I couldn't risk it. Everything got so out of hand—"

"My God, Lucy, how could you even think of trusting Craig?" Henry asked incredulously. "I know he's your father, but shouldn't that mean you know him better? How could you even entertain meeting him alone? You must have suspected it'd be some kind of trap."

Lucy confessed, "A part of me was hoping he had changed

and I could trust him again. That we could work something out."

"With Craig? Fat chance."

"No," Lucy said. "Not Craig. I lied to Gwen and Will. It sounds stupid, but I was too embarrassed to tell them the truth. I didn't come to New York to see Craig. I came to meet Paul."

22

Two years earlier, when Lucy Montgomery had snatched her little brother and fled Oakdale, she'd understood that she'd be entering into a life of deception, a life of constantly looking over her shoulder, of never being able to trust anyone or let down her guard. She'd been prepared for all that. What she hadn't anticipated was the loneliness.

In theory, Lucy had understood what being on the run meant. It meant false names and sneaking away in the middle of the night. It meant looking in the eye people who'd reached out to her and offered friendship, and blatantly lying to them. It meant forged papers and nerve-shattering border crossings. It meant becoming mother, father, extended family, and playgroup to a little boy who had no idea what exactly was going on but still harbored the sense that something wasn't quite right and, as a result, clung to Lucy even more tightly.

Lucy loved Johnny. Her path into unexpected motherhood might have been more unconventional than most, but she knew she was doing the right thing, that Johnny was better off with her than he ever would have been as the subject of a tug-of-war between Craig and Paul. And, besides, a majority of the time, she enjoyed hanging out with a three-year-old, rereading her favorite children's books, watching Disney's latest releases, building cities out of cardboard scraps, making balsa-wood airplanes, and drawing endless rainbow-surrounded smiley faces. The problems started in the rare times when Lucy allowed herself to face the fact that *Charlotte's Web, Dumbo,* and a skyscraper held together with glue was all she had in her life.

And that it wasn't enough.

Lucy tried to deny it to herself, but there were things she was missing. From Montega to Sweden to New York City, she was missing friends. Real friends. People she could confide in and laugh with and share and be herself with. Lucy couldn't be herself with anyone anymore. There were too many lies to keep straight, too many inadvertent slips to guard against. Any and all relationships by necessity had to be kept surface and glib and tightly controlled. Especially ones with men.

Lucy wasn't just missing friendship in her life. She was missing love, too.

There had been a few potentials over the years. Men who had made her smile a little broader, take a bit more time with her hair in the morning, laugh a little harder at something they said. A good portion of the time, her subtle signals had been reciprocated. Why not? Lucy was a beautiful young woman, with shoulder-length, honey-blond hair, wide brown eyes, and a fluid way of carrying herself that recalled a glass of water being poured from a crystal pitcher into a tall, frosted glass on a lazy summer afternoon. She had every reason to attract potential suitors. And even more reason to, ultimately, turn them away.

Which was why Lucy supposed she'd ended up so vulnerable to the email that had popped up in her in-box several weeks after she and Johnny, with a little help from the Russian Mafia, Swedish division, had snuck back into the United States.

To: Cindy.Bryant@gmail.com
From: FriendInDeed@gmail.com
Subject: Enough is Enough
I know you're Lucy Montgomery. I know you're in New York City. You're tired of running, I'm tired of chasing. Let's end this once and for all.

To: FriendInDeed@gmail.com
From: Cindy.Bryant@gmail.com
Subject: Re: Enough is Enough
You know who I am. Who are you?

To: Cindy.Bryant@gmail.com
From: FriendInDeed@gmail.com
Subject: Re: Re: Enough is Enough
An old friend who wants to help you.

To: FriendInDeed@gmail.com
From: Cindy.Bryant@gmail.com

Subject: Re: Re: Re: Enough is Enough
If you're really an old friend of mine, you must know I'm not stupid. I'm not doing anything until I know exactly who you are and what you want from me.

To: Cindy.Bryant@gmail.com
From: FriendInDeed@gmail.com
Subject: It's Paul
I want to help you, Lucy. You must be dead tired of life on the run. I know I'm tired of looking for you, and I am most certainly tired of dealing with Craig. I know you thought you had no choice but to take off with Johnny, but if you'd given me a chance, we might have been able to put our heads together and come up with a better solution for all of us. Please give me a chance. Meet with me. Let's talk. For old times' sake, if nothing else. Give me a chance to make this right for you. It's the least I can do.

To: FriendInDeed@gmail.com
From: Cindy.Bryant@gmail.com
Subject: Re: It's Paul
First things first. I need proof you are who you say you are, and this isn't a trick.

To: Cindy.Bryant@gmail.com
From: FriendInDeed@gmail.com
Subject: Re: Re: It's Paul
Name it.

To: FriendInDeed@gmail.com
From: Cindy.Bryant@gmail.com
Subject: Terms
If you're really Paul, send me as an attachment a
photo of you holding today's newspaper, sitting at the
Lakeview, drinking a Mojito and wearing a lavender,
buttoned-up shirt. I figure if you're not Paul, you're
not exactly going to have a picture of him with today's
paper, drinking something he hates in a shirt he vowed
never to wear despite his designer mother forcing it on
him.

To: Cindy.Bryant@gmail.com
From: FriendInDeed@gmail.com
Subject: Re: Terms
You are an evil and twisted young woman. That said,
I hope you find the attachment herein to your satisfac-
tion. I got a lot of strange looks at the Lakeview. I hope
you'll be home soon to explain it to everyone.

To: FriendInDeed@gmail.com
From: Cindy.Bryant@gmail.com
Subject: Where do you want to meet?

Lucy insisted on a public place in broad daylight, so they
agreed to get together at Bryant Park, behind the grand old
building housing the New York City Public Library's main
branch.

An hour before their scheduled meeting time, Lucy found
herself taking extra care with her hair and her makeup and

her clothes, smiling as she recalled all the funny and interesting and profound things she'd credited Paul with saying
back in the days when she'd been a mere high school senior
with a mad, inappropriate crush on the older man who'd
shown her some kindness.

Lucy realized this was not the correct attitude with which
to enter a situation that was potentially fraught with manipulation and deceit. She realized that she was, most likely,
playing right into Paul's hands. But she couldn't help herself.

And she knew that couldn't possibly be good, either.

Still, when Lucy first caught sight of Paul, sitting behind
one of the rickety metal tables set out for New Yorkers to
take a break, sip a cup of coffee, and read a newspaper at the
end of a lawn surrounded by trees and the towering library,
her heart did a pirouette. It wasn't just that she was happy to
see Paul. It was the fact that Paul stood for home. He stood
for a time when Lucy had been able to worship her father
freely and believe that he could do no wrong. He stood for
an unlimited future and he stood for being young. These
days, Lucy felt very, very old.

When Paul finally spied her, when he stood up and
folded his newspaper and smiled and held out his arms to
her, Lucy rushed into them with gratitude. Not because she
didn't know that she was being played or that there had to
be more to this meeting than Paul was revealing to her, but
because, just for a moment, she had given herself permission not to care.

She stayed in his embrace for perhaps a beat longer than
would have been considered merely friendly. Because, in

that beat, Lucy was seventeen years old again, and Paul was the hero who'd rescued her from an attempted date rape, then let her down so gently when, after a retrospectively laughable seduction attempt, she'd finally spilled about her crush.

"It's good to see you," Paul said.

"How did you find me?"

Paul linked his arm through Lucy's and steered her for a walk across the lawn, toward the merry-go-round on the opposite end of the grounds. "Your friend Valentina back in Sweden. She contacted both your father and myself, offered to sell info about your whereabouts to the highest bidder."

"Thank goodness you won," Lucy said, making a mental note that perhaps, in the future, she should refrain from trusting people who lied and backstabbed as a career choice.

"Not exactly," Paul said. "She ended up selling both of us the information."

"That does sound like Valentina."

"But when I went back to complain to her about it and mentioned that such treachery might motivate me to use my connections as nominal heir to the nominal Swedish throne to make life a bit difficult for her and her base of operations, she threw in your email address. As a show of good faith."

"So Daddy knows I'm in New York, too."

"Not only that, he knows you went to Chicago to see Gwen and Will, and he knows that you returned to New York without Johnny. Craig is on your tail, Lucy. It's only a matter of time before he tracks you down. Unless you allow me to help you."

Paul took Lucy back to his hotel. He was staying at the Ritz-Carlton, which, Lucy had to admit, was a step up from the one bedroom in Brooklyn she and Johnny had been sharing. As they crossed the threshold to his room, Paul was saying something to Lucy, something about how they needed to work together to protect Johnny from Craig. But she couldn't focus on his words, because she was too distracted by the suite's full bath, complete with Jacuzzi tub. Her current place only had a shower the size of a drainpipe.

Paul saw where Lucy was looking.

"I'm an idiot," he said. "You must be exhausted from all the traveling you've been doing. Go ahead, use the tub. They put in fresh towels and robes this morning. I'll wait. We can talk afterward."

Lucy didn't have to be asked twice.

She luxuriated in the tub through two complete cycles of hot water and what seemed like half a bottle of bath oils. She washed her hair, dipping under the surface and staying there as long as her lungs could bear it, letting the white noise of waves beating against her ears clear her mind. By the time she finally got out and toweled off, wrapping herself in a luxurious robe, Lucy felt both more energetic and more exhausted than she had in months.

When she stepped out of the bathroom, Paul was waiting for her next to a three-course meal. Pappardelle pasta, watercress and endive salad, salmon in beurre blanc sauce. All of it on gleaming white china atop silver trays, none of it needing to be cut into small pieces or moved out of the way of tiny, grasping hands.

"You've really thought of everything, haven't you, Paul?"

"I try my best."

He also did his best, over lunch, never to let the words "Craig" or "Johnny" cross his lips. Instead, Paul filled Lucy in on all the Oakdale gossip. He told Lucy about her friend Alison and her former boyfriend Aaron. He explained in detail how and why Dusty had ended up dead, and he stroked Lucy's hand sympathetically when she couldn't stop the tears.

"I thought I had dealt with it," she admitted. "Back when my mother first told me about it, I cried and I wondered why and I cursed whoever I could think of. But that was over a year ago. I thought I'd moved on. And now, hearing it from you . . ."

Paul said, "I know. I've had feelings I was sure I'd analyzed and identified and put in their proper places, never to be heard from again. Except, at the oddest moments, there they are. My parents, for instance. Do you have any idea how many times I've told myself, 'Enough. Okay, so I'm the spawn of the most evil man to walk the earth. But that's not my fault, and I don't have to give in to it. I am my own person. My father doesn't control the decisions I make.' So I'll be going along, convinced I've got the Stenbeck in me fully under control, and then pow! Out of nowhere, I'll get the chance to take the low road. And it starts to look real tempting."

"I worried about that," Lucy admitted, digging into her salmon. "Right after I kidnapped Johnny, a part of me kept saying, 'Isn't this exactly the sort of thing Craig would do? What makes me any better than him?' "

"How about the fact that you put your own happiness on the line for Johnny's, instead of vice versa? That's one big difference right there."

"But the thing is, my father doesn't get up in the morning twirling his silent-movie-villain mustache and thinking of ways to make other people's lives miserable."

"Are you sure? Because I'm pretty certain mine does."

"Craig always thinks what he's doing is for the best. Just like I did."

"Well, he's wrong. And you're right."

"I bet you didn't think so at first. I kind of doubt your initial reaction upon hearing that I'd taken off with Johnny was, 'Oh, that Lucy, she did the right thing!' "

"Are you making fun of me?"

"Maybe a little."

Paul smiled. "I've missed that."

They finished the rest of their lunch talking about happier things. Lucy filled Paul in on his nephew, his likes, his dislikes, how smart Johnny was, how verbal, how loving, how stubborn.

"I swear, even his hair is stubborn," Lucy laughed. "Just these masses and masses of red curls that grow any way they want, in any direction they want, any length they want. Every month when I sit down to cut his hair—and by 'sit down' I mean plop him in front of a video with a lollipop in one hand, a pretzel in the other, and it helps if he's half-asleep, too—it's a completely different animal. Whatever styling worked last time isn't guaranteed to work this time. It's a good thing he's a boy and too little to care how he looks, because I've done some hatchet jobs on the poor kid."

"Don't worry about it. Jennifer's hair was the same way when she was Johnny's age. It used to drive my mother crazy. Because not only is Barbara a designer, so the idea that she couldn't manage her little princess's do was anathema to her, but also because Jennifer being a girl— and an equally verbal one, at that—Jennifer did care how she looked. And she and Barbara rarely agreed on the style."

"I'm sorry I robbed your mother of the chance to see Johnny grow up. I know she was sick last year. Oral cancer. Will told me. The thought that Barbara might have died without seeing Johnny and knowing that he was okay—"

"My mother understands. She was married to Craig. She knows what he's capable of. She does not want him raising Jennifer's little boy."

"I wish there was some way to make this right for everyone."

"There is," Paul said blithely.

"What?" Lucy felt twinges of the uneasiness and the suspicion she'd buried earlier.

"I'll tell you in a bit," he assured her. "But right now, you look beat. Why don't you stretch out on that big, comfortable bed over there and take a nap. We'll talk when you wake up."

This time, Lucy did need to be told twice.

But twice was all it took.

Before becoming an instant mother, Lucy had harbored the naïve notion that sleep was sleep. You closed your eyes, and you either drifted off or you didn't. Then, courtesy of what she'd learned in medical school, she'd expanded her definition of sleep to entering a state of a rapid eye movement. In either case, one eventually woke up and proceeded to join the conscious world. That, it turned out, was not exactly how it worked for everyone. When it came to sleep, there was the rest of the world, and then there were parents.

Parents, Lucy had discovered, did not technically sleep. Sure, they closed their eyes, they drifted off, they might even hit REM cycles once or twice. But that was just for appearances' sake. What they were really doing was closing their eyes, drifting off, and REMing while simultaneously listening for their children. Was someone crying? Falling out of bed? Getting up to explore? The first few times it had happened, Lucy had been amazed when she'd realized that she'd actually been waking up a split second before Johnny had burst into tears, or before his little pajamaed feet had hit the ground. Which meant, as she'd said before, that she hadn't technically been sleeping at all.

That probably explained why, to any casual observer, Lucy looked as if she'd been out cold, whereas the minute her subconscious mind registered the faint peep of a cell phone being opened, it quickly sent a message to her spinal cord, which in turn hammered her brain, shouting, "Cell phone! Cell phone! Johnny's gotten into your cell phone!"

Lucy's eyes popped open and she saw Paul sifting through the outgoing and incoming calls in her cell phone.

Lucy lay perfectly still. In fact, as soon as she registered what Paul was doing and instantly surmised why, she shut her eyes again and made a big show of turning over—eyes still closed. The noise was enough to distract Paul momentarily. He instantly stopped scrolling and shoved the phone back into Lucy's purse. But her closed eyes led him to believe that she hadn't seen what he was doing.

Once she'd heard the rustle that indicated Paul had put her phone back in her purse, Lucy lazily opened her eyes, yawning for extra effect.

"Good morning, sleepyhead," Paul greeted her.

Lucy smiled groggily, continuing the charade that any nonparent was destined to buy—the idea that one actually needed time to awaken, as opposed to leaping up fully alert and ready to slay dragons.

"So what now?" Lucy asked Paul innocently.

"Get dressed," he said. "We're going out."

Lucy thought Paul might take her out to dinner—somewhere lush and romantic—the better to soften her up for whatever proposal it was he'd spent the bulk of the day already softening her up for. But, instead, he swept Lucy away to Rockefeller Center, where, as the snow fell in gentle, couldn't-have-been-better-if-he'd-ordered-them-from-a-special-effects-shop flakes, the two of them whipped around on rented ice skates through the throng of seemingly enraptured tourists. Paul gripped Lucy's hand—even though she actually was the stronger skater. And he gazed into her eyes—even though that meant he couldn't watch where he was going and twice crashed into the barrier. It was all a bit much, and Lucy would have ended things right then and there, except that she was truly curious to see where Paul was going with all this.

Afterward, they drank hot chocolate under the stars, and, when Paul suggested a moonlit horse-drawn carriage ride, Lucy went along. The sheer hokiness of his romantic gestures made her wonder if Paul was aware that time had passed and she was no longer seventeen years old. She decided not to enlighten him.

Because here was the problem. Lucy understood that he was being hokey. She could articulate it in words with no trouble whatsoever. The trouble stemmed from the fact that while she understood he was manipulating her, she didn't feel that at all. What she felt, while wrapped in a warm blanket with Paul, under a full moon, the click-clop of the horse's hoofs in her ears, Central Park in all its glory before her eyes, and Paul's arm around her shoulder, was exactly what Paul wanted—nay, expected—her to feel. She felt good. She felt safe. She felt happy and taken care of and cherished. And she hadn't felt any of those things for a long time.

Lucy struggled to remember that Paul was playing her. That just a few hours earlier he'd been going through her cell phone, looking for information on where she might have stashed Johnny. And yet, she couldn't help thinking,

What would be so wrong about telling him? What would be so wrong about stopping the running, about settling down, and picking up her abandoned life? What would be so wrong about giving in when Paul kissed her? And what would be so wrong about kissing him back?

Nothing, that's what.

Nothing in the world.

When she opened her eyes, he was smiling down at her, their lips still inches apart, their bodies pressed together beneath the blanket.

"Hi," Paul said flirtatiously.

"Hi," Lucy repeated.

"Should I be apologizing?"

"You tell me."

He leaned back a little. "Are you teasing me again?"

"What would you like me to say?"

"I don't know," Paul admitted. "I wasn't expecting—this."

"No?"

"No! I mean . . . here's the thing, Lucy. I've been thinking about you a lot. Not about you and Johnny; just you. I don't know if anybody filled you in on what happened with me while you were away from Oakdale. Your father's wife, Meg—did you know about that?"

"It's pretty hard to keep up with all my father's wives, but, yes, my mother told me he'd married Meg."

"Well, Meg was really in love with me. She was pregnant with my baby, but your father couldn't stand that. He tried to give her a drug that would make her miscarry. He backed out at the last minute, but the fact that he even thought about it, well, it shows what he's capable of."

"I thought Meg lost the baby after she fell."

"It was an accident. I was going after Craig and Meg tried to step in and stop us, and, anyway, it doesn't matter. She lost the baby, and Meg blamed me. Rather, she blamed my obsession with Craig. It was the second child I'd lost. My little girl with Emily was stillborn. I don't know what's wrong with me. Maybe I wasn't meant to be a father, I don't know. The only thing I know for sure is that I really, really want to be one. I know it's stupid, but I've always thought if I ever got the chance to raise a child, and to raise him right, it would kind of be like me thumbing my nose at James Stenbeck, you know? Like, 'Hey, man, you tried, but you didn't get me. I learned right from wrong in spite of you. And here's the proof: my kid.' You must know what that's like. Because that's you and Craig. He's a son of a bitch, you're not. You didn't let him pull you into his sick, twisted, lying view of the world. You broke free. You're your own person."

"I'm sorry about your baby, Paul. But I'm not sure what that has to do with me."

"You and Johnny, Lucy. You could be my chance. You know I have feelings for you. I've had them since you were a kid. The problem was then you were too young, so there was nothing I could do, I couldn't act on them. You're not too young now. You and me and Johnny, we could be a family. From a legal standpoint, we'd have a hell of a case against Craig. I'm the biological uncle, you're the biological sister, plus you've been his primary guardian for over two years. No judge would take a kid away from the only mother he's ever known and hand him over to a convicted felon like Craig—especially not when Johnny's real mother's family is behind

you. It would be perfect. You could stop running. We could
be together like we were meant to be. We could be a family.
We could be each other's salvation."

It was a wonderful speech.

It was a terribly tempting speech.

Stop running. Be together. Be a family.

But, unfortunately, it was also an untruthful speech.

Because Lucy knew better. Paul might have hoped that
the combination of kisses and moonlight and loneliness
would have turned Lucy's head—and it had, up to a point.
Though not so far that she'd forgotten how things had really
been between them. Despite what he proclaimed now, the
only feelings Paul had ever harbored for seventeen-year-old
Lucy had been friendship mixed with a good deal of sympathy because of who her father was. It wasn't Lucy's jailbait
age that had kept them apart then; it had been the fact that
Paul had been utterly and thoroughly not interested. In fact,
if Lucy remembered correctly, the woman Paul had really
wanted all those years ago had been Rosanna Cabot, another wife he and her father had ended up having in common. The tale he was spinning might have been a good one,
but it hinged on revisionist history. And that never worked
out in the end.

Just as she'd both dreaded and pragmatically suspected,
the real issue at hand was that Paul wanted control of
Johnny. Peripherally because he loved and missed his sister.
But primarily to piss Craig off. And, hey, if he could add to
his enemy's overall aggravation by reeling in Craig's daughter as part of the arrangement, so much the better. But this
wasn't about her, and it wasn't even about Johnny. It was

about Craig. Which was why Lucy had taken off with her brother in the first place.

She made up her mind. She looked Paul in the eye and she leaned in, kissing him herself this time. Before he'd had the chance to shake off his surprise, Lucy said, "Let's go back to your room."

She kissed him again, all but pinning Paul against the wall, as soon as they stepped through the doorway. He seemed scandalized, but game.

She whispered, "I've been waiting such a long time for you."

"Oh, yes, me, too," he agreed.

"I can't believe it. I daydreamed about this when I was a kid—"

"Well, you're no kid anymore, I'll give you that."

"Absolutely not. I can't wait to prove it to you."

"Sounds great."

"The tub," Lucy urged him. "It was heaven alone. I can't imagine what it'll be like to have you with me."

"Now?" Paul asked.

"Right now. Hurry."

She started undressing Paul, insisting when he hesitated, pressing herself against him, pushing him toward the tub first gently, then firmly. He had his shirt off, and Lucy was working on the buckle of his pants, loosening it to the point where they couldn't stay up any longer, when she turned suddenly, shoved Paul inside the massive tub, and turned on the overhead shower. She grabbed the clothes she'd managed to get off of him; leaving Paul dazed and thoroughly drenched, she tore out of the bathroom, sticking a chair under the knob to keep him inside for at least a few minutes.

Lucy grabbed her own purse and coat, plus Paul's overnight bag, and ran down the hotel hallway.

She ditched his things in the lobby, slipping the bag unobtrusively onto a departing guest's luggage cart as it headed toward a waiting taxi.

And took off into the night.

23

"When I realized that both Craig and Paul knew I'd left Johnny with Gwen and Will, I knew I couldn't risk contacting them," Lucy told Henry and Vienna. "I didn't know what the exact situation was, and I was afraid to make it worse. I figured if either Paul or Craig had managed to already get their hands on Johnny, Gwen and Will would have let me know. Since they didn't, I had to assume there was a reason, so I kept my distance. I came here to the UN. Bianca was kind enough to sequester me away while we thought of what my next move should be."

While Lucy had been telling them the story of her New York rendezvous with Paul, her aunt had unobtrusively slipped into the room. Unlike the rest of the Walsh women — Lucinda, Sierra, Lily, Lucy — who all fit in somewhere along the tall and various shades of blond/dirty blond/brunette-with-blond-highlights spectrum, Bianca was actually on the petite side, with dark eyes and wavy, ebony hair down to her shoulders. However, in the way that she held her head straight up, the way she looked people directly in the eye, and even the way in which she crisply leafed through the official-looking papers waiting on her desk before tossing them authoritatively aside, there was no doubt about what family had adopted her and, literally, made her one of their own.

Bianca said, "I've made arrangements for Lucy to join the next expedition of Physicians Without Politics. They're headed for Tibet. Even Paul Ryan and Craig Montgomery can't reach them there. All we needed was Johnny."

"I can't thank you enough for taking care of him," Lucy said warmly to Henry and Vienna as the little boy giddily buried his face in her hair, then peeked through and pretended the strands were his mustache and beard.

"It was . . . interesting," Vienna said.

Lucy gave Johnny a sideways glance. "Why did the lady say that, Johnny?"

"You're pretty," Johnny told Vienna.

"Hey," Henry cracked. "At least the kid's got taste. Anyway, listen, since it was your grandmother who hired us to find you, we're going to need to tell her where you are." He decided to leave out the part about her grandmother also firing them.

"Go ahead," Lucy reassured them. "I realize she's been very worried. She's called Bianca twice just this week, screaming for the UN to send out the troops to look for me. Grandmother insists that since America is the largest contributor to the United Nations, they should at least be entitled to some personalized service. I felt bad for Bianca, having to take it—"

"It's all right," Bianca reassured. "Next to Hugo Chavez, Mother doesn't even seem all that blustering."

"—but I'd sworn her to secrecy. I was afraid Grandmother would tell my mother. And I couldn't risk that as long as Craig was still blackmailing her."

"Oh, that," Henry said offhandedly. "We took care of that."

"You did?" Lucy asked, surprised.

"Yeah, yeah, didn't anybody tell you? Vienna and I, we popped on down to Montega, had it out with Craig. He's not a threat to Sierra anymore. So go ahead, drop Mom a note, let her know how you're doing. No worries."

"I don't believe it!"

"We're a full-service agency," Henry said proudly. "Your grandma would only hire the best."

"As far as I'm concerned, you two are worth every penny Grandmother is paying you."

Henry and Vienna exchanged looks.

"We'd better go," Bianca said. "Finish making arrangements for your trip."

Holding Johnny, Lucy walked over to Henry and Vienna. She kissed Henry on the cheek and offered Vienna a one-armed hug. "Thank you again. Johnny and I would have been lost without you." Detaching the boy's fingers from her hair, Lucy winced, "I hope he wasn't too much trouble."

"He missed you," Vienna said, searching for a neutral yet honest statement. "I am sure that if we had met under different circumstances, the circumstances, they would have been . . . different." Goodness, but it was easy to run out of words when one was striving for truth without insult.

Lucy said, "Don't hesitate to put all the repair, dry-cleaning, and noise violation tickets in your expense report.

Though I wonder if even Grandmother has the means to cover every last one."

"You mean," Vienna said cautiously, "Johnny misbehaves with you, as well?"

"He's a three-and-a-half-year-old boy," Lucy shrugged. "It's what he does."

"But he loves you!"

"I know. And I love him. Doesn't mean I'm unaware of what he's capable of."

Bianca stuck her head out the office door and looked both ways. She told Lucy, "The coast is clear. Let's go."

Lucy urged, "Say good-bye to Henry and Vienna, Johnny."

He pursed his lips and glared at them for a moment. "No."

"All right, then. How about say, 'Thank you for taking care of me.'"

"No."

"Johnny . . ."

"No, no, no, no, no . . . I'm hungry."

"All right. We'll stop and get you a muffin."

"My socks are too big."

"You're right. How did that happen?"

"I want to get down."

"In a minute."

"Where are we going?"

"On another adventure!" Lucy put on her best enthusiastic-adult face.

"No! I don't want to!"

Lucy shrugged apologetically, waved for the last time,

and stepped out the door. They could still hear Johnny complaining even when the three of them had turned the corner and disappeared out of sight.

"That is amazing," Vienna said.

"Such a little body, such big lungs?"

"She loves him."

"He *is* her brother. That's got to count for something. They're not total strangers like we were to him. They're family."

"I know you can love a child that is not yours by blood. Look at Gwen and Will, and Hallie. Or Lucinda and Lily. What I meant was, she loves him not because he acts differently with her than he did with us. She loves him in spite of his acting the exact same way. He is as much trouble with her. But she loves him."

"I think it's kind of the parents' code. Got to love them no matter what. Through upswing and upchuck. Through naps and nags. Through jaundice and jail. Through . . . could you please stop me, I'm running out of alliterations."

"Stop," Vienna said.

"Thank you."

"No. Truly, stop. Listen." Vienna indicated down the hall. Though Johnny's cries had faded in the distance, coming from the other direction was the sound of two male voices arguing. Two very familiar male voices.

"I swear to God, the next time I see you plunging off a cliff into a raging ravine, I am diving in after you to make sure the lethal plunge sticks."

"Next time I replace blank bullets with real ones, I'll make certain you take the entire cartridge in the chest."

"Next time I put a bomb in your car, it'll be of the nuclear variety."

"Next time I try smothering you with a pillow, I'll really put my back into it."

"Paul, Craig," Henry said when they rounded a corner and ended up face-to-face. "Funny running into you two. Again."

"We know Lucy's here," Paul said.

"Are you looking to reclaim your pants?" Vienna asked innocently.

Craig turned his head slightly as he took a moment to peer curiously at Vienna in response to her query. But the rest of his body was focused on the task at hand. He used both arms to shove Henry out of his way, then he sprinted down the hallway, leaving the rest of them with no choice but to hustle double-time and follow.

Craig's height gave him an advantage. He was able to catch up in time to see Lucy, Johnny, and Bianca as they were about to step into a private elevator at the end of a long, out-of-the-way corridor. Bianca shoved her key into the lock, jiggling it to make the doors open faster. She and Lucy, who was still carrying Johnny, ducked inside, and Bianca repeated the frantic action with the key, this time to shut the door before Craig could reach them.

"Lucy!" he bellowed while charging at top speed toward them.

"Daddy."

The way she said the word made it both a warning and a question. She sounded calm and in control but also very young and uncertain. She made Henry think of all the meaning and history and expectation that could be gerrymandered into one simple, but in no way insignificant, word.

Lucy and Craig locked eyes as the doors closed. She bit her lip and looked at him apologetically. And defiantly. And longingly. And resolutely.

"Daddy?" Johnny repeated. The boy was obviously asking what Lucy had meant by calling Craig that. Well, it was obvious to everyone but Craig. Hearing his son utter the word "Daddy" so innocently was enough to break Craig's stride. He tripped and went down on one knee. He scrambled up instantaneously, but the stumble still granted enough time for the elevator doors to shut just as Craig's fingertips attempted to wedge between them.

Frustrated, he slammed the bulletproof metal with his fist, then darted from one corner of the hallway to the other, frantically looking for any means to follow them. Finding none, he spun around and seethed at Paul, who was approaching them, "This is all your fault. I'd have gotten here in time if I didn't have to worry about you dogging me every step of the way."

"I know the feeling," Henry mumbled.

"Excuse me?" Paul smacked the side of his head, as if he'd been hearing things. "*You're* the one who's been following *me* around like a lost and rabid mongrel, Craig. You would still be looking for an Anglo-Argentinean dictionary if you hadn't hijacked my search."

"Oh, yes." Craig caught his breath and struggled to regain the flip and detached control he was otherwise famous for. "Did I ever thank you for fingering me as a Nazi sympathizer to the Buenos Aires authorities? I'm sure it was just an honest mistake on your part."

"You do have an abnormal appreciation of Wagner."

Craig turned on Henry and jabbed a finger in his face. "Tell me where the hell Lucy is taking my son now."

"In the words of your son"—Henry crossed his arms across his chest—"no."

Craig softened. "Johnny talks?"

"Of course he talks," Vienna said. "He is three years old."

"In my mind he's still a baby," Craig confessed, "like he was the last time I saw him. I try to imagine him now, but I've never thought of him talking. What sort of things does he say? Is he intelligent? What sort of boy is he?" If Henry hadn't known better, he might have actually thought that Craig, in that moment, seemed, well, normal. Paternal. Vulnerable.

Human.

Vienna must have gotten that feeling, too, because she sincerely answered, "He is a very smart boy. He talks a great deal. He loves to get his own way, and, when he does not, he makes his displeasure most clear."

Craig smiled, "His big brother Bryant was like that when he was Johnny's age. Once he'd made up his mind, he refused to budge. And he would argue his side no matter what. Sierra and I called him our little Johnnie Cochran: If I don't quit, you must acquit. We used to say that was his motto . . ." Craig's voice trailed off. And then it hardened as thoughts of the first son that he'd lost reminded him of the second. "Tell me where Lucy and Johnny are going before I rip off that obnoxious smirk of yours and turn it into a grappling hook," Craig threatened Henry.

"Listen to you!" Vienna exclaimed. "Johnny is supposed to be the child in this situation!"

"My child," Craig stressed.

"My sister's child," Paul reminded them.

"This is not about Johnny," Vienna said. "This is about the two of you. The two of you are the reason Lucy took Johnny in the first place, and the two of you are the reason that poor girl has not had a moment's peace since."

"There's an easy way to rectify that problem," Craig pointed out.

"Leave Lucy alone!" Vienna ordered.

"Just as soon as I get my son back," Craig said.

Paul considered the implications of his actions and shrugged. Nonetheless, he felt forced to agree with the man he claimed to despise, "Lucy started this. I'm just looking to end it."

"I was afraid of this," Vienna sighed.

"Just tell us where they're going and we'll gladly leave you alone. I told you back in Sweden, guys, this isn't your fight. You don't have a horse in the race. Why do you want to be stuck in the middle of somebody else's family feud? Don't you two have enough domestic issues of your own to stress over?"

Vienna said, "I have had enough of this. If no one else agrees to bring this Byzantine bickering to an end, then I will."

"Your girl speaks some sense there, Coleman," Craig said as he nudged Henry in the ribs. Then to Vienna, he said, "Finally ready to spill the beans?"

"Yes," she said. "I feel I have no choice in the matter."

"Vienna!" Henry hissed.

But she pointedly ignored him. "It is up to me to end this. So, Paul, here is the situation: If you go to the Montegan consulate, you will find there a man by the name of Mr. Fazendiero. In Mr. Fazendiero's possession is a list. On that list are the names of several international criminals who paid Craig Montgomery a most generous amount of money to provide them with new identities and illegal Montegan passports. If you can get any of those men to testify against Craig—and I am sure that between you and your father some sort of deal can be worked out—then Mr. Fazendiero, not to mention one Sierra Esteban, will happily issue a warrant for Craig's arrest. It should prove rather difficult for him to stalk Lucy and Johnny from a Montegan prison, or while perched on an International Fugitive list. And that is not even counting what those whom Craig's customers cheated might want to do to him in payback."

"You little bitch!" Craig exclaimed, then made a menacing move in Vienna's direction.

Sensing this was his moment to play hero, Henry gallantly stepped between them, though, to be honest, he wasn't exactly thrilled with Vienna's actions, either. Granted, Paul was the lesser evil of the two men, and if one really sat down and thought about it, neutralizing Craig was the more logical action. But it did mean that Paul would now have carte blanche to pursue his nephew.

From behind him, Vienna gently rested her fingers in the crook of Henry's elbow and moved him aside so that his heroics proved superfluous and she was now facing Craig head-on.

"Craig," she said calmly, "if you travel to Sweden, you may wish to visit the home of Gjord and Martina Hyatt. They will tell you about Paul Ryan's kidnapping of their daughter, as well as personally lead you to the location where she was held and almost murdered."

"Hey!" Paul yelled, prompting Henry to shift his chivalry in the other direction by now stepping between Paul and Vienna. "You two got out okay. And anyway, your parents were in on the whole thing."

"Of course they were," Vienna agreed sweetly. "Good luck explaining that to the authorities. In Swedish."

"What are you doing?" Henry demanded.

"It is called mutually assured destruction. I learned it from the Americans and the Russians while growing up. If both sides have ample evidence to destroy the other, then both sides end up in perennial stalemate. If Craig pursues Lucy, Paul can have him put in jail. If Paul pursues Lucy, Craig can do the same thing."

"How about if I kill him?" Paul suggested.

Vienna shrugged. "Go ahead, risk it if you must. Though I would suspect Craig possesses the ingenuity to orchestrate your downfall, even from beyond the grave."

"My little pepperkakor . . ." Henry was flooded with pride, shock, and awe. Not to mention a healthy dose of fear. Which, in its own way, was the most exciting emotion of all. His girl could kick some serious ass!

"All right then," Vienna said. "We are through here." She waved her hands in Paul and Craig's direction. "Now be gone, both of you. Leave the United Nations. They have enough of their own petty conflicts to settle."

"Talk dirty to me," Henry panted to Vienna later that afternoon as they lay in bed together, having run out of other Plaza Hotel furniture on top of which they might express their exhilaration with the afternoon's events. "Tell me how you've got me backed up against the wall — and how I'd better like it or else."

"Now, now, Henry. You know I am not really that tough and ruthless. That was just an act I created to be rid of Paul and Craig."

"I'm disappointed. Here I thought we'd unleashed a previously unseen side of you. The one that comes with whips and chains and safe words."

"Oh, that," Vienna yawned. "I suppose if you are truly interested in such old-fashioned entertainments, I could ring my parents and ask them to send along the box of my old high-school things."

"Are you saying we could have whips, chains, *and* a schoolgirl uniform?"

"Catholic school uniform . . . ," Vienna teased.

"Be still my heart."

"Only if you fail to follow my instructions."

"Vienna Hyatt, you are a woman of unending surprises," Henry said. "Which reminds me, speaking of surprises: How are we paying for this room? Still on the Gjord and Martina Hyatt grant?"

"Oh, no," Vienna snuggled back into the comfy pillows. "That ran out ages ago. I believe lunch at the Mona Lisa did us in."

"Then how, my pet? Because, you see, while I would love to ravish you several more times before the checkout hour, I fear the presence of irate bill collectors and house detectives might well dampen my ardor."

"Surely, a man like you can rise above it all!"

"I'm not as young as I used to be."

Vienna giggled. "Do not worry, Henry. I put the room on a credit card, just like you taught me to do."

"That could be problem. Ours are maxed out. Several times over."

"Henry?"

"Yes?"

"Did you know that when you enter one of the boutiques downstairs and purchase an item such as this fine negligee that you are now admiring, if you sign up right then and there to receive their personal credit card, they hand you the pretty little thing on the spot? And you get 10 percent off your purchase?" Vienna wiggled a little to offer Henry an optimal view of her lucky purchase.

"So you used a brand-new credit card to pay for a room we can't afford because we don't even have the money to pay off our previous credit cards?"

"That is correct."

"I love you."

"A wise choice."

"And yet, I'm still stuck with this nagging need to know how you imagine we might—maybe not today, maybe not tomorrow, but soon and for the rest of our lives—pay for it all?"

"Lucinda," Vienna said. "She is a fair woman. Once we tell her how we located Lucy and reunited her with Johnny, not to mention how we cleverly diffused both Craig and Paul's relentless pursuit of the poor girl, Lucinda will have no choice but to reward our efforts handsomely. Which means that in no time at all, you and I shall be living happily ever after."

"Yes," Henry said. "About that. Since it appears we've run out of excuses for putting off talking about that vague, amorphous happily ever after and what it may—or may not—include . . . I've been thinking—"

"Oh, no!" Vienna exclaimed.

"What?"

"It appears that the negligee I purchased for 10 percent off is also 10 percent too big. I cannot seem to keep it on myself no matter what I do." Vienna sat up and demonstrated. "Look."

Henry looked.

In the words of Oscar Wilde, "Women are to be loved, not understood."

So Henry did his best.

EPILOGUE

OAKDALE

"Of course you deserve a reward," Lucinda said as she offered a magnanimous sweep of her arm that, for all Henry and Vienna knew, might encapsulate her entire estate and grounds. "One perfectly fitting the situation."

"You see, Henry," Vienna beamed. "I knew that Mrs. Walsh was a fair and magnanimous person. She is not one to hold grudges."

"Of course not," Lucinda said. "Why should I hold a grudge? Merely because I hired you to find my granddaughter and you managed to get her more lost than ever?"

"Now wait a minute," Henry interjected. "You wanted to know where Lucy was. We got you that information."

"She is in Tibet! Surrounded by dilettante celebrity do-gooders and pandas! Is this supposed to put my heart at ease?"

"At least she and Johnny are free of Craig and Paul."

"Let me ask you something, Henry. Am I missing something? Was it not your sloppy sleuthing that brought Craig and Paul to my Lucy's doorstep in the first place?"

"Not exactly," Vienna said in their defense.

"Not exactly," Lucinda repeated. "Well, in that case, I feel moved to give you your reward—only not exactly."

"Uh-oh," Henry said.

"Your reward, my darlings, is the most valuable thing there is: Life experience."

"How's that trading on the open market these days?" Henry wondered aloud.

Lucinda ignored him. "Thanks to me, the two of you have learned something. At the very least about the detective business, if not about your own selves. My reward to you, Henry, Vienna, is the gift of self-reflection. An unexamined life is not worth living, isn't that what they say?"

"Who are 'they'?" Henry wondered. "And why do they talk so much?" Then he recalled what Oscar Wilde had said: "I always pass on good advice. It is the only thing to do with it. It is never of any use to oneself."

"I will not be giving you a monetary reward," Lucinda said. Then, in response to the sheer devastation on Henry and Vienna's faces, she softened long enough to add, "But perhaps I can be convinced to pay off the expenses you incurred in the course of your investigation. Never let it be said that Lucinda Walsh is not fair."

"Oh, thank you, Mrs. Walsh!" Vienna clapped her hands. Lucinda arched an eyebrow. Vienna stopped clapping.

"Besides," Lucinda went on, "one never knows when one might once again need the services of an experienced investigative team."

"Is this your way of saying we did a good job?" Henry clarified.

"It's my way of saying . . . it could have been worse." Which, for Lucinda Walsh, was about as close to a compliment as anyone could expect.

Back at Al's Diner, Vienna observed, "Well, if Mrs. Walsh pays off our expenses, we will no longer be in debt. We will merely be broke." She sighed. "None of this went the way I expected."

"Welcome to my world."

"I like your world," Vienna said. She settled down on a bar stool and removed her coat. As always, Vienna simply let it slide off her shoulders toward the ground, confident that somewhere, somehow, some man would catch it. As always, Henry did.

"What's your favorite part?" he wondered. "The perennial poverty or the continual sense of loser-dom that settles around me like the fine mist of cheap cologne?"

"My favorite part is you."

"You know, Vienna, it's very difficult for me to cling to my lowered self-esteem in the face of your unearned adoration." He sighed and sat down next to her. "We're broke. Two well-connected sociopaths have sworn revenge upon our persons. And our last job actually ended up costing us money, which I think I remember reading in *The Seven Habits of Highly Effective People* is not one of them."

Vienna shrugged.

"That's it?"

"That is it."

"Would you care to elaborate on that shrug?"

"I would not."

"Jesus Christ, Vienna, what is the matter with you? I dump you at the altar, I insult your parents, I cause an international incident, I stick you with a kid who makes "The Ransom of Red Chief" read like a documentary, I bankrupt the diner, and you still put up with me. What is that, some kind of Swedish neutrality thing?"

"Switzerland. They are the neutral ones."

"What's going on here?"

"It is very simple, actually."

"Fill me in."

"I am happy with my life."

"Beg your pardon?"

"My life. Our life. I am happy with it. I am happy with you. I love the diner. Even if you do lose it periodically in a poker game, you always manage to win it back in the end. I loved our most recent adventure. If it were not for you, I would have never engaged in a car chase in Montega. That was very exciting. And my parents: obviously it was time for us to come to a new understanding. You helped to facilitate that. As for Johnny; Johnny was the best part of all."

"Uh-oh. That's not good."

"No, I think you will like it."

"Listen, Vienna, I'm sorry I had that little meltdown back at the consulate. Going without socks does that to me. I overreacted."

"No. You did not. You were right. Having a child, taking

care of a child, it is a monumental responsibility. It is not a game, it is a life-changing commitment. I do not think I saw it in such a light before. You are right. We are not ready to have a child of our own . . . yet. Our life is wonderful and exciting the way that it is. I have no desire, at this point, to change it."

"Vienna!" Henry leapt out of his chair, swooping her into a hug and spinning her around and around. "That's fantastic!"

"No, it is not," Vienna said primly.

Henry stopped the spinning. He set Vienna carefully down on the ground and stepped back, as if she was a ticking time bomb that might go off at any moment. "Explain."

"I am an awful person."

"Not from where I'm standing."

"I am. I am shallow and selfish. Look at Lucy Montgomery. Look at everything that she has done and sacrificed for a boy who is not even her own. She is a good person. Look at Gwen and Will Munson. So young, and already taking care of that little girl they adopted. Look at everyone in Oakdale. Everyone but us."

"I'm looking," Henry agreed. "And I'm liking."

"What is the matter with us? Why do we not want to be like everyone else? Why are we not willing to make those same sorts of sacrifices?"

"Because we're not idiots," Henry said. "Everyone else you mentioned, they went into the whole parenthood thing with the same starry-eyed blinders you had on up until yesterday. They thought it was all cute booties and Christmas pageants and mother-daughter fashion shows. They didn't know what they were getting into. They didn't have a dry run, like us. Plus, they had other reasons to reproduce. Carly Snyder? She conceived Parker in order to cash in on a fifty-million-dollar trust fund. Gwen Munson? She got knocked up while she was still in high school."

"So why do they have more than one child now?"

"Once your life is over, what else are you going to do? Just keep on reproducing. God knows, that was my old lady's modus operandi. Keep on popping them out, maybe eventually you'll end up with one who isn't a holy terror. Didn't work so well for her. Don't think it really works for anyone."

"But it is all so empty, living a life where you do not have someone you would sacrifice everything for."

"Who says?" Henry challenged. "You and me, we do have someone we'd sacrifice anything for. We've got each other."

Vienna leaned back to survey him from a distance. "You thought I was willing to sleep with Craig Montgomery."

"You didn't care that Sierra was coming on to me," he countered.

"She was not."

"Besides the point."

"We did not exactly exhibit a great deal of trust toward each other."

"So what? When push came to shove, I pushed and you shoved. Together. It was a beautiful thing. You didn't side with your parents against me."

"And you were willing to sleep in subzero temperatures. For me."

"You didn't berate me for losing all our money."

"You were willing to accept charity from my parents."

"That one doesn't count. I'm always happy for a handout."

"I am sorry that I did not realize before how seriously you took the concept of child raising. And how traumatized you were over what happened to Maddie and Eve."

"And I'm sorry I didn't stick you with a redheaded terror sooner. We could have settled all this months ago."

"You know, Henry, I am not saying that I will never want a child. Just not now."

"Vienna, my darling, you have made me the happiest man in the world."

"We are still broke."

"Piffle."

"And while I may have put motherhood on the back burner for now, I would still like to get married."

"Let's do it, then," Henry said. "Right now. Right here. You deserve it."

"Do not be silly."

"I'm serious. You know I'm licensed to perform weddings. God knows I've officiated at enough of Katie's. Why shouldn't I perform my own for a change?"

"Well, one reason is because I believe your license to officiate came from a website that also promised a free set of martini glasses with every ordination."

"I really needed a new set of martini glasses."

"And two—I do not believe that even if your credentials are authentic, you are allowed to marry yourself."

"Double piffle!" Henry cleared his throat. "Vienna, my darling, what's a wedding? It is a ritual wherein two people pledge their eternal troth to each other."

"What is this troth?"

"I have no idea. I always pictured a large, woolly-mammoth type thing. It fits, don't you think? Troth, troth. Here comes the big, hairy troth . . . anyway, where was I?"

"Pledging a big hairy mammoth."

"Right. A wedding is two people promising to love each other forever. Everything else is just window dressing. And flexible window dressing, at that. For instance . . ." He hummed, "Here comes the bride/All dressed in white . . ." as he reached past Vienna, plucked a paper napkin from a dispenser wobbling on a nearby table, and reverently placed it over her head. "Your veil."

"It is lovely," Vienna laughed.

"And biodegradable! Let no man say that Henry Coleman doesn't love the environment almost as much as he loves his blushing bride."

"Why am I blushing?"

"I'm guessing it's because you're wearing a napkin on your head."

"That makes sense."

"So what else do we need to make this official? Rings? Rice?"

"Vows?" Vienna guessed.

"Vows. Right. Vows." Henry cleared his throat and began, "Vienna Hyatt, you are the most wonderful, miraculous, exasperating, surprising, challenging, sweet, sour, hot, cold, beautiful, kinky, sexy thing that has ever happened to me. For you I would brave the heat of the tropics, the cold of the Arctic, the kowtowing of a monarchy, and the brutal prohibition of European socialism. I will honor your every wish, grant your every whim, and worship your every step. You wanted a guy who would die for you, Vienna? I submit that any man can make such a claim. Instead, right here, right now, with the power vested in me by the state of Illinois and in the presence of you, the only witness that matters, I do hereby make the following vow: I, Henry Coleman, do solemnly swear to not merely die for you; I swear to live for you, too."

Wow! Henry thought. *Where did that come from? And if this is what he was capable of, who needed Oscar Wilde?*

The scariest part was that, after a lifetime of hiding behind clever tongue twisters and other people's copyrighted quips to keep his real feelings at bay, Henry now meant every word he'd just said.

Vienna swooned. She really did. Thirty years of reading novels of high adventure and bosom-heaving romance and, for the first time, Henry was actually witnessing a real-life woman swoon. What was more, she was doing it in response to his words. Words that he actually meant!

Vienna went weak at the knees, so that Henry had to hold her up with his manly arms. She leaned against him, and she caught her breath. Vienna's arms snaked around Henry's neck. His own hands cupped her back. She closed her eyes and leaned in to him. He pulled her closer.

As her glorious lips sought out his, the besotted girl sighed, "Oh, Henry . . ."